She blinked, focus  lifted her hand to wave

"There are no more chances, Emma. Make something happen."

With a grunt, she stood on the highest spot of the log. The man was lifting something shiny and black from under a pile of branches. She called, but her voice seemed to fall straight to the ground. She coughed until she bent at the waist. Maybe he'd hear her coughing?

A whistle. That's what she needed. How many times had Mom suggested that, and she had scoffed? But even if she had a whistle, did she have enough energy to blow it?

"Help." Her hoarse voice crackled in her ears. A dizzy spell hit, and she tilted. She gripped a branch sticking off the tree and stared at the boy, willed him to see her.

"Help." She waved her arm. Why wasn't her coat bright red or yellow, not this drab gray? She had to do this for Mom. She grabbed a bushy twig lying across the tree. She waved it like a flag. She swung it over her head. She swirled it in a circle. How long could she keep this up? Not long.

The guy stopped what he was doing and turned his face toward her. Had he seen her?

When the man dropped the shiny, black thing, her brain buzzed. He raced across the field in her direction, and she sank onto the log.

"Thank all the goddesses and stars."

The Incident

by
Avis M. Adams

The Incident

Cover Art by *Tina Lynn Stout*

The Wild Rose Press, Inc.
PO Box 708
Adams Basin, NY 14410-0708
Visit us at www.thewildrosepress.com

Publishing History
First Edition, 2022
Trade Paperback ISBN 978-1-5092-3848-4
Digital ISBN 978-1-5092-3849-1

Published in the United States of America

Dedication

To Sylvia, a mentor, a friend, and a good writer.

Acknowledgments

I'd like to thank Mary Aquino, who read this book in its rawest form, found the message timely, and encouraged me to keep writing. Thanks to Jody Segal and Anthony Warnke who read a less-raw version and gave feedback and further support. Thanks to Trevor O'Hara, who tore the book apart and helped me build a better version that started to sparkle.

Thank you to The Baker Street Critique group: Ardi Butler, Harvey Homan, Skeeter (Tim) Wilson, and Gary Habenicht who have supported me and helped me grow and stretch as a writer and gave me constant encouragement about the importance of this novel. And to the Flamingo Writers: Carl Lee, Catherine Brugger-Brown, Wendy Kendall, Melanie MacDonald, Jacquline Kang, and Preeti Gopalan who kept me writing and pushing forward on this arduous journey to publication. For me the learning curve was steep, my friends.

I'd like to thank Alicia Dean for her editing session and encouragement to submit this novel, and Ally Richardson for promoting this book for publication. Thank you so much for the opportunity. I'd also like to give my thanks to PNWA and their president, Pam Binder, who provide the resources that help novices like myself reach their publication goals. To anyone I've forgotten, friends, family, and fellow writers, thank you from the top and bottom of my heart.

Chapter One

Josh

Josh sat at the dining room table and glared at the calculus problem on the worksheet. He ran his fingers through his hair. Why couldn't he get it? He pushed away from the table, the chair squeaking over the wood floor, and moved to the dining room window. A sign swung on its post at the end of the driveway, "Woolf Farm," organic milk and vegetables, until Grandpa passed away. A For Sale sign hung beside it. How could his dad sell Grandpa's farm? He stuffed his fists into his back pockets.

"Grandpa was the farmer, and with him gone, it doesn't make sense to stay anymore," Dad had said.

Why sell the farm, though? Where would they go? Grandpa had been married here, and so had great grandpa. Did *Woolf Family est. 1908,* as carved in the sidewalk, mean nothing? It meant something to Josh.

Sold. That meant—forever.

He plunked in the chair, laid his head on his arm, and hummed a bar from Pachelbel's Canon in D. He shuffled through his precalculus papers scattered over the table, dropped his hands to his lap. What was the use? He couldn't concentrate. He walked to the window and plopped on the window seat, glanced around the yard for Fergus. He put his hand to the glass.

Both Grandpa and Fergus gone in one week, and soon the farm?

A golden maple leaf floated by the window, one of the last on the tree. November winds would clear off the rest, nature's scrub brush. He rubbed his fingers over the polished oak of the window seat, smooth as glass, perfect, made so by Grandpa's hand. Couldn't his dad see what he'd be selling? They would never find a house like this in town, not one where stories hid in every corner, on every step, behind every door.

Tears pricked his eyes. He wiped them on the back of his sleeve. Mom said, "grief takes time," but how much time? Why couldn't Fergus have hung around for another year at least? Fergus would have made it kind of bearable. Grandpa doted on his Irish wolfhound for twelve strong years, two years beyond the expected lifespan. It was a double whammy, for sure.

Scrubbing his hands over his face, he shook his head. It was time on his own that did this, gave him time to think of all he'd lost. If he could only get past the grief.

Dr. MacMurray said it was normal to be distracted and unable to focus, but that didn't stop his grades from suffering, or his violin practice, or his soccer game. He wiped his nose and scanned the tabletop. Where'd he put the stress ball?

A package with his grandpa's test strips sat on the buffet. Diabetes. That word ate at him. He had fussed and fumed at the hospital as Grandpa disappeared before his eyes. He'd been helpless to do anything.

"Diabetes runs in the family," Grandpa had said. "Fine one day, in the hospital the next, just like my old man."

Hospice. Josh winced. Why couldn't he turn off this loop that wound through his brain over and over? He'd be a doctor one day, and then he'd find a cure. But who would do his homework in the meantime? He scooped up the precalculus papers and forced himself to pick up a pencil.

He stared at the problem on the sheet, but his mind wouldn't focus. If they moved, where would Dad keep all his equipment? This farm was perfect. Everything had its place.

He crossed his arms, his thoughts drifting to summer evenings on the front porch, watching for bats flitting in the dusk. Grandpa would ask about soccer as the chickens clucked on their way to roost. Maybe that was why his dad wanted to sell. Grandpa was everywhere.

He set the pencil on the stack of precalculus homework and picked up his violin. He drew the bow over the strings. Somber notes drifted through the living room, like some fluent and soothing language, calming him. As he played, the birds would sing along, but where were the birds today? He drew the sheers back to reveal a row of steel gray clouds to the southwest. Was that why? The sky was still blue over the farm. Was that the storm Dad had predicted? It looked like a billowing black wall rushing toward them, and all the NOAA reports said it was supposed to be a big one.

Mom raced down the driveway, dust billowing behind her car. The branches on the giant maple by the barn swayed in the light breeze, and golden leaves floated to the ground. The fir trees swayed in the distance, and the dark clouds raced toward the farm across the November sky. The apple tree creaked in the wind. Another reason to stay, the applesauce.

Mom skidded to a stop and hopped out of her car, dragging her book bag with her. She clomped up the front steps and burst through the front door.

"Pretty spectacular, right?" She nodded toward the clouds, setting her bag on the dining room table.

"How's Dad? Is he ready for his big speech?"

Dad loved a good storm. He studied irregular weather patterns, and monster storms were his specialty.

"Almost ready. He's the keynote, first thing in the morning this time. I have to make a couple of quick revisions, and he'll be all set." She ran her fingers through her curls. "This storm couldn't come at a better time. Maybe this will convince the doubters of changing weather patterns, right?" She gave him a shrug.

He nodded stuffing his hands in his pockets. Dad's team at Vandby U had predicted a storm phenomenon originating in the Pacific Ocean. El Primo was all he talked about. "This storm pattern will come in a series of storms. They'll hit the West Coast with such intensity they'll wash out roads, topple trees, and destroy power grids and infrastructure." He'd grinned. "You know, the usual monster storm stuff."

"Good thing we're solar powered." Josh leaned against the table.

"Another thing to thank your grandpa for. He believed in his son, but he also believed in self-sufficiency and a well-stocked root cellar." She shot him a quick glance.

Since the funeral, she'd avoided mentioning anything to do with Grandpa. Josh gave her a shrug.

"Did Dad say anything about this storm?"

"He agreed with the NOAA forecast. This one will be a whopper. A little help?" She jogged back to her car, and he followed. She must have broken every speed limit on her way home. Dad always did this to her, last minute changes, but mom let him do it. She'd work through the night if she had to.

His belly grumbled. He'd heat a can of soup for dinner. She stopped, and he bumped into her.

"Sorry," she mumbled, staring at the sky.

Was she having trouble focusing too? "No. It was me." He turned his attention to the clouds stacked into a thick mass that seemed to press down on the barn and house.

She sucked a whistle of air between her teeth. "This storm is moving fast." She bent into the car and snatched her briefcase from the front seat.

He glanced at the skyline, and his neck tensed. The black mass seemed to boil as it moved across the sky. He lifted a box of books from the backseat and followed her to the house.

The sky started to rumble. He struggled against a sudden gust of wind, the heavy box making him top-heavy. The for-sale sign banged in a frenzied rhythm, and lightning flashed across the sky. Thunder boomed, vibrating the air.

"Less than a second." He took the porch steps two at a time. "It's right over us."

A gust of wind pushed him through the front door, and his homework blew off the table. The scent of fir trees filled the air. He dropped the box on the dining table and grabbed at his homework as it flew in all directions. The last thing he needed was another zero in pre-calc.

Thumps on the roof startled him. Branches and pinecones hit the house as though blasted from a bazooka. This storm was moving fast.

Mom handed him a roll of tape. "Windows, quick."

Her phone rang from inside her purse. "Ed? Ed?" She held her phone away from her ear. "Stupid phone." She slipped it back into her purse, her brows furrowed. "He'll call back, right?" She stared at the fireplace, her blank eyes sending a chill down his spine.

"Is this El Primo? Is that why he called?" He waited for her to answer, but she didn't, and he couldn't read her face.

Another gust hit the house, shaking the windows and doors. He lifted a curtain in the dining room. She rushed to his side, scanning the sky. He had the urge to put an arm around her bent shoulders but didn't. A cold shiver tingled from the back of his head down his spine.

Chapter Two

Emma

A typical Saturday at the Tate house, yelling optional, slamming doors required. Why did Mom have to freak out every time a storm rolled through Vandby?

Emma slid her bedroom window open. Her hands shook. With the steady movements she'd learned in gymnastics, she climbed onto the porch roof and sat on the edge, rolled onto her belly, and stretched her foot over the edge until it reached the trellis.

Hand over hand, she climbed down, jumping the final three feet. She jogged to the corner and glanced back at her house. She loped around the corner to the bus stop. She had to catch this bus. If she didn't, she'd get caught, and mom would never trust her again, and she'd miss the march. She faltered a step, glanced one last time at the house, and drew her phone from her pocket.

No bars? "Hm." She slid it into her back pocket. She could use Megan's support right about now. Anything to drown out her mom's voice in her head.

"What happens if you get stuck downtown, Emma? How will you survive? Who will you trust?" Mom was like a broken record.

No trust, that woman. What was the big deal? She was fighting for the planet, doing this for Dad. Stupid storms. Stupid car crashes.

She glanced down the street for the bus. It rounded the corner. The 102 to Vandby/Founders Square screeched to a stop in front of her. She covered her ears. Geez. Get a brake job, bud. The doors swished open, and she climbed aboard.

Four passengers? That was odd for a Saturday afternoon. She plopped in her usual seat. The bus radio sputtered unintelligible static. A guy with a leather satchel sat toward the front, his knee bouncing up and down. He must be running late.

The radio volume squawked louder, and she gritted her teeth. Was he deaf? The bus driver slowed the bus.

"High winds expected. All buses, finish routes and return to bus barn. Repeat. Finish routes—"

"10-4 dispatch. 102 out."

"Wait. Does that mean I'll have to walk home from downtown?" The guy clutched his bag, no longer tapping his feet. The driver pressed his lips into a thin line and nodded.

She'd have to walk home too. She glanced at the blue sky filling with dark clouds. This wouldn't be a walk in the park.

The bus stopped at 10th and Main, and the doors whooshed open. She rose and followed a mom and her toddler son off the bus.

She stepped onto the curb and jogged across the street. The First Bank sign flashed:

Vandby, Washington
1:16 pm
Saturday
November 9
Storm Alert — High winds

Clouds sailed overhead so low they seemed to brush the tops of buildings. *That's not right. This must be Mom's storm.* The angular lines of the bank building seemed so out of place next to the squat, old brick and stone buildings of Founders Square. Dad had been the lawyer who fought against building the high rises, yet there they stood. Emma clenched her fists. First the environment, then city hall.

Why couldn't Mom understand? This was for Dad. The storm, the car crash, weren't they reason enough to march? Someone had to save the environment, right? Then what was that throb at her temples? Guilt?

Note to self: No more lies—after today. She'd show Mom.

She held her phone. If she hurried, she might just make it on time. She glanced at the screen, no service. "Still?" She shoved it in her back pocket and sprinted down the street. The protest started at 1:30. Where was everyone?

Her phone vibrated. Megan, at last. She stopped and read the text.

Protest canceled

"What? No." They couldn't cancel the protest.

but im here

A gust of wind whipped her hair into her eyes. It stung, and her eyes watered.

Idiot big storm coming

Idiot? What the—

She tapped her response, hit send, and waited. She gripped her silent phone. No bars and a dead battery? Note to self: upgrade friend and phone.

She scrambled for balance as another gust hit her, pushing her against a building. She leaned into the wind

9

and took several steps. Wow. These winds were intense.

Squaring her shoulders, she adjusted her backpack. She had to do something. She only had two blocks to go, and she'd be at Founders Square. Should she risk it?

Mom could not be right this time. There would be someone at the protest, and she'd be there to hand out flyers.

Gritting her teeth, she pressed on. There'd be another bus, and she'd be home before Mom even noticed she was gone. The wind picked up, and her knees buckled. It whistled over her, around her, through her thin hoodie. She glanced at the sky churning with dark clouds. When had they turned black?

Her phone vibrated, and she checked her phone. Bars. Finally.

get inside quick
Ill catch next bus

She hit send but her battery icon was red. Why did she always forget to charge her phone? Another gust of wind bumped her into a wall.

A woman struggled down the street wrestling with her umbrella. She didn't even glance at Emma, and from her high heels and tight skirt, Emma knew she wasn't headed to the protest.

Another blast of wind hit her, and she stumbled into the wall. Her hands flew out for balance, and her phone sailed from her fingers and across the sidewalk. It landed next to the curb in the street. Pushing against the gust, she fell to her knees and scrambled to grab it. A taxi screeched to the curb, right over her phone.

No.

The wind kicked up particles of dirt and grit,

stinging her cheeks. The force of it took her breath away, whipping hair out of her ponytail. She clung to the edge of the curb and tried to stand against the wind, but it forced her to her knees.

She searched under the taxi where her phone should be. The driver leapt out, leaving his door open. Over the roar of the wind, his radio squawked: "All drivers, park immediately, seek shelter. This is not a drill."

"Where's your mom, kid?" The driver's words hit her like a slap. He skirted around her and into a building. She sat stunned. Wasn't he supposed to help her? She was just a kid.

The air was heavy and damp. She opened her mouth wide to pop her ears, pushed herself to a crouch. Megan was right. She needed to get inside. The taxi driver had disappeared through double glass doors, but what about her phone? A fat raindrop hit her forehead and rolled down her nose. Rain, really? She swiped at it.

A glint from something under the taxi made her reach under the cab. She wrapped her fingers around her dripping phone.

"Yes." She held it to her face. "Oh no." The screen was cracked in two. "No." She slipped it into her pocket and struggled to her feet. The wind caught her and pushed her beyond the doors the taxi driver had disappeared through. It pushed her into Founders Square. Large raindrops pelted the top of her head, and she scanned the brick buildings for an alcove, some sort of shelter.

"Help!" The wind drowned out her voice and blew the rain sideways. The next gust swept her book bag off her shoulder. She clutched it to her chest, but the zipper had opened, and flyers scattered across the square.

She rushed toward a building and yanked on a door handle. Her wet hair slapped against her face. Locked? Was this a joke? She pounded on the glass. "Help, someone, anyone!"

The wind howled, and the rain pelted her like bee stings.

A sliver of light cut across a marble lobby floor. Emma pressed her nose against the gold lettering on the glass. A woman raced across the lobby. She unlocked the heavy wood door, and it flew open, hitting Emma's shoulder. Emma flew back, and the woman's mouth dropped open, her eyes round. Everything happened in slow motion. Another gust of wind knocked her against the front window, unbalanced her, and she rolled along the slick sidewalk like an empty paper cup.

"Oh my God." The woman's voice faded into the roar of the wind.

Emma grasped at the smooth granite foundation stones, the wind whistling down the city street. Her hip, elbow, wrist banged the sidewalk, the wall, the light pole. Her vision blurred. She reached an alley and grasped the corner of the building. A side wind caught her, and she tumbled on.

"Help!" She screamed, skidding out into the road.

Rain pelted her body, and her clothes and her hair clung to her. She dug in her heels, but nothing could stop her.

"No, no—no." Emma tumbled down the sidewalk until down became up and a loud crack burst in her ears.

Chapter Three

Josh

Mom stood at the window. Her gaze was frozen on the clouds bunching over the farm. He could read her mind but couldn't assure her that Dad was safe. Josh reached his hand out to her but let it drop at his side. He had to try.

"Dad will be safe at the conference." He kept his voice soft and steady. If Dad were here, she'd be bossing him around, not fretting like this. She nodded, put her hand to her lips, dropped it to her side. She reached out to button his shirt, and he took her hands in his. Her eyes met his, her face a blank. Did she even know he was there? She wasn't telling him something, but what?

"Right. Sure, he will." She buttoned her own sweater with trembling fingers. "You're just like him, calm in the midst of chaos." She pressed her fingers to the side of his face, her lips in a thin grin.

"Mom." How would he stop the panic brewing behind her eyes?

"It's just… Why did he have to ride his bike?" Her voice trailed off, and her face lost its color.

"It was a perfect second-summer morning, as Grandpa would say." Josh shrugged. "He did mention this would probably be his last ride of the year, if that helps?"

"It doesn't." She wiped her nose on her sleeve. "If he makes it back, he's going to get a piece of my mind. This *will* be his last ride." Color returned to her cheeks as she shook her fist.

And she's back. Parents.

Dad always said, "Our love was written in the stars." Their connection baffled him, but what did he know? He'd never even dated.

He combed his fingers through his hair. "Grandpa's emergency plan is bulletproof, right?"

"Sure. I mean, yeah." She turned to him and smiled. "Let's batten the hatches. I left all the kitchen windows open. It was a pretty great day."

He watched her back disappear down the hall then hurried to a living room window, checked the barn, a haunting silhouette against the dark stew of storm clouds.

The hair on his arms stood on end. Lightning would strike and soon. Humidity had swollen the wooden sash windows, and he grunted as he tugged. The window shut with a bang.

He turned the lock. "Ow." He jerked his fingers back, stung by the static. Branches pelted the roof, and pinecones pinged against the gutters.

"Hurry," Mom called.

She slammed the dining room window shut and latched it, then dashed to the den. He closed the windows lining the front of the living room. His great grandmother had wanted a light-filled house, but today they seemed extravagant and dangerous.

He raced up the stairs to his bedroom. Four bedrooms meant four windows, four too many. The wind howled. He spun around his room. Maps on the wall, laptop on the desk, twin bed that he'd outgrown three years ago.

"If this gets any worse, we're heading to the basement." Mom's muffled voice came from a back bedroom.

Would it get that bad? His mind raced through the list of things his grandpa and dad would do if they were here: prep the generator, check the solar panels, connect the well pump for running water. Grandpa always stacked firewood to get them through the winter, and food and water to survive for month. They would be fine, and he could take care of everything, but he'd never had to do it alone.

He picked up the dirty clothes he'd left where they fell around the room. Mom had asked him four days ago to bring his laundry down. He kicked his clothes into a pile in the middle of the room. The winds roared outside, and mom appeared at his door, her pinched lips and hollow eyes unsettling him. She didn't glance at the dirty clothes.

"This has to be El Primo." He shouted over the winds.

"No. It can't be." She shook her head but raised her fingers to touch her lips.

"Dad will stay in Vandby now, for sure." He clapped a hand over his mouth. Too late to stop those words. Mom's haunted expression left him kicking himself.

"This was supposed to be the conference that changed everything. Are we already too late?" She raked her hands through her hair and paced in a circle. "Climate experts, government representatives from around the globe, even the vice president is slated to attend and hear Dad's lecture. El Primo is the main event."

Was that what was raging outside right now? Was this dad's storm? "No one can predict the future," Grandpa had always said. But his dad was trying, in the hope of saving lives and the planet.

Josh's temples throbbed, and he massaged the wrinkles on his forehead. Why would El Primo hit now with Dad gone? Mom struggled to maintain a blank face, but her jaw clenched and unclenched. The winds blew stronger as she ran into the spare bedroom. His shoulders tied in a knot.

He lifted his phone from his back pocket and sent a message to his dad, but it failed to send. He hit retry three times, but no luck. He slipped the phone in his pocket.

A crack like a gunshot rang through the house, then a thump shook the walls. He raced to his window. A Douglas fir lay sprawled across the front yard, missing his bedroom by only a couple of feet. In the distance, the silhouettes of trees waved like tall grass in the high winds. Then another crack split the air. Another tree hit the ground, then another. They left a view of the sky and a dark swarm of clouds.

He opened the window, sliding the screen out of its track, but the wind tore the screen from his hands and flung it into the gathering darkness.

"Whoa." The force of the wind took his breath away.

"What are you doing?" Mom appeared in his room. "Close your window and help me."

He slammed the window, his heart pounding in his

chest. This was bad—very bad. He joined Mom on the landing and waited for her scold. She grasped his hand, and she pulled him down the stairs into the living room.

The wind whistled through cracks he didn't know existed, and the walls shuddered. He grabbed his violin, threw it in its case, and slid it under the window seat. Another tree fell, and the whole house shook with a loud boom. A large branch crashed through a living room window, and he stepped back, bumping into a bookcase. The tart scent of fir blew in with the wind. Shards of glass sprinkled across the floor.

"My God." He stared at the chaos.

"Come on." She ran to the dining room table.

"I'll take the papers. You get the books."

He lifted the box, clutching it to his chest. Another crash and the crackle of breaking branches joined the roar of the wind. The lights flickered, dimmed, and then popped out.

"Mom."

A loud screech filled the air. No. Not the solar panels.

"Basement. Hurry."

He could barely make out her words. The near-deafening winds muffled her voice and seemed to bombard the house with more debris than air. The complete darkness disoriented him. He collided with her, and the box flew from his arms. The rustle of books and papers flying followed.

"Oh no. His lecture. Quick." She climbed to her feet, gathering what papers she could reach in the dark.

He scrambled to throw books back in the box, but it seemed hopeless. There were so many, and it was so dark. His mind raced. The wind thundered.

"Let's go." She clutched Dad's lecture notes to her chest.

They dashed to the basement door. Holding the box in one arm, he tugged it open. The house groaned as though it would fly off its foundation, and the cracks and thumps of more trees falling to the ground filled the air. His head spun.

His mom stopped at the top of the stairs and turned to the dining room. What could she see through the darkness? The wind blew through the broken windows and whipped hair into his eyes.

"This is off the scale." She froze at the top of the stairs. "Your father—"

What was she waiting for? "Go!" He yelled over the howling winds.

She dashed down the stairs. He followed, slamming the door behind him. He grabbed a rechargeable flashlight from the wall, the box balanced on his hip threatening to fall again. The storm noise grew quieter with the door shut, and he could hear himself think.

He switched on the flashlight. Mom shrieked and disappeared out of the beam of light into the darkness, papers, like ghosts, flying.

He directed the light to the bottom of the stairs, but the figure sprawled on the floor made no sense to him. His eyes adjusted, and he could make out his mother's form. She groaned, and he flew down the steps, the box weightless under his arms. She didn't move.

He dropped the box and panned the light over her arms and legs but stopped on her left arm. It was bent, but not at the elbow.

Chapter Four

Emma

Emma woke, a metallic taste in her mouth, and tried to sit. Someone pressed down on her chest. She pushed against the hands, but they pressed harder. She opened her eyes. Grit scratched them, and she clamped them shut, pushing at the hands.

Where was she? How did she get here? Flashes of a woman's face, the sidewalk, her backpack. The march?

A roaring filled her ears. It came from above. Was she underground? She stopped slapping, and the hands stopped pushing. Someone was talking to her, but the voice was tinny and distorted. Was this a dream? The hands seemed real enough.

"Where—" she mumbled. She lifted her head, and a shock of pain surged through her skull. She fell back. "Ow," she moaned. Note to self: No sudden moves.

"Be still," a voice said, clearer now.

"Who are you?" She squinted and saw candlelight, pressed her lids closed again. More images crashed through her brain, the sidewalk, the wind, her phone.

She dropped back on the pillow. Through a blur of tears, she eased them open, could make out a woman's form sitting next to her on a couch. She had muscular arms and something dangling from her lips, a pen?

19

Was this her rescuer? A rescuer wouldn't hurt her, right?

Another woman mumbled something—two of them? Great. Her eyes watered, and she kept her lids closed. Tears would wash the grit out. She dabbed at her lashes with her fingertips. "Ugh."

"See. She's not dead."

"Dead?" She sat and cracked her eyes open. Another woman stood in the shadows beyond a candle that flickered on a kitchen table.

"Fine. She's not dead. Are you happy now?"

Did she detect a Southern drawl?

The woman ran her fingers over a faded scar that ran from her shoulder to her elbow. Star and swirl tattoos surrounded the scar.

"I told you she was tough. Just like us." As she spoke, the pen bobbed between her assailant's teeth.

"Lilli, you're a bleeding heart. Anyone ever tell you that?"

Lilli? The one with the pen was Lilli.

"I'm with you, aren't I?" The woman in the shadows took her hand from the tattoo and shoved it in her pocket.

"Mmhmm." Lilli held out her hand.

Emma blinked and wiped her eyes with her sleeve. Her vision cleared. A set of stairs rose into the darkness on the other side of the candle-lit room. Was that the only way in and out? She lay on a tattered, brown couch, the aroma of lavender and cigarette smoke rising from the fabric.

"Okay. I owe you fifty bucks." The woman pulled out some bills and handed them to Lilli.

Emma stared then looked away, heat rising to her

face. The lace-like design of her scar blended with her tattoo, making it look like the Milky Way.

"Thanks, Jade, honey." Lilli pocketed the money. She placed her hand on Emma's back, and Emma didn't resist, shifting her gaze from Jade's scar to Lilli's pen.

The couch was pushed against a rough brick wall. Founders Square, she was close to where the protest was supposed to be.

"What happened?" Emma tightened her ponytail and smoothed her loose hairs against her head.

"Try 911 again, Jade." Lilli stood all of five feet tall, four inches shorter than Emma, but she had the voice of a drill sergeant.

"No bars." Jade put her phone in her back pocket.

"Hmm." Lilli slipped the pen out of her mouth, balancing it between her fingers like a cigarette. "Trying to quit." She grinned at Emma and wiggled the pen.

Her hair, shaved at the back and around her ears, spiked on top with short bangs parted on one side, a cut Emma coveted, but not Mom.

The candle on the table filled the air with a musky scent. Vanilla? The light kept the shadows at bay. Emma counted the tattoos covering Lilli's arms, across her chest, and up her neck: hearts, diamonds, swirls. She stopped at the one on her chest, *"J'aime…"* She turned away and cleared her throat. Lilli loved something.

She glanced at Jade, whose long braid hung down her back, her fingers tracing the scar on her arm again. Was she nervous? Emma glanced down at her own damp, stained, skinny jeans and torn T-shirt. At least Jade's plaid shirt over loose jeans and black combat boots were clean.

Emma tried not to stare at Jade's other tattoos, the sunburst rising from her chest to her throat. "So, you saved me from the storm?"

Jade tensed. Tall and lanky, like Mom, but Jade stood with her shoulders rolled forward as if trying to make herself small. Lilli stood ramrod straight, hands on hips, like Mom when she wanted answers.

"Who are you guys?" Emma tried again, her lips slow and thick.

"First of all, we're not guys. This is my partner, Jade, and I'm Lilli." She motioned to Emma. "And you are…?"

"Emma." She shook Lilli's hand. Why had Lilli corrected her? Of course, they weren't guys. Her belly cramped. "I don't feel so good." She held her abdomen.

"Concussion." Lilli picked up a wastebasket from beside the fridge. "I told you. If I hadn't gone out to get her, she'd be in the river by now."

Lilli placed the basket in front of Emma. She stared at it, not wanting to use it, but her tummy rolled. She spewed her lunch into it. A sheen of sweat emerged on her upper lip and forehead. Dizziness left her weak, and tears trickled down her cheeks. With a ragged sigh, she fell back against the couch.

This was not good. Note to self: No sudden moves.

Lilli stuck the pen in her mouth and chewed. Jade's fingers moved up and down her scar. Both women seemed unsure of what to do now that she was awake.

She pushed loose strands of hair from her face. "What's happening outside?"

"Oh, honey, only the storm of the century, after

Katrina that is." Jade's accent grew stronger, and she cradled her scarred arm.

"And it's not over yet." Lilli pointed at a window set high on the wall. It reflected the glowing light from the candle, and outside a plastic bag whizzed past, then a paper cup. The wind shook the glass in the frame.

She glanced to the kitchen cabinets that stood open, revealing cans of soup and pasta boxes. A door at the end of the cabinets revealed a toilet—a bathroom. Good, she'd need one, soon.

"I heard some scientist guy over at Vandby U talking about this new monster-storm thing," Lilli said. "It was on the news, just before the power went out."

"Monster-storm? Was it Dr. Woolf?" Emma wiped her fingers over her forehead, winced when they met the bump. She jerked her hand away. Blood stained her fingers. She scanned the room and stopped on a kitchen table and chairs, moved to the bed behind a beaded curtain, the TV on a stand in front of the couch—all the comforts of home, where she should be right now.

"Just sit back. You hit your head pretty hard," Jade said.

"I heard it crack."

"Lilli, shush now." Jade put her hand up to stop whatever Lilli was going to say next, but Lilli ignored her.

"We didn't know if you'd make it. You slept fo—"
Jade took Lilli's hand. "You're scaring her."

Emma raised her hand to her chest.

"Sorry. You'll be fine, kid. We were worried was all." Lilli swung Jade's hand.

Emma was not fine. What weren't they telling her? Had her mom noticed she was gone yet? Her scalp tingled. If she could only get to her backpack, she could make her escape, but the storm raged outside in full force, so leaving wasn't an option.

"Where is this?"

Lilli cleared her throat. "You're in our shop, the Little Shoppe of Colours. Get it? Like Little Shop of Horrors, only colors has the British spelling with 'ou.' "

"No one gets that, Lilli, seriously." Jade held a cloth under the faucet and dabbed Emma's forehead. "Our shop is on 10th near Founders Square."

Jade's lips curled up in a grin, evidence of her pride. Emma's Aunt Beth owned an antique shop, which she talked about nonstop. Emma always avoided her aunt, but with Jade, talking about her shop didn't seem like boasting. It obviously meant everything to her.

"We were open late, of course." Jade's voice shifted to monotone, like she was reciting a dream or something that happened to someone else. "Almost had to tie Old Freddie to a chair because of the storm."

"Couldn't keep Freddie, though. He hopped on his motorcycle and sped off. I watched him until he sped around the corner. That's when you blew across the street, just like a rag doll."

Emma shuddered, pushing that vision her from her mind. Would they ever stop talking?

"Man, you were flying—weird, right? I mean, a hurricane in Vandby? So, I ran out and picked you up." Lilli chewed her pen.

"She's the big hero." Jade sniffed. She placed her hand over her scar, which up close resembled a map of Italy. "She ran out before I could stop her. We carried you into the cellar, and here you are."

Breaking glass crashed above the roar of the storm. Emma gripped the blanket.

"I got you on the couch just before the lights went out."

"You got lucky this time, Lilli."

Emma glanced from one to the other. She clutched her abdomen.

Jade's forehead creased. Lilli chewed her pen.

"Thanks?" Emma wasn't sure how to respond. Her throat tightened. They looked tough and wild, but they'd rescued her, saved her life. The window rattled. A hamburger wrapper flew by, and she cringed. She was stuck here until the storm was over.

"You need tea." Lilli leapt up and darted to the kitchen.

"She needs a doctor, brave-heart," Jade said.

"What?" Emma leaned forward, her head in her hands. "I'm sitting right here."

"Right." Lilli walked toward the stairs, raising her phone to get reception. "Still no signal."

"The cell towers are out, and with no power, no tea."

Emma lay back. Was she invisible, or were they deaf?

"The thermos has hot water. Where is it?"

"Upstairs, but ya ain't going up until the storm's over. Now chill."

"I don't want anything, really." Emma's head pounded, and she could barely follow their conversation. Her fingers hit a lump the size of a golf ball on her forehead. "Oh man. Mom is going to kill me."

"Wait until the black eye sets in." Lilli grinned at

her.

Emma moaned and swung her legs off the couch.

"Do you want to pass out again? Don't move."

Emma sobbed and clamped a hand over her mouth. Jade eased her back into the pillows. Emma couldn't look away, Jade's soft eyes warm, like Mom's.

She fought back her tears. Mom. Was she okay? Why hadn't she gotten Megan's text twenty minutes earlier? Why didn't she listen to Mom?

"We should put ice on that bump." Lilli opened an old mini fridge. There was no light. She rummaged through the little freezer section.

"Peas." Lilli held up a plastic bag.

"Peas?" Jade frowned.

"From our Paleo diet, remember? Here, this will help the swelling." Lilli placed the bag on Emma's lump.

"Mom uses peas, too." Emma shivered, and her stomach tied in a painful knot.

Lilli hauled a worn blanket out of a dresser drawer and draped it over Emma.

She drew the scratchy blanket to her chin, scrunching into a corner of the couch and let her heavy lids close. Why didn't she listen to mom? She could be home right now, not here with complete strangers. She curled up on the couch. The storm trapped her here, but once it was over, she was gone.

Note to self—

Quit saying note to self.

Chapter Five

Josh

Josh hovered over his mother's body, the blood pooling on the floor beside her bent arm. He couldn't move, let alone breathe. What did he do first? Think.

He checked her pulse as she lay sprawled on the floor. She had one. A gash in her forehead oozed blood. He stood rubbing his face with shaking hands.

He sank to his knees, eyes closed. "Calm. Focus." He ran his fingers over her right arm, her legs, and torso for other breaks or cuts, found a cut behind her left ear. Concussion and a broken arm were the big problems. He brushed his fingers down the bicep of her broken arm. She moaned as he reached the break. He froze, a boulder sized ache in his belly. He didn't want to hurt her, but this would hurt.

"Mom." He knelt by her side, but she didn't open her eyes. He gritted his teeth and lifted her sleeve to reveal jagged bone protruding through her skin and blood, lots of blood. His head swam, and he gulped air. He drew his phone from his back pocket. No bars? No 911.

No. No. No. No. It was fully charged. This couldn't be happening.

He scanned the floor for her phone, but she'd brought his father's papers, not her purse. He moved to the desk and picked up the landline Grandpa refused to disconnect. Silence. A chill settled in his chest. He was on his own, and mom needed more medical attention than he could give. His mind raced.

Think, compound fracture—what should he do?

He panned the flashlight around the dark basement, looking for an answer, revealing only dust and cobwebs. He pointed the light into the kitchen area over the cabinets and sink. He checked the worktable.

He needed a pillow to elevate her head, that would help. He lit on the overstuffed couch in front of the fireplace. He'd stabilize her arm, stop the bleeding, then move her to the couch.

His beam landed on a stack of wood by the fireplace. He'd start a fire, too, later. He shone the light into every corner of the basement. Bingo. He snatched a cushion from a chair and, lifting Mom's head, slid the cushion under her.

Now for her arm. He glanced at her sleeve stained red from wrist to elbow. These mistakes weren't supposed to happen. The plan was to start a fire, to stay warm and heat food cooked over the flames. He wasn't prepared for compound fractures. This wasn't part of the plan…

He sat back on his heels, shoulders slumped. His lack of medical training sank like a wedge in his chest.

He inhaled through his nostrils and exhaled. Calm. Focus. He knelt over mom and lifted her sleeve. The skin bulged where white bone broke through her skin. He closed his eyes and sank back on his heels. His gut churned.

He needed more light. He moved to a cabinet, found matches in a drawer, and lit a couple candles.

They illuminated the papers mom had dropped and a red cross hanging above the sink. Red cross.

The first aid kit, Uncle Carl's cheesy birthday gift, but Josh appreciated it now. It might not be 911, but the *Emergency Medical Manual* was priceless.

He opened the kit and took out the *EMM*, searched for "Compound Fractures" in the index, and flipped to page 230: "An injury where broken bone pierces the skin, causing risk of infection."

Infection? No. Please. He read the list:

"1. Stop bleeding."

He reached out and lifted the sleeve. The blood was coagulating. Coagulating was good.

"2. Splint the break. 3. Look for swelling."

Her hand wasn't swollen, which meant no blood vessel was broken. His neck muscles pinched, and he rolled his head from side to side to release his tension. Being a doctor was stressful, especially when he wasn't one.

"4. Call 911."

What? He turned the page. It said nothing about what to do if he couldn't call 911.

"Splint over the break."

He could do that, but what could he use? Grandpa's desk under the stairs.

Tugging open the drawer, he grabbed two wooden rulers. The length should work. They clattered in his hands. A moan came from the floor, and a sharp pain shot through the center of his gut.

He stepped over Mom, filled a large bowl at the kitchen sink. A moan came from the floor. Mom was grinding her teeth. He wiped his brow. This would hurt him as much as her.

He reached for a bottle of ibuprofen for inflammation and acetaminophen for pain. Should he give it before or after? He'd wait until she woke.

Scissors. He stuffed them in his back pocket and carried the pot of water to Mom. She moaned, and her eyes fluttered open. He elevated her head and fed her the pills with sips of water. She fell back on the cushion, and he lifted the fabric of her sleeve, cut it open with shaking hands revealing the full extent of the damage—the grotesque lump, the angle of the bone. He leaned back on his heels and rubbed his hands over his face as though that would wipe away the image.

So much blood.

Get a grip. He poured antiseptic over the wound on her arm. His mother's eyes rolled back in her head. He placed a towel under her arm and swabbed the wound with gauze, then more antiseptic, then more swabbing. She glared at him, her gaze boring into him. She hadn't spoken yet, and the silence left him hollow.

"It's broken." He returned her steady gaze. She nodded.

She pressed her eyelids shut. "I can't feel my fingers. Compound?"

"Yes." His voice cracked, and he cleared his throat. Did she know he couldn't reach 911? "I'll splint it, but the bones are exposed. I might have to set it if I can't get ahold of 911."

She frowned but nodded, clamping her jaw, her teeth showing. He took hold of her hand and her elbow, his shoulders tense.

"Is it a clean break?" she asked.

He couldn't answer. She remembered more from the first aid course they'd taken together than he did.

She understood what was happening, blood loss, bone fragments, shock, and infection.

"You are the calm in this chaos." Her voice hummed low and steady. "You can do this."

No, he couldn't do this, but he had to. "When the power comes back on, we can call for help." He crossed his fingers behind his back.

She eased back on the pillow. He swiped his brow with his sleeve, picked up the rulers, and placed them on her arm. The bones clicked, and she cursed under her breath. He winced and dropped the rulers. She never swore. Her arm started bleeding again. He poured more antiseptic over her arm and laid a gauze pad over the wound. Splinting could wait.

He wanted to comfort her. Instead, he held her arm as still as he could. She'd fallen unconscious again, and he almost joined her.

"Hang in there, Mom," he whispered.

The wind blasted through the rooms upstairs. Another window broke, but the crash didn't faze him. He opened the *EMM*, and reread page 234, Splinting.

Lifting the rulers, he placed them against her arm. He wrapped, and she winced, even unconscious. Why weren't his fingers ten inches longer? Why hadn't the power come back on yet?

She moaned again, and he fumbled the bandage. She opened her eyes and tried to smile through her clenched teeth.

"Sorry." He pressed his fists against his rolling belly.

"I know." Her eyelids slipped shut.

He pressed his hand over his mouth. Doctors didn't puke on their patients. He stared at the bandage in his other hand. If he didn't finish now, she'd only be in pain longer. He swallowed and continued wrapping.

He pressed the wrap on the end to fasten it then pushed himself onto weak legs. Mom tried to sit, but slumped back with a gasp, cradling her arm.

He dragged his finger down the index of the *EMM* for Head Injury. Page 126: "Call 911 if the person loses consciousness, even briefly."

Why did it always say, "call 911?" Wasn't there any useful information in this book?

He took the *EMM* out, laid it on the floor, and opened it. He read the list for head injuries.

Breathing— she was.

Pulse—strong and steady.

Bleeding—a towel.

He worked as fast as he could without applying too much pressure or bumping Mom's arm. For such a small cut, it bled a lot. She lay still, eyes closed, pulse regular. He, on the other hand, couldn't seem to get enough air.

"I'm going to get ice. Don't move."

"Really? No laps around the basement?"

Humor was good. He headed to the freezer, grabbed an ice pack, and carried it to her. With great care, he placed the pack on her head. The blood was starting to dry on the floor and in her clothes, drying on his hands and arms, Mom's blood.

She grimaced but let the ice pack rest on her head where he placed it.

"Mom?" The wind rumbled above them like a locomotive.

"I still can't feel my fingers." His mother's thin voice was barely audible over the storm. He leaned on the arm of the couch.

"Why was I in such a hurry? I panicked." She glanced around the room, books and papers still scattered at the foot of the stairs. "No electricity?"

"No. Does anything else hurt?"

"Just give me a day, and I'm sure everything will hurt, but for now, just this." She pushed the ice pack off and touched her fingers to the bump on her head.

"Ah." She reached up, and he grasped her hand and placed it in her lap. He shook out a wool blanket from the back couch and covered her. A bloodstain grew through the gauze on her forehead. She squeezed her eyes shut. He swallowed hard. Even in the dim glow from the candles, her face glowed white as her blouse. Shock, page 26.

"You need a real doctor, Mom."

"You're all I need." She gave him a nod, and the corners of her mouth lifted. "I guess I won't be arm wrestling anytime soon." She cradled her arm and shut her eyes.

She was putting him at ease, being Mom, but her words were exactly what he needed right now. "I want to get you onto the couch and elevate that arm." He calculated the distance of the couch to where she lay, ten feet

"Okay, but I don't feel so good."

Nausea. Concussion, page 131. He drew a scarf off the back of a chair and tied the corners to make a sling. He slipped it over his mother's head and, with steady movements, lifted her arm. He gripped her elbow to cause the least amount of pain. She lifted her arm a fraction.

"Agh." She hugged her arm to her chest, her breath

quick and shallow.

He jerked away, jiggling her arm. She ground her teeth and hissed air over her clenched teeth. She shot him a glare that startled him, but with her help, he slid her broken arm into the sling. Sweat beaded her forehead, her gray face pinched.

"Get me to the couch before I pass out or puke." She cradled her arm. "Or both."

He pushed to his feet and helped her sit. Her moan hung in the air between them. She got to one knee, panting, her teeth gnashing together. She nodded, and he placed her good arm over his shoulder.

Calm. Focus.

He shuffled her around the old kitchen chairs to the couch, half carrying, half guiding her to the couch. It was a hide-a-bed, but the bed would have to wait. She needed to lie down now. He eased her onto the cushions. She groaned.

"Okay?" he asked.

"Mm." Her thin face was grayer, but she no longer panted or ground her teeth.

"I'll mix some Rejuvelyte."

"I could use the electrolytes." She gripped the bicep of her broken arm.

He placed his hand on his abdomen. Was he calm in the midst of chaos, really? He glanced at the blood on her forehead, and his calm evaporated.

Tears glistened on her cheeks, and a frown drew her eyebrows together as the candlelight flickered. Josh glanced away, not sure what he should do. She worried about him, and he worried about her. What a pair. But if infection…?

He wiped his face with both hands and stood his

full six feet two inches. He wouldn't let that happen. They'd prepared for everything, food, water, shelter, everything, but not a compound fracture.

Where was Dad now? Stuck downtown at the conference, most likely. Dad had a plan for any emergency, and Josh did, too, but he'd never had to do it all alone. Mom lay on the couch, pale and still. He had to face facts. The longer the phone was out, the more likely infection became.

The wind howled outside. Could this be El Primo? Would it go on for days? He wanted to yell, but that wouldn't help. His other option was to crawl into a ball in front of the fireplace. That one might work, but right now Mom needed him. Focus.

He ran down the emergency list: start the generator, check the radio, keep the water pump running, start a fire. He knelt by the fireplace, wadded paper, and stacked kindling around it. The paper lit with one match, and the kindling began to snap. He added larger pieces of wood, and the room filled with light and grew warm. She seemed to doze, and his nerves settled. He poked the fire and laid another log on top.

"Cozy," Mom mumbled from the couch.

He spun around. "You're awake."

She managed a small grin. "Can't sleep. How are you doing? Any news on the radio?"

She would ask that. "No electricity, no radio." He combed his fingers through his hair. "No phone, no 911. I can't get to the generator until the storm dies down. I know how to do all this, but not without Dad. It's too much." Josh paced between the floor and the couch.

"You're doing fine. We're safe and warm and

there's light." She adjusted herself on the couch. "Think of Uncle Carl. He's probably up to his eyeballs in emergencies, running his ambulance."

Uncle Carl would know what to do. Would he come? Josh shoved his hands in his pockets. A loud crack split the air. In two steps, he was at the black window, peering into darkness. Lightning? A dull thump added to the blare of the wind.

"Must be a tree." He moved to his mother's side and adjusted the blanket over her small form. "That was close."

"Sounded like the old apple tree," she said.

"No." He stood and paced the floor. Not that tree, the one with the tire swing and crunchy, sweet apples in August.

"It'll be okay." Her teeth chattered.

Shock? He reached for the *EMM*.

Page 26: "Elevate the legs and feet slightly."

He put a cushion under her calves. She pressed back into the pillows.

"Your fa—" she mumbled.

"He's fine."

"But these winds are off the charts. He wouldn't have left us here if he'd known." Was she in so much pain she couldn't think straight?

What could Josh say to comfort her? Lie? Trees fell and winds blew through the house, leaving every muscle he had tensed and his concentration scattered. This was the worst storm he could remember. The hands on the clock above the sink pointed to 6:03 pm. She had fallen at 3:27, and the winds hadn't died down at all.

He adjusted the ice pack on her head. It was

thawing fast.

"How long does it take to walk from the U to Cedarville?" he asked.

She didn't reply. She lay so still he leaned in to check her pulse. She twitched but didn't open her eyes. No one had ever died from a compound fracture. It was the infection that killed them. She needed antibiotics—the real stuff, not antiseptic ointment.

She dozed, and he paced, his fingers itching for his violin. Why hadn't he grabbed it? Because he'd chosen his dad's books instead. He needed the motion of drawing the bow over the strings, the melody to fill the air with soft notes.

Gusts of wind blasted through the house in a steady rhythm, like waves hitting the shore. The steady roar lulled him into a memory. He and his dad had been in the barn repairing one of the weather stations. It brought heat to his cheeks. He should have paid closer attention.

"Dad?" He had loosened a screw but kept his dad in view to gage his expression as he worked. "About that new laptop. Mine can't even run the calculator for my precalculus class." He owned the calculator, but his laptop was eleven years old, and he wanted a new one.

Dad grunted and stood his full six feet three inches. "Use your brain."

"Brain?" He bit his lip. Too late.

"You know. That gray matter that sits between your ears. Use it or lose it." He pounded on a metal leg in a vise, inspected it, and blew off metal chips. "Besides you need to practice working out those problems on paper for later when you're in the field. Pens don't use electricity." His dad screwed a bracket onto the metal leg, avoiding eye contact. The conversation was over.

But Josh couldn't let the argument drop. "Dad—"

"Look, when the electricity goes out, what will you do then?"

"But the electricity always comes back on."

"When El Primo hits, monster storms will come one after another. We won't be able to repair the damage and restore the electricity fast enough. It will take months, maybe years, to recover and rebuild."

Dad turned back to his weather station, and Josh didn't get the new laptop, not until Christmas.

Now the electricity was out, and if this was El Primo, he could only guess for how long. They'd rely on the solar panels if he could even repair the circuit. At least his grandpa had installed them in frames on the ground and not the roof. Grandpa had always believed in his son and prepared for the worst.

Josh stared into the flames in the fireplace. He'd have to keep the fire going, but when would he sleep? He glanced at the couch. The steady rise and fall of Mom's chest were a comfort as debris hit the walls and roof in constant thumps and bangs. He placed the back of his hand on his mother's forehead, and his belly tightened into a knot.

Fever, page 80.

Chapter Six

Emma

The storm tore through the streets of Vandby, but the cellar in the Little Shoppe of Colours was protected. Emma glared, unblinking, at Lilli.

"I told you, I don't want a tattoo." She slapped at Lilli's hand.

Lilli hopped back to avoid being hit and released Emma's sleeve, a grin splitting her elfin face.

"Not even a little butterfly right there on your shoulder?" Lilli leaned in and poked Emma. Her eyes flashed, and she stepped back again.

"No." Exhaustion hung on Emma like a weighted vest. She wanted to curl in a ball under the blankets and sleep until the storm was over, not spar with Lilli about tattoos.

Lilli chewed her pen, grinning. Emma needed a wall with a door between her and Lilli, a door to slam. She needed her room. What would Megan do?

Stand up to her, but Emma slumped against the pillows. "Where do you get your energy?"

"Welcome to my world, hon." Jade grinned. Her eyes followed Lilli's erratic dance around Emma.

"Not even a little flower here?" She poked Emma's ankle.

Emma pressed her lips together and shook her

head. She didn't want a butterfly or a flower. She wanted a dragon or a constellation of stars, like Lilli and Jade had. The ink marks seemed to whisper an ancient language of protection. She wanted to wear that protection, but Mom, hand on her hips and her flashing eyes, stopped her.

Dad had come home with a tattoo. What a disaster. It was a tiny compass on his ring finger.

"It's a compass, always pointing to you." He'd grinned and shrugged, twisting the ring he wore on a chain around his neck.

He said he couldn't wear his wedding band for two weeks. Mom's silence had cut through the air and etched that day in her memory.

She had slammed the door to their bedroom so hard it shook the window in Emma's room. The floorboard in the hall squeaked as he trudged down the hall. He made a bed on the couch and slept there two weeks.

No. Emma was in enough trouble without returning bruised and tattooed.

Lilli flopped on a chair, joining Jade at the kitchen table. "Your loss, hon."

Emma drew her cell phone from her pocket, caressed the cracked screen. "You are dead, my precious." She glanced at Jade, who raised her brows, a small grin on her lips.

Of course, she'd read Tolkien. Emma slipped the phone in her pocket, its bulk and Jade's grin a comfort.

"How long are we going to be stuck down here?" Emma raised her hand and pressed her temple to stop the ringing, but nothing seemed to work. Between the storm and her throbbing head, she would go crazy. She wanted hot cocoa not tea. Mom would make it without even asking.

The storm was still storming. Was this the climate change the flyers warned about? Emma sagged against the pillows. She'd failed before she even began. Was this Mother Nature's revenge?

She rubbed her eyes. Instead of marches, she should have been learning how to survive. If this was climate change, it sucked. She took her phone out again. She needed to let Mom know she was alive. She held the power button, but her phone didn't even flicker. She wanted to scream, to punch something. So much for getting home before mom noticed.

Lilli turned in her chair. "Not even a—"

"Leave her be, Lilli." Jade's frown could have stopped a bulldozer. She stood and hauled a blanket off the back of her chair and billowed it over Emma. "Sorry, hon. She's bored." Jade rolled her eyes. "She'll chew her own leg off if we don't get out of here soon."

"Well, I'm not going home with a tattoo because she's bored."

Lilli needed to back off. Emma glanced at her under half closed lids. Lilli acted like Brian, Megan's cousin, but he was only fifteen. Brian never missed a march and came up with the slogans. His deep voice carried over the heads of marchers, so he was asked to lead them.

Lilli was old, though. She was annoying and funny at the same time. Emma raised her fingers to the throbbing bump on her forehead. Why was she complaining? At least she was safe and inside, which was way better than lying unconscious in an alley behind the Save-a-Dollar.

Jade's fingers moved to her scar, searching the

length and width of the proud flesh. The storm rumbled outside, a white noise to their confinement, but it was having its effect on Jade. Emma wanted to take her hand and tell her everything would be fine. Instead, she sank deeper into the couch.

Lilli cleared her throat, as if Jade suddenly came into view. "So, is anyone keeping count of the days? I think today makes three."

"It has been seventy-five hours and thirty-three minutes." Jade glanced at her watch. "This is our third afternoon of storms."

"She's my numbers girl, that one," Lilli said. "Our bookkeeper, CPA, business manager, and marketing guru combined." Lilli winked at Jade who grinned and let her hands drop to her sides.

"If the Little Shoppe of Colours ain't open, it ain't making dough," Jade said. She raised an eyebrow at Lilli, clasping her hands in her lap.

"No one is making any dough, not even the bank." Lilli tipped back in her chair.

Crossing the room, Jade wrapped Lilli in a hug. Emma glanced away.

The space around Emma seemed to push into her, the room getting smaller and more confining. She bit her lip.

"Don't fret, hon. We have insurance to cover the damages and the loss of income."

They were losing their shop? They had their own problems, and still here she sat, on their couch, in their shop. How did she thank them for saving her?

Emma cleared her throat. "I guess I could get a little tattoo if you need the money?"

"No. Now look what you've done, Lil." Jade

perched on the edge of a recliner next to the couch. "You're a guest, not a customer. Lilli needs to mind her manners."

"I thought this was like a break room, or something, but you guys live here." Emma scanned the cellar, took in the couch and TV crammed in beside a small kitchen table and chairs, a bed with patchwork quilts behind a beaded curtain.

"Ha. Break room. Good one. We lost our apartment two months ago." Lilli perched on the arm of Jade's recliner.

"Wait. Listen." Lilli leaped from the recliner and stood at the foot of the stairs.

"What now?" Jade perched on the edge of the chair.

"You're right. It's quiet." Emma pushed the blanket off her legs, swung them to the floor. "The storm is over." Emma rose from the couch.

Lilli put a foot on the first stair, but Jade held her back. Lilli pushed Jade back and ran up the steps.

"Wait." Emma pressed her hand to her head to stop the dizzy spell and scrambled after Lilli up the stairs. Lilli pressed her ear to the door, and Emma joined her. She grabbed Lilli's arm as her vision blurred.

"It's over," Lilli whispered.

Emma pressed against Lilli who cracked the door. The sun burst through, hitting Emma's eyes.

"It's over." She blinked as her eyes watered adjusting to the brightness.

Could she finally go home? A bubble of laughter rose in her throat. She swallowed it down.

"It is over," Lilli said.

Emma squinted and followed Lilli into the shop.

The front window was shattered. Broken glass littered the floor. The racks of T-shirts and shelves of lotions and dragon figurines still stood, though.

"No, no, no." Jade's voice drifted up the stairs like a moan. The hair on the back of Emma's neck stood on end. Jade rushed up the steps.

"Bless the goddess." Lilli floated across the shop, the sun beckoning her.

"Lilli, no." The tremor in Jade's voice stopped Emma, but not Lilli.

Jade lunged for her, but Lilli slipped out the door into the street.

The door stood open, sun glinting off the golden lettering, Little Shoppe of Colours. Jade clung to the door frame, and Emma inched in beside her. Jade's whole body shook, and Emma stepped back. This was bad, but she wasn't sure why.

Lilli, arms spread eagle in the middle of the street, performed what appeared to be her victory dance. Jade's body had turned to stone.

A man approached Lilli. He pointed as though asking for directions. Lilli laughed and twirled, pointing toward Johnson Park on the next block. The man staggered off. Then more people appeared in the street. Emma took a step, but Jade clasped her by the shoulders. What was it that she saw that Emma didn't? Emma grabbed the doorframe as she swayed.

"I better sit down."

Jade helped her to a chair covered in black pleather next to the door. Did this mean she was a customer now? Emma sank into the chair.

"Lilli," Jade whispered, her voice hoarse. "Come back, hon. Oh my—she doesn't see it."

"What? What doesn't she see?" Emma lifted one of the blinds covering the window. Nothing that happened outside made sense. The people in the street came into sharp focus, but they seemed confused.

"Shhh." Jade held a finger to her lips without taking her eyes off Lilli. "Look at 'em."

"What's wrong with everyone?" Emma stared at the people. "They look—"

"Like zombies." Jade's eyes were glued to Lilli.

Emma's mom hated zombie movies, so they weren't allowed, but Megan's mom was addicted. Emma had seen *Zombie Revolution*, and *Triumph of the Zombies*. But these people were not extras in a movie. They did have the vacant stares, disheveled hair, and wrinkled clothes.

"People are running out of water and food. The looting starts now."

"What?" Nothing Jade said made sense. "But it's only been three days. You guys have food and water. Doesn't everybody?" Was this what the flyer meant about disaster preparedness?

The sign for 10th Street stood at the corner, the pole leaning like the Tower of Pisa.

"Lilli," Jade called, louder this time. "If she'd only think for a second."

Lilli's arms swung wide as she danced along 10th Street. She approached a woman who staggered as though she hadn't slept, showered, or eaten since the storm began. A scream tore through the air, startling Emma.

"Lilli?" Emma jolted forward, but Jade grasped her hoodie and hauled her back into the shop.

"What are you doing?" Emma spun to face Jade.

"We need to help her."

The woman in dirty clothes, the scream, Jade holding her back, none of it made sense.

"That wasn't Lilli. She never screams. She fights."

"We need to get her back, right?" Emma pressed the heel of her hand to her forehead. Why didn't Jade help her girlfriend or at least warn her? Jade gripped the scar on her arm.

"It's too late." Jade lowered the tattered blinds over the broken window with a shaking hand and peered through the slats, her eyes wide as she scanned the street.

A chill tingled down Emma's back like ice. She'd stayed with these women for three days, but Jade had never acted like this before. Broken glass crunched under Jade's boots, and Emma wanted to scream. She cleared her throat.

"I can't lose Lil." Jade's voice warbled as she peered through the blinds.

"She'll come back," Emma said.

Lilli had to come back, or Jade was going to…

What was Jade going to do? A cool breeze blew through the broken window, and Emma shivered. She put a hand on Jade's shoulder to steady herself as much as Jade, but Jade kept scanning the street with wild eyes.

Emma kept watch for Lilli, too, but saw only Zombie-like survivors. Was this "Maslow's hierarchy of needs" like her psych teacher talked about? People didn't have basic survival stuff, so they acted without thinking, going back to basic instincts, acting primal.

This was survival of the fittest. A river of blank-eyed people stumbled past the Little Shoppe of Colours, and Emma scanned the street for Lilli.

A woman with gray hair stooped to pick through a pile of debris then lurched toward the next pile as more and more people emerged from apartment buildings, condos, and shops. Maybe if she yelled, "Cut!" everyone in the street would stop this chaotic dance and start walking and talking like normal. What was normal anymore?

Three bristle-faced men pushed their way into the grocery store across the street. Its front window had shattered, and a young boy climbed out of it carrying a bag of rice or dried beans. He bumped into an old lady with a cane, who fell onto her hands and knees as he raced away without a backward glance.

Jade scratched her scar until it bled, and Emma slipped her fingers around Jade's, clasping them to her chest. Jade's hollow eyes met Emma's, and Emma hugged her as she gazed out at the street.

Jade gasped and reached out her hand, as though she could help the old woman, or stop a man from hitting a little girl with a broom handle and grabbing the loaf of bread she was clutching to her chest. Emma leaned against the window frame for support and rubbed her eyes, unable to wrap her head around the violence and brutality.

"Shouldn't people be helping one another? This is against the law." Emma's voice caught in her throat. She patted her fingers over her tangled ponytail. Did she look like them?

A boy her age emerged from the store, his arms filled with milk and bags of oranges. A woman followed behind him, cradling a case of bottled water. Two women with mops attacked a man with two carts of canned beans, carrots, and tuna.

Jade's finger shook as she pointed. A man lurched by, tears steaking his face, in his arms a small child, maybe three or four. The corners of his mouth drooped as he stumbled along 10th. Emma could not tear her gaze away from the child's curly blond hair bobbing with each step the man took.

"Is he… "

"Dead." Jade finished.

Emma couldn't draw air into her lungs. The man and child disappeared around the corner as Lilli staggered into the shop. She eased the door shut, and Jade wrapped her in a hug, rocking her.

"I swear to all the goddesses," Jade mumbled between kisses.

"Sorry. I didn't—"

"Think?" Jade held Lilli at arm's length. "Don't you ever do that to me again."

"I'm sorry, hon, but the cellar was stifling. I had to get outside, but I had no idea it would be so—people fighting over food—water."

Emma shuffled her feet while Jade embraced Lilli, patted her arms and legs for broken bones or wounds, then hugged her again.

"You're bleeding." Lilli's fingers stroked Jake's scar. Jade took her hand and kissed it.

Emma cleared her throat. If she could ignore the fact that she was invisible sometimes with Lilli and Jade, she'd survive.

"What happens now?" Emma glanced at the door as the voices outside grew louder.

"We have to leave this place," Jade said, her voice husky. She guided Lilli down the stairs and sat her on the bed behind the beaded curtain and plopped beside her. "This is our Michael, our Dorian, our Katrina."

Emma clung to the railing as she took one step at a time. "Our what? The hurricanes? Didn't they destroy cities? Kill people?" Tightness rose from her chest and into her throat, her mind racing. Jade wasn't helping. "We don't have hurricanes here."

"Category 5 hurricanes kill people. The ones who are left run out of food and water, then the looting begins, just like now."

"Is there any good news?"

"Sorry, Emma, but you have to understand. Jade was a kid in New Orleans when Katrina hit. She lost her mother and grandmother on that day." Lilli wrapped her arms around Jade, who stared into the dark corner as though trying to block out some vision she didn't want in her mind. "She got her scar when she was swept away in a flood of water."

"I was hoping to get away from hurricanes. That didn't work very well, did it?" Jade patted the bed beside her. Emma sat, and Jade put her arm around her, pulling her into a hug. Lilli leaned in on her other side, and Emma sat sandwiched between them.

The front door rattled.

Jade's body went taut. "Someone's testing the door to the shop."

A man's voice on the street said, "It's just a tattoo shop, stupid. No food in there."

"The front window is shattered." Lilli's eyes scanned Jade's face. "They could just climb through."

A loud bang echoed in the street, and Lilli hugged them into a tighter knot.

"Firecracker?" Emma asked.

"Gun," Lilli's voice dropped low, became monotone. "We have one too."

"We do?" Emma clutched her hands to her middle as bile rose in her throat.

"Yes." Jade yanked open a drawer in the nightstand and rustled through the drawer. Jade's shadowed face in the flickering candlelight gave Emma a start.

Lilli stood and brushed aside the beaded curtain to the sleeping alcove. She glanced up the stairs, her face as white as a ghost. Emma followed Lilli's gaze. The cellar door stood open.

"Lilli? You promised." Jade reached out but did not stand.

Lilli rushed to the top of the stairs and eased the cellar door shut. She locked it behind her and listened at the door.

Emma stood unsure which way to go, up the stairs or under the bed. Jade sat on the bed, clutching the revolver. Lilli tiptoed step by step until she reached the bottom. Emma's arms and legs tingled. Was this fight or flight or both?

Jade stood and pointed the gun at the door.

"They're climbing in."

Chapter Seven

Josh

Time dragged as the storm raged on, a constant roar. He was trapped in the basement with Mom, a fire snapping in the fireplace. It illuminated her sleeping form on the couch.

He climbed the steps one more time and put his ear to the door. If the storm would only stop, he could go outside and work off some energy. He'd tried running steps, but Mom woke and began a contestant stream of worry for Dad, the storm, Uncle Carl, everyone but herself. She'd dozed off finally, and Josh welcomed the silence.

He ran his fingers through his hair. This had to be El Primo. The wind had been blowing for hours. He climbed down the stairs, his nervous energy draining from his arms and legs like someone had let air out of a balloon.

He poked at the fire, and the flames grew. Brushing his hands on his jeans, he sat at the worktable to write. He found Dad's stock of Mead notebooks and opened one, cataloguing the conditions of the storm:

Two days of strong winds from the southwest. Barometer reading? Rainfall?

He needed to get to the barn and check Dad's equipment for those readings. Would Mom be okay?

Who was he kidding? She wouldn't let him step foot outside. Where was that stress ball?

Dad and Grandpa had prepared for this. He should be able to survive anything, solve any problem. He was registered for the amateur radio license exam next weekend.

"A day late, and a dollar short," as Grandpa said. The storm hit before he was ready, and since Mom's fall, he questioned every move he made. Mom's fretting didn't help, and his resolution to keep the farm safe seemed impossible.

Was Dad still at Vandby U? If anyone knew his way around a storm, Dad did. Josh needed to make his own way around this storm. He needed his own plan with the knowledge he possessed.

He jotted down his mom's symptoms:

Compound break. Could be bone fragments in wound. Sleeps most of the time. Pain makes her restless. No infection—yet.

The knot in his gut tightened. He rose and crossed the floor to the desk. Grandpa hadn't used it since Christmas two years ago. His Norwegian friend Hilmer wanted some airtime with Gramps. He flipped the switch on the ham radio, still nothing. The switch clicked, but there was no static, nothing. He jotted one last note:

No electricity, no phones, no 911.

He dropped into the upholstered chair by the couch, reached for the stress ball. It wasn't his violin, but it would have to do. He rolled it over his fingers and spun it around his thumb, sank back into the chair and watched Mom's abdomen rise and fall. She was alive. The candlelight shone on the waxen sheen across her forehead.

Warmth from the fire filled the basement. At least he'd done that right. He could boil water on the grate for tea and heat soup until he could start the generator and use the stove. What was he forgetting?

He set the ball down on the coffee table. He'd write one more entry. Crossing the room to the worktable, he sat and tapped the pen on the table. He gave himself a goal: write one positive thing. He chewed on the inside of his cheek then wrote:

Wind still howls. Maybe the for-sale sign blew away.

Josh snorted, and Mom moaned. Was she waking? If she didn't ask the same question about Dad all the time, he'd welcome her company. She sighed and rustled under the blanket.

He glared across the room at the radio, but staring at it wasn't going to make it work. Where was Dad, Uncle Carl, anyone?

He craved the sound of another voice.

He pushed back in his chair. "It's quiet." He clapped a hand over his mouth. His voice seemed to echo off the ceiling and walls. Mom slept on.

He moved to the stairs.

"Where do you think you're going?"

He spun around. She was wide awake and trying to sit, and her mom-superpowers were in full force. He rushed to her side and helped her, but she grimaced and flopped back against the pillows.

He knelt beside her, and she grabbed his arm.

"What are you thinking?" Her words slurred together.

Delirium from infection would be next.

Infection, page 236.

How could he get a message to Uncle Carl without the radio? Uncle Carl—the survivalist, the EMT driver, mom's older brother. He might have penicillin or something to fight her infection.

He could jog the three miles up Crooked Creek Road. He'd do it for Mom, but would she let him go? If she passed out again, he might have to. He needed a plan.

"Any word from Dad?" Shock was affecting her memory. She uttered those same words every time she woke.

He gritted his teeth. "No, so no radio either." He held a glass of water to her lips, and she sipped. He'd better mix a pitcher of Rejuvelyte and have it ready to go. Dehydration was the last thing she needed.

"Where is he?" She fiddled with the edge of the blanket.

Why couldn't she just relax? He stood and paced the floor. Why hadn't he thrown his violin on top of the books?

"He's waiting for the storm to break. Just like everyone else." He clenched his fists. "Sitting here doing nothing is driving me crazy." He turned his back to her. Why couldn't she just sleep?

"Try Zumba. I've got a DVD." She chuckled, which turned into a cough.

"Hmm." A sense of humor was good, right? "We have to get you to the hospital. It wasn't a clean break."

"We're not going anywhere in this storm." She rolled onto her right side, her lips twisting into a frown.

"This is the storm Dad predicted, isn't it?"

"It could be. He couldn't predict when it would hit,

though. We prepared food, water, generator." She stroked her arm above the break.

Could she read his mind? They weren't ready, no matter how much they'd prepared. Her dark eyes sought his.

He threw another log on the fire. It burned brighter than the candle.

"Ugh." He squeezed his eyes closed and opened them. What a mess, books everywhere, and Dad's papers scattered across the floor. He picked up some books, stacking them on the table.

"Let me blow out the candle, make it all disappear again." She chuckled.

He snorted, and soon they were both laughing, but his mother's laughter turned to sobs, and with her good hand, she lifted the blanket over her face.

He sat on the edge of the couch and put his arm around her. "We'll figure this out."

She leaned into him, heat radiating off her body.

Fever, page 80.

"We planned for this." She wiped her eyes. "The solar panels, the root cellar, the radio. But look at me. I'm useless, and I forgot Kleenex."

"Kleenex? That's your big worry?" He hugged her to him. "We can do this, Mom."

She placed her hand over his, a slight tremor in her fingers.

"Once the storm is over, I can start the generator and radio Uncle Carl. He'll have the meds you need in his truck."

She nodded. "Dad will be here by then, right?"

"Sure, he will." He tried to keep his voice steady. "Hey, you remembered paper towels. I'll bring you one in case you spring another leak." He grabbed the roll on the kitchen counter.

She smiled at him, and he placed it in her hand. Closing her eyes, she dabbed the tears.

He glanced away. She never cried.

A loud boom shook the house as another tree fell. She jerked. He turned to check the dark window. It reflected the room, and he cringed as winds whipped through the house upstairs. The crashes and thumps could be anything, his Gran's Danish plates, the crystal vase, pictures blown off the wall.

"We should get some sleep." He sank into the overstuffed chair next to the couch.

"Right," she said, her face pale, her voice soft.

Chapter Eight

Emma

Jade stood at the foot of the stairs the gun clutched in her hand.

"What are you doing?" Emma flipped the tip of her ponytail in her mouth. Her lips trembled. The candle on the table cast shadows on the wall, like this year's haunted house, but this was worse.

Jade jerked around, bumping into Lilli, who drew Jade into a hug, trapping both her arms. She somehow got the gun from Jade's hand. Glass crunched on the floor above them, and Jade stepped back, her hand flying to her scar. Using two hands, Lilli pointed the gun barrel at the cellar door.

"Not the cash register, Bubba." Lilli ground her words between clenched teeth.

Did whoever was up there have a gun too? Emma pulled her hood over her head.

Footsteps thudded across the floor in the shop. Every hair on Emma's arms stood on end. The shaking in her lips had moved to her hands, and she clamped her eyes shut to stop the spinning. She clung to the back of Jade's shirt. The man carrying the small, limp body looped through her mind like a horror film. She pressed her free hand against her middle.

"Not the ink cabinet." Lilli swung the gun across

the ceiling, following the sound of the footsteps.

A loud crash shook the walls. Jade raised her hands as if in prayer. "Not the dragon figurines."

Emma clamped her hand over her mouth to stop her scream. The footsteps clumped toward the door. A slam shook the beaded curtain. Emma sagged to the floor, her knees quaking. Lilli kept the revolver trained on the cellar door.

Jade placed her hand on Lilli's forearm. "They're gone, hon."

Lilli lowered the gun to her side and bent over her hands on her knees, her chest heaving as though she'd sprinted a mile. "Thank all the goddesses they're gone. I need a drink."

"I'm on it." Jade rustled through a cabinet and grabbed a bottle, like Grandpa's special Christmas whiskey. She lifted a glass from the cupboard and splashed amber liquid into it.

"How will that help?" Emma winced. The words were out of her mouth before she could stop them, and heat rose from her chest to her eyebrows. Why did she always ask the dumb question?

"Takes the edge off." Jade handed the glass to Lilli. "For clients who love tats but not needles so much."

Lilli took a sip and scrunched her eyes. "Yowzah."

Jade chuckled and rubbed Lilli's back. Emma shuffled from foot to foot. Lilli and Jade focused on each other, and she was invisible, once again.

"Here." Lilli handed the glass to Jade who finished it in one gulp.

"That'll cure what ails ya," Jade said, her voice husky. She glanced at Emma. "Sip?"

"What? No." Emma shook her head. Did they think

she was a nerd? She didn't care. She preferred nerd to this foreign world of tattoos and whiskey.

"We need a plan before I actually have to use this thing." Lilli waved the gun, and Emma ducked.

Lilli's actions grated on every nerve Emma had. She wanted to go home, not plan. Her vision blurred, and she swayed.

"It's been a long year, today," Jade said.

She led Emma to the couch. Emma plopped into the cushions, but sleep was the last thing on her mind. Why hadn't mom just locked her in her room? The fighting and looting in the streets, the gun in Lilli's hand, the curly headed child, is this what standing up for yourself got you? If so, she didn't want it. Who were Lilli and Jade, really?

****

Emma cracked her eyes open, but she wasn't in her bed. She pushed herself up and fell back, her head woozy. She was in the Little Shoppe of Colours. How did she fall asleep? Two figures sat at a table. Lilli and Jade, it was coming back to her. They must be making that plan Jade talked about. Emma yawned and rubbed her eyes.

"Wakey, wakey," Lilli said.

Emma put her ponytail into her mouth, then spit it out and folded her hands in her lap, unsure where to put them as Jade moved to the couch to sit next to her.

"The storm's over. I need to get home," she said.

"That's what…" Jade tilted her head, a frown forming on her smooth brow.

Emma didn't wait for Jade to finish. She pushed the blanket to the floor and marched to the steps. Jade reached for her, but she pushed her hand away.

"I'm going, and that's that."

"Emma, wait." Jade held her arm.

"No." Emma yanked away and ran up the stairs. She yanked the door open before Jade could stop her.

"Looters," Lilli hissed from the foot of the stairs.

Emma froze her hand on the cellar door. She dropped to the floor, putting a hand to her head. What had she done? The pounding in her head caught up to her feet, and she wobbled.

"Well, what do we have here?"

A man stood behind the counter. Blood rushed from her head, and the room spun. This was it. This was how she was going to die. She scrambled on hands and knees behind a rack of T-shirts lying on its side. She glanced behind her. Lilli peered out at her and blinked once. Was that a sign not to move or run for it? She gripped the cool metal bar of the rack and scrunched lower. Lilli held a finger to her lips.

The man behind the counter rustled through another drawer. Emma's thigh muscle cramped. She dug her fingers into her leg and rolled onto her side. This was it. She was going to die lying under a rack of Harley Davidson T-shirts.

"Whatcha got, Mikey?" one of the men asked.

Were they blind? Emma pushed the T-shirts aside, revealing a man behind the counter holding something in the air.

"A puka shell necklace. I got one of these from Gina Zombarski my senior year."

How had they not spotted her? Thank all the goddesses. She scrunched farther under the T-shirts, clenching her teeth to stop the groan. Her thigh muscle spasmed. She glanced back to the cellar door, but Lilli was gone.

"Jinx, you and Gus, check the cellar. The cash box might be down there. I'll check the rest of these drawers. This register is empty."

"Empty? Mikey, you said—"

"Just hit the cellar," Mikey growled.

The sound of shoes on broken glass sent shivers up her spine, and she lowered her face to the floor, her breath quick and shallow. Three men: Mikey, Jinx, and Gus, and they all had guns. Someone had torn the blinds out of their brackets, and the shop window let in full sunlight. She'd be spotted for sure. She scanned the shop for a better hiding spot. A curtain hung separating a chair at a workstation from the rest of the room. Could she make it?

No.

The wall on her left was plastered with posters of tattoos from around the world. She curled into the smallest ball she could and covered her head and shoulders with T-shirts. Gus and Jinx walked around two other racks still standing and stopped at a cabinet right beside her. She chewed her fingernail, tasted blood.

Lilli's face appeared behind the rack of dragon figurines. Emma gasped. Lilli held her finger to her lips. Emma nodded.

"Jade?" Emma mouthed.

Lilli pointed to the cellar door.

A drawer screeched as it was opened, and Emma gritted her teeth.

"Careful," Mikey called. "Those bitches are crazy."

"The cash better be down there," one of the other men said.

They tromped past Emma, to the cellar door and down the steps. Emma's pulse pounded in her ears. Jade had the gun, but she was alone.

The clatter of booted feet on the steps was interrupted by a blast like a shock wave hitting her brain. Two more shots followed.

"Jade." Her voice echoed inside her skull.

One set of footsteps pounded up the stairs. Emma hunched in the T-shirts, her lips and fingers numb. A figure emerged from the cellar.

"Jinx is down." Gus ran past Emma. "You didn't say she had a gun!"

"I told you they were crazy!" Mikey gave the box a final shake before throwing it across the shop, shattering a mirror. Glass sprayed over Emma, and she crouched lower, pressing her eyes closed.

Boots crunched over broken glass, and she followed Mikey's form as he ran after Gus, slamming the door behind him. The patter of their footsteps faded down the street, and Emma sat on the floor, rubbing her thigh.

"That rat, Mikey. I'll slaughter that guy!" Lilli scurried to the cellar door.

Emma sprinted after her. "You know those guys?"

"Mikey owes us money." Lilli disappeared down the steps. "Jade!"

Chapter Nine

Josh

A cinder in the fireplace pinged, and Josh jolted upright. He unwedged himself from the overstuffed chair and rubbed the knot in his neck from hours cramped in a lumpy chair. He searched the dark windows for signs of morning light. Mom rustled under her blanket, and Josh glanced at Grandpa's clock on the mantel. No one had wound it since grandpa fell ill. The man loved himself some wind-up clocks, that was for sure. Dad had wound the gold pocket watch and put it in Grandpa's pocket during his funeral.

Josh pushed against the arms of the chair and stood. The clock over the kitchen sink read 6:48. Stretching his arms over his head, he waited for the thump of a tree or the whack of a branch.

Embers glowed in the fireplace, and he stirred the ashes. He threw on some kindling. A flame leapt up, and the wood snapped. He added a larger piece then another. Flickering light filled the basement.

Coffee. He shuffled toward the sink for water. He'd French press a pot and have water left for mom's tea. The creaks of the old house as it settled heightened his senses.

"Silence?"

The quiet sucked the air from the room. His ears

rang with it, or was that the rush of his blood through his veins?

"Mom?" He bent, checked her pulse. Her chest rose and fell in a slow regular pattern. "Mother?" He jiggled her shoulder, but she didn't moan or stir. He brushed the back of his fingers across her forehead, dry and hot. He lifted the bandage, and a sour odor hit him.

He rushed to the bathroom and checked the medicine chest for antibiotics, knocking over a bottle of milk of magnesia. A pair of toenail clippers fell into the sink. He slammed the medicine chest door. The hospital would have what she needed. He sure didn't.

How would he get her there? All he could do here was keep the wound clean, but it wouldn't be enough. He crossed the room and knelt at her side. Heat radiated from her still form.

Fever, page 82.

He shook her shoulder harder, but she didn't even moan. Rushing to the sink, he wet a cloth under a cold faucet, wrung it out, and turning, knocked into a chair. It skittered across the floor, hit the rug, and crashed on its side.

"What a klutz." Great, now he was talking to himself.

Her eyes flickered, and she moaned. He hurried to her and placed the cool rag on her burning forehead. She didn't stir. Dehydration. No, no, no.

Rejuvelyte, how could he forget? Dashing to the sink, he reached for a packet knocking the whole box on the counter. He gripped the edge of the sink and gulped in air.

He could do this. He had to.

The electrolytes in the drink would help stabilize

her. How much water? He read the box; one packet per quart. He filled the pitcher, splashing onto the counter. His fingers trembled as he tore open two packets and dumped them into the pitcher, the tinkling of Mom stirring a pitcher of Rejuvelyte flashed through his mind. She called it R and kept a pitcher of it in the fridge for the first signs of flu or colds. This had to work. It was the only plan he had.

He pressed the glass to her lips. She sipped a small amount at first then drank deeper from the glass. She needed to be in a hospital. He lifted his dead phone from his back pocket. Where was Mom's? A knot formed at the base of his skull. She'd dropped it in her purse and grabbed dad's papers instead. It was still upstairs. He climbed the steps.

He eased the door open, and sunlight burst through. A fresh breeze washed over him, and goosebumps rose on his arms. He blinked until his eyes adjusted. The quiet pounded in his ears. Bird song came from outside, and the tang of fir trees hung in the air. Branches, insulation, glass, wood, and papers covered the floors, but he couldn't find the purse.

He climbed over chairs, bookcases, and tree branches, scanning the floor, opened the front door and wandered into the sunrise. He stood on the front porch then like a sleepwalker stumbled out into the yard.

Trees lay on the ground, stacked three deep in places, branches, bits of paper, plastic bottles, and shingles covered the lawn. But the sunshine warmed him, and the blue sky gave him hope. Mom needed to see this. The warm sun would do her good, but how did he get her up the stairs?

Light filled the yard where trees had once cast

shade. He smoothed his fingers over his hair. The number of trees that had snapped in half or been uprooted stunned him. They lay sprawled on the ground. Root systems fanned out like enormous plates of tangled hair, clods of dirt clinging to them. Many of the trees had stood sixty to eighty feet tall, their branches the size of small trees.

Grandpa's barn still stood and so did the apple tree. Several branches dangled and some lay on the ground, but the main framework of branches and trunk stood strong and upright. Josh drew from that strength. He scanned the yard for the for-sale sign and chuckled. The farm was officially off the market.

He glanced at the house. This must be dad's storm. One of the fingerprints of El Primo was high winds blowing in from the southwest. They'd rush over the Pacific Ocean bringing warm temperatures and moisture. He squinted in the direction of the highway, but fallen trees now blocked his view. How would an ambulance get in?

He climbed over branches and debris to the barn, took inventory of the house. The roof looked solid, but all the windows on the west side were either cracked or broken, glass and fir needles covering the porch. The front door had deep gouges where branches, pinecones, and other debris had hit.

He jogged across the driveway and into the living room to the window seat, reached underneath until his fingers hit the familiar case. Opening it, he inspected the violin. Not a scratch. Tears sprang to his eyes, and he wiped them away with the back of his hand.

He drank the sweet air, so refreshing after the dusty basement. Mom needed another drink. He clutched his violin to his chest and headed down. All he could do was keep her comfortable, but how long would she last now that infection had set in?

****

The warmth of the sun did not reach the basement, and the firelight did not match the sunshine outside. Josh slumped in the lumpy chair and stared at Mom. She never got sick. How could this happen now when help seemed as far away as Mars? He needed to stick to Grandpa's plan. He'd start the generator. That would keep the water pump and radio running until he got a solar panel circuit running, then he'd make sure the ham radio antenna was still attached so he could listen to NOAA and keep track of the storm.

Why had he waited to get his license? Grandpa had harped on it until he got too sick. Grandpa had always said, "If the power goes out and things are really bad, fire up the emergency radio." Once he was gone, Josh had lost interest. Without his license, if he got caught, he faced fines by the FCC, but this was an emergency, right? Mom needed help.

His mom lay on the couch, flushed but otherwise unchanged. He offered her the glass of R, and she sipped. She'd need a steady dose of R every half-hour or so. He grabbed grandma's windup timer by the stove. He set it for a half-hour, slipped it into his jacket pocket, and, tucking the blanket around her, he headed to the generator.

The full effect of the storm hit him like a blow as he emerged from the house. There'd be another storm soon, if this was El Primo, so he'd have to work fast.

The electrical grid would take weeks to restore with all this damage. A glint in the driveway under the branches caught his eye, a solar panel. He'd find them all and repair the circuit.

The kitchen windows and porch had escaped the high winds. He yanked the tarp off the generator and folded it. He brushed his hand over the dusty, red metal, added fresh gas to the tank, then turned on the generator. It roared to life. He plugged in the cord and ran it to the circuit box hanging inside the kitchen door. He plugged it into the manual transfer switch and flipped the switch for the basement circuit to generator.

He caught the distinct odor of gas and checked the sides until his fingers located a dent near the bottom of the metal tank. It didn't seem to be leaking. He'd just filled the tank. Maybe some had spilled. If the generator had a leak, the solar panels would be a priority. He had about two gallons of gas left in the tank. How much was in Mom's car? Bugger only had enough to get him to the gas station. The real question was, how long would the power be out, and when would another storm hit?

One storm would follow another, Dad said, each with high intensity, which meant even if this weren't El Primo, the well pump and the radio had to be running, maybe long-term.

He flipped a light switch at the top of the stairs. Light filled the stairwell. Such a simple thing to flip a switch and have light. He pursed his lips and blew out a hiss of air. Their emergency plan was working, except for Mom's arm. He took the timer out, two minutes. He jogged down the steps and gave her a sip. She didn't open her eyes. Was she in pain? He let her sleep.

He set the timer again and, with a lighter step, headed outside. He threw branches and kicked debris out of his way, creating a trail around the house to the chimney. He located the wire antenna running up the side. It hadn't been knocked down.

"Yes." He raced into the basement. The radio would work, and he'd call for help. With a final glance at the blue sky, he entered the house.

He headed down the steps, and the timer rang. Mom drank.

He sat at the desk and bumped the hidden door with a loud crack. He glanced at Mom. She rolled toward the back of the couch. He pushed the wall panel, and the door popped open, but it hung loose in its frame. The storage room let in dust, and he sneezed. The apples from the root cellar beyond made his mouth water. He'd grab one for lunch.

He closed the door and removed the plastic cover from the radio. He flipped the power switch, but the dials didn't move. He tapped the glass, nothing. He opened a desk drawer and pulled out the crank handle. He fitted it on a cog and cranked. Still nothing. Now what?

He laced his fingers behind his head, glaring at the radio, willing it to work.

He turned the radio around and checked the connections between the power supply and the radio, flipped the switch, nothing. He leaned back in the chair.

"Could I please get a break right now?"

He stood and paced. How would he send and receive messages? How would he let Uncle Carl about Mom? He dropped into the chair and flipped the switch on and off several times.

The crunch of footsteps on the floorboards upstairs brought him to his feet, and all his muscles tensed.

Chapter Ten

Emma

Emma pressed her hands over her ears, her whole head still vibrating from the gun shot.

Focus. Center. Her mom's mantra? Where did that come from? But it didn't help. Jade sat on the bed in a nest of blankets, blood staining her left pant leg. Her gun sat on the blanket beside her.

"I'm shot."

Lilli hurried to her side, lifting an old T-shirt from the floor. Her gaze never left Jade's as she applied pressure with the shirt. Jade grunted but let Lilli apply pressure. The room spun, and Emma place her hand on the wall. She shook her head and stared at the corner, the ceiling, anywhere but Jade's leg.

"What about him?" Jade's voice was slow, heavy.

Emma glanced at the floor and leaned against the wall. He lay on his back in a pool of blood, the beaded curtain rested across his belly. Where was his gun? His dirty pants bagged around his legs on one side of the curtain, his torn jacket and spiked hair lay on the other. He was just a kid, her age. His revolver lay by the curled fingers of his left hand. Left-handed? Jinx was someone, or he had been. A pain in her gut shot to her head and blossomed. She held her face in her hands.

Lilli bent down and pressed two fingers to his

carotid artery. Jade leaned forward. Lilli shook her head and took Jade in her arms. "Oh, hon."

Jade's gritted teeth glowed in the candlelight. Jinx did not stir, and Emma's tummy lurched.

Jade scratched at her scar until Lilli took her hand with her own. "Hon, leave it be."

"No." Jade stared at Jinx's body.

Lilli took Jade's face in her hands, turning her away from Jinx. "This was self-defense. You have witnesses."

"You weren't down here. It was just me and— Damn it. I need a drink." Jade sank back into the pillows.

"I need a cigarette."

"No, you don't." Jade grabbed a pen from the drawer in the nightstand, bullets clanking as she shut it. She blanched and dropped the pen. "You've chewed through them all but this one."

Lilli picked up the pen and clamped it between her teeth. Her eyes never left Jade's. "Emma, two fingers." Lilli applied pressure to Jade's leg

The whiskey bottle glowed amber on the counter. "Golden Rose" shone on the label. Emma pushed through the beaded curtain. Her hands shook as she grabbed a glass from the cabinet. She dropped the glass. It clattered on the counter but didn't break.

"Better make it a double." Lilli held Jade's hands. Jade squeezed her eyes shut.

"A double?"

"Half full." Lilli held Jade closer. "Be still, now."

"Half full, that's how you see life, isn't it?" Jade pushed Lilli away. "It looks half empty from where I'm sitting."

"Oh, hon." Lilli took the pen from her lips and kissed Jade's hair.

Emma splashed the whiskey in the glass and handed it through the beads to Lilli who held it to Jade's lips.

"I killed him." Jade took the glass, raised it in Jinx's direction, then tossed back the contents in one swallow. She lifted the gun off the bed with her thumb and forefinger, passed it to Lilli. "I'm a murderer."

"No, hon." Lilli placed the gun on the nightstand.

Jade handed the glass back to Emma, and she poured. Lilli took it and sipped.

"He looks pretty dead from where I'm sitting." Jade crumpled into Lilli's arms. Lilli held her while she sobbed.

Emma shifted from one foot to the other, not certain what to do. "Lilli's right. He would have killed you." The words were out before she could stop them. Jade glared at Emma then sobs shook her shoulders.

Now she'd done it. Emma plopped onto the bottom stair and lowered her head to her knees. She'd set out to save the planet, not sit in a cellar with a dead body. She couldn't save anything, not even herself.

The room grew quiet, and dust motes hung in the air.

"I'm going to have to see that wound."

Lilli's voice startled Emma.

"Of course, you are." Jade clamped her eyes, her face pinched and white.

Emma's neck knotted. "Maybe 911 works now?" She checked her phone, still dead.

"Already tried." Lilli helped Jade ease her jeans over her hips and settled her in the nest of blankets on the bed, while Lilli examined her leg.

The room rotated, and Emma closed her eyes, her woozy head sagging. Jinx lay on the floor. He hadn't even made it through the beaded curtain before he got shot. Emma jerked a blanket off a chair and threw it over his body. The beaded curtain rattled, and his hazel eye glared at her.

With a shudder, she adjusted the blanket over his face and stepped back. The second dead person she'd seen today, but this one wasn't going anywhere. If she could drain her throbbing head of all the chaos, maybe she could think. A sob escaped her. She glanced at Lilli, who spoke in hushed whispers to Jade, her face inches from Jade's thigh. Lilli poked and prodded the wound, and Jade bit into a pillow. Lilli lifted her leg, checking the circumference, and Jade groaned, blood seeping from the wound. Emma covered her eyes and turned her head away.

Lilli brushed her hands together and stood. "The bad news is the bullet ruined your new jeans. The good news is it went all the way through the muscle, thank the goddess."

"It still hurts like hell. Which goddess did you thank?" Jade asked.

Lilli rolled her eyes to Emma. "I thanked them all, if you must know, and watch your language."

Emma's cheeks burned, and she put a hand to her face. "I've heard worse." How old did they think she was? Eight?

Lilli snatched a clean towel off the back of a chair and pressed it to the wound. "Emm, grab me the antiseptic ointment in the cabinet above the sink, along with bandages."

"Got it." Emma turned away from Jinx's form on the floor, but she watched for movement. There was none.

Lilli pressed, and wiped, and wrapped, and kissed, and fussed over Jade, while Emma gathered bloody bandages and threw them in a garbage bag. Lilli had called her "Emm." No one had ever called her that. She liked it.

"That wasn't so bad, was it?" Lilli screwed the cap on the ointment. "More whiskey?"

Jade nodded.

Emma took the glass without being asked and poured out a double.

They sat, Jade sipping, Lilli rubbing Jade's back, Emma waiting.

Emma pictured Mom in the burgundy chair, Sarah cradling Cuddles, Mom reading to her by candlelight. The walls of the cellar came into focus, replacing the warm image of home. The chill of the damp cellar seeped into her bones, and her teeth chattered. She had to go.

"Better?" Lilli asked.

"Better," Jade said, "but now I'm mad." Jade glowered at Lilli. "Was that Mikey's voice I heard?"

"Yep." Lilli ran her hand along Jade's scar before she could.

"If he thinks we have cash here, he'll be back. We gotta get Emma out of the shop, and we gotta get out of Vandby."

Lilli's mouth dropped open. "Oh?"

"We need to get Emma home. People are already looting, and that—" Jade nodded at Jinx. "—happened."

Home. The word enveloped Emma like a warm blanket.

Jade started barking orders, as though someone flipped a switch and she had become the sergeant major.

"We need water. We have a case on the shelves in there. Don't leave any." She pointed to a folding door beside the fridge. "Lilli, grab the first aid stuff and all the food we got. We'll need those puri—"

"Purification tablets?"

"Right. Then we get the hell out."

Lilli found a tiny bottle of red ink in the cabinet and held it in her hand. "I forgot to put this upstairs." Her arm dropped to her side, and she glanced at Jade. "I hate to leave all our ink. This shop..." Lilli's mouth opened and closed like a fish gasping for air.

"We can't stay, hon. I was her age when—" She nodded her head at Emma.

"I know, but—"

"No buts. We're out of here." Jade stood, her hands on her hips.

"But help will be here soon."

"You don't know that, hon. Now, Emma, where do you live?"

"What?" Emma was dizzy trying to keep up with their conversation. She choked out, "Wilson Street."

The last three days blurred together, the storm, the looters, the gun, the death, and Lilli's reluctance to leave her ink, which was her life, behind. Were they making a mistake leaving the cellar for the unknown in the streets? If it weren't for looters who had guns like Jinx...

Home. She had to get home.

"Wilson? That's all the way out in northeast?" Lilli planted her hands on her hips.

Emma nodded, her pulse pounding in her ears. "I've never walked that far before."

Jade glared at Lilli before Lilli could speak. "It's not that far. What do you say, Lill? We have to do this—"

"For Emma." Lilli shrugged and frowned at Jade. "Fine. I guess we're hitting the road."

****

Lilli grabbed packs from coat hooks by the stairs, Emma's among them. Emma gathered the water bottles and divided them between the packs. Jade tossed the bottle of purification tablets and extra bandages into her pack. Lilli slapped together sandwiches, ripping the bread in her rush. Emma opened a cabinet and found a jar of strawberry jelly.

"Forget something?" She handed it to Lilli who shrugged, the pen bobbing between her lips. She had become part of Lilli and Jade's world.

What would she say to her mom when she got there? "Sorry?" What would she say to Lilli and Jade for saving her? "Thanks?" Both words seemed inadequate since the storm.

Opening the cabinets, Emma found apples, instant oatmeal, and saltines. None of it looked appetizing, but she divided everything in the bags, anyway. Lilli stuffed two sandwiches in each pack then brushed her hands together.

"That's it. You ready, babe?" Lilli lifted a pack to her shoulders.

"I was born ready." Jade wobbled, favoring her left leg.

Lilli took one side and Emma took the other, and they climbed the stairs.

"So, we're really doing this?" Every muscle Emma had, and a few she didn't know existed, tensed.

"Don't jinx it," Lilli said.

Jade paused, almost toppling Emma, who clutched the railing.

"Sorry. Of course, we're doing this." Lilli gripped Jade as she wobbled. "First stop Emma's, then on to Franklin."

"Franklin?" Emma stood on a step. "My Gran and Papa live near Cedarville, really close." She looked from Lilli to Jade. "Maybe I can come visit sometime. If we ever go to Gran's, that is."

"Sure, kid." Lilli helped Jade up another step. "Over the river and through the woods to Gran's house you go, right?"

Emma shook her head. Sarah's favorite song, as of two weeks ago, sang in Lilli's monotone voice sounded wrong. Emma's foot caught the step, and she grabbed the railing again. Why did everything have to be gray right now? She wanted a rainbow.

"Your folks will be so happy to see me again, won't they?" Jade's voice quavered.

Lilli raised her eyebrows and squeezed Jade's shoulder.

"Who knows, maybe this time will be different?" Lilli said, but her voice rose at the end, like a question. "Emma, you're leading the way."

"I am?" Emma jerked her head up. "I mean, okay."

She rubbed the back of her neck. Easy-peasy, right? At least it would be if she could tell north from south and left from right.

Chapter Eleven

Josh

Bootsteps clomped through the living room and into the dining room. Josh grabbed a hatchet leaning against the fireplace and held it like a weapon. He tiptoed up the stairs, his heart banging against his ribs.

He stopped halfway and gripped the handle. What was his plan? Chop whoever it was? He braced his feet. The basement door was cracked open, and he glimpsed blue jeans and cowboy boots. The hatchet slipped in his grasp.

"Anyone here?"

Josh froze on the stairs.

Someone yanked the door open, and a man stood there. Josh took a step backward, gripping the handle. He peered at the form. "Uncle Carl?"

"Josh? I wasn't sure I'd find you here."

Josh dropped the hatchet and took the steps two at a time. Carl crushed him in a bear hug.

"Is Dad with you?"

"No, and I'm fine. How are you?"

Josh pushed away. "Sorry. I just—"

"I know. Aunt Jan sends her love." Uncle Carl winked.

"Have you been to Cedarville?"

"Yep." He placed a hand on Josh's shoulder. "It's

getting bad fast. Looters hit the Stuart's place. Martha ended up in the hospital. Squatters broke into the abandoned farm on Belly Creek Road, burned it to the ground."

"What?"

Uncle Carl wiped his face with his hands. "Enough of that. How are you guys? Where is Sis?"

Josh winced. How did he tell him? Just tell him. His tongue was thick as he tried to speak. "We were headed to the basement. She fell." Josh fought against the pressure pounding between his ears.

"Hurt?" Uncle Carl's gaze bore into Josh.

"Her arm—it's bad." Josh struggled to keep his voice steady.

"Well, let's have a look-see." Uncle Carl used his country drawl, the same one he used on heart attack victims or people with broken legs. It calmed them, and it calmed Josh now.

Josh led him down the stairs, but he jerked to a stop at sight of her still form.

"Mom, Uncle Carl's here."

She moaned but did not open her eyes. Josh's neck tensed, and he moved to the fireplace to give Carl room.

"Hey, sis." He bent at her side, leaned over, and lifted the sling. "Trying to fly, were you?" He glanced under the bandage. His frown deepened.

She didn't respond.

"No antibiotics, I suppose."

Josh shook his head, his middle quivering. Infection, page 236.

"Antiseptic and gauze then, quick."

Uncle Carl slid her arm out of the sling and removed the bandage. Mom sucked air through her teeth in one hissing breath.

"I need more light."

Josh grabbed the flashlight and pointed the beam on the wound. The long silence that followed stretched on. What did Uncle Carl see? Gangrene? His stomach tightened, and he gripped the flashlight with both hands.

"Carl?" she mumbled.

"That's my name." Uncle Carl held her arm in one hand, his banter bringing a grin to her lips. He poured antiseptic solution over the wound. "I've got you right where I want you."

"Ha," she snorted, clenching her eyes shut as Uncle Carl worked.

How could they joke? She was in danger, right? Josh held a towel underneath her arm to keep the antiseptic from her clothes. The bleeding had stopped, but the edges of the wound were an angry pink.

Uncle Carl nodded to the corner, and Josh followed him to the far side of the room. "It's a pretty nasty break, but you've done a fine job of cleaning and splinting it. Still, infection has set in." He looked Josh in the eyes. "We're going to have to set the bone. Then we'll get her to the hospital."

"Wait? Set the bone before you go? But isn't that dangerous?"

"I have to try, son. She'll travel better with it set." Carl's drawl had disappeared, his voice quick and sharp. "I need your help. You okay with that?"

A cold chill settled over Josh even though the fireplace crackled. His neck muscles pinched, and he reached up to massage the tension. Setting the bones would cause her more pain. Using his right hand, he rubbed his neck. He stood pressing his shoulders back. He'd be faced with decisions like this every day as a doctor. How did they do it?

Josh gulped. His mother's moans paralyzed him, but they had to get her to the hospital. Infection led to sepsis. He glanced at her form lying on the couch, gray and small.

"Okay. Let's do this before I chicken out."

Uncle Carl's forehead grew smooth as he smiled. "We better wash up."

He went through the motions on autopilot. Josh waited for instructions, wiping his damp hands on his jeans.

"You sit on the couch behind your mom and wrap your arms around for support, got it? I'll set the arm, but it's gonna hurt like-a-mother-bear. You have to hold her."

Josh clenched his teeth and nodded. He raised mom's shoulders and slipped in behind her. He wrapped his arms around her right arm and torso, leaving her left arm free. He shut his eyes and buried his face in her shoulder. The scent of her lavender shampoo filled his senses. Her body stiffened, and Josh tightened his hold.

Uncle Carl held her upper arm in his left hand and her lower arm in his right. She gritted her teeth and nodded. He pulled. She shrieked then went limp in Josh's arms. It was over before Josh could say, "mother-bear." He sat, his arms wrapped around her, holding her. Uncle Carl poured more antiseptic solution on her wound then examined her arm.

"It looks better with the bone set. We need to get her ready to travel. The sooner we get her to the hospital the better." Uncle Carl went to the sink and washed the blood off his hands.

Josh eased his mother back onto the pillows and scooted off the couch. He joined Uncle Carl at the sink.

"How do you that? I mean it's your sis…"

Uncle Carl's eyes never blinked, as if removed from this basement and Mom's broken arm. Josh wiped his hands on a towel.

"We need to re-splint now. Hold these while I wrap."

Josh nodded and held the rulers. With sure and steady hands, Carl took them and placed them on her arm and began wrapping. Josh sat mesmerized watching him work.

Uncle Carl fastened the end of the wrap and stood. "She'll be out for a while. Do you have any pain meds?"

"Just acetaminophen and ibuprofen. I checked the medi—"

"That'll work. I have a stretcher in my truck." Carl headed for the stairs.

"Truck?"

"Yep, four tires, steering wheel—you know the kind."

Josh shook his head. Uncle Carl seemed unphased, and he was a mass of quivering jelly. "Yeah, I do." He followed Uncle Carl up the stairs. "What were the roads like?"

"Pretty much like your driveway. I brought the chainsaw, had to cut through a dozen or more trees just to get here."

Uncle Carl, the survivalist. Of course, he had a stretcher and a chainsaw. Josh watched from the porch as Uncle Carl disappeared behind a tangle of trees. He'd left the trees in the driveway so looters couldn't see the house. He knew everything, and Josh couldn't even take care of mom…

Uncle Carl climbed through the branches carrying the stretcher, and Josh grabbed one end. They stomped into the basement. Mom's eyes sank into the dark circles above her cheekbones. Dehydration. He grabbed the ibuprofen and acetaminophen from the bathroom cabinet and filled a glass with R. He handed it all to Uncle Carl. "Easy now. Little sips." She nodded, her eyes shut.

Uncle Carl motioned his head toward the corner, and Josh followed.

"Hey. You were a big help," he said.

"I just did what you said." Josh shrugged, but a warm glow filled his chest.

"We have to get her up the stairs and to the truck. It's going to jostle her quite a bit, so be prepared."

"Okay, but I'm not going with you."

"What?" Uncle Carl did a double take. "Of course you are."

"No. I'm not leaving the farm or dad's equipment. Someone needs to take readings and record them." He quivered inside, but stood his full height, his face a mask.

"Your mom probably needs surgery. We can't wait any longer, and you are going."

Josh glared at Uncle Carl. "No. Someone has to stay so it doesn't get burned to the ground." He scanned the kitchen floorboards. He had to convince Uncle Carl. "Dad needs the data for his research." Josh frowned and clenched his fists. "I'm almost seventeen, remember?"

"How could I forget." Uncle Carl ran his hands over his buzz cut, looking Josh up and down. "I hear the generator. Is the radio receiving messages?"

"Well, no," Josh swallowed hard. He could have lied, but Carl would have checked.

"Thank you for telling the truth. I knew your radio didn't work because I sent you three messages with no response. You can't stay without a radio."

"But—"

"No buts."

"Uncle Carl, please."

Carl's frown deepened. "Let me double check your generator then see what's up with the radio. Then I'll decide."

Josh nodded, crossing his fingers behind his back. Grandpa would never leave the farm in such a state, but he would have had the radio running by now. Josh tagged behind Uncle Carl.

The generator rattled and roared. Uncle bent down, and Josh leaned over his shoulder.

"I smell gas." He ran his hand over the dent then sniffed his fingers and stood and wiped his hands on his jeans. "This old thing runs like a top, but you got a leak. If you can get a solar panel circuit connected, you can swap over and save gas. I expect your dad will be home before that."

"Yes, sir." Josh rolled his shoulders easing the stiffness. "With the storm over, Dad will probably be here by nightfall."

"All right, all right." Uncle Carl chuckled and held up his hands. "I still have to look at that radio. No promises."

Josh nodded. "I'm sure it's a simple fix, but I don't

have my license."

"This is an emergency, so use it. Besides, the messages you receive are as important as what you send."

Josh nodded, trying to suppress a grin. "So does that me—"

Uncle Carl scowled at Josh. "I haven't decided yet."

He marched into the basement. Josh hung over his shoulder as he turned the radio around to expose the back and unscrewed a panel. He checked the wires inside, mumbling to himself. Josh kept track of all the checks he made. He'd been as prepared as he could be, but he still didn't know enough. Would he ever?

"Did you get a reading on those winds yet?" Uncle Carl asked.

"I haven't had time to get out to the barn to check. How big is the outage area?" Josh clamped his jaw shut. Had he just given Uncle Carl a reason to change his mind? Josh wiped any emotion from his face as Uncle Carl stood and scratched his head.

"NOAA clocked the winds through Vandby Valley at 120 miles per hour. Explains all the downed trees, right? In Alaska they got up to 175."

Josh's mouth went dry. How did he stop this train wreck before it got any worse? He had to stay.

"The messages so far report power outages up and down the West Coast. Could this be Ed's storm?"

Josh shrugged. He shifted from foot to foot.

"NOAA says there's another storm moving in."

Now he'd never let Josh stay. Josh rubbed his pounding temples. "It might be."

"I figured as much."

Why had Josh opened his big mouth? If he didn't change the subject his head might just explode. He focused on Uncle Carl's hand working on the wires at the back of the radio.

He pointed. "Is that a loose wire? Could it be the problem?"

"That wire's fine, but your bushings are tarnished. No wonder it doesn't work."

Josh shrank. Of course. The bushings.

"Easy fix, though. I told your dad he should upgrade this equipment. At least it's got a crank if your generator goes out." Uncle Carl wiped his hands on his jeans.

"The crank is in the drawer."

Uncle Carl took the crank, fit it on the knob, and turned it once. "Once the bushings are cleaned, you just turn until the dials come to life. You'll get the hang of it."

Josh nodded. Was he leaning toward letting Josh stay?

"Got an eraser?"

"Eraser?"

"To clean the bushings. I got one in the truck. Your radio will be as good as new, well almost."

Josh nodded and trailed after Uncle Carl. Mom slept on the couch oblivious, her cheeks flushed.

"Fever," Uncle Carl said. "Hurry." He dashed up the stairs.

Josh ran after him but stopped on the porch and scanned the horizon. Clouds were building in the southwest, and all warmth drain from him.

"I'll drive the truck around so we can load up Sis."

Josh jogged to the barn and to the backside. He

rolled the heavy door open, and Uncle Carl drove his truck down the center aisle and to the porch. Josh left the doors open for his departure.

"This will just take a minute." He climbed the steps, a pencil with an eraser in one hand.

Josh would be alone if this worked, and Dad might not make it home before the next storm hit. A sharp pain pinched his neck, and he rolled his shoulders.

He cleared his throat. "What more could I have done?"

Uncle Carl stared at his boots. "I'm not going to sugarcoat this. Your mom must get to the hospital before the next storm. It's a good thing we get this window of time. But you saved her life with your quick thinking. She's going to be fine." He cocked one eye at Josh. "Still want to be a doctor?"

The weight of what it meant to be a doctor hit him like a wrecking ball. "I just feel like I could have done more."

Carl took Josh's shoulders in his large hands and held his gaze. "That's what will make you a great doctor. We all feel that—paramedics, doctors, nurses. You did everything you could with what you had. Now I'll take her to the hospital, and she will be fine."

"Yeah. You're right. Thanks." The pain in his neck released, and he nodded.

"Let's get that radio working. Maybe you'll have time to get a circuit repaired. That will set you up for the next storm, and by then your dad will be home. Just keep that radio on, and I'll always be in touch."

"Wait. So, I can stay?" Josh stared at Uncle Carl's back.

"I haven't decided." He disappeared down the

stairs chuckling.

****

Uncle Carl tipped the radio on its side and started rubbing the bushings with the eraser. He blew off black eraser pieces and tightened a loose wire with some needle-nose pliers. He checked several wire connections and pushed the plug into a socket.

"Ready?" He motioned to Josh.

Josh turned the knob, and the dials leapt. "Yes."

Uncle Carl grinned.

"That's it?" He should have known how to fix this, but he did now. He dialed in the NOAA channel. "It's like magic."

"No magic here." He held up the eraser and pliers. "They don't make radios like this old set anymore. It's in good shape, but you'll need the solar panels connected and running before the generator runs out of gas. Who knows when the power will be back on, right? It pays to have a backup plan."

"I saw several panels in the yard. I can get that sorted out, no problem."

Carl nodded. "Remember to stay hydrated, don't work too hard, and keep your eyes on the weather. I want to hear as soon as your dad arrives."

"So, it's official? I can stay?"

Uncle Carl nodded. "Sure. Now, let's get your mom ready."

Uncle Carl grabbed the stretcher, and Josh dragged the coffee table out of the way. Carl laid it on the floor next to the couch. The fireplace lit the space with a cozy glow.

"She'll have to ride in the back seat. She'll be more comfortable than sitting up front."

"What roads are open?"

"Thomas Road is clear for the most part. I've already cut a way through. We'll have to cut through some fences and drive through a couple pastures. Not ideal, but we'll get there."

"Poor Mom." Josh glanced at her, his belly tightening at the sight of her chapped lips. "This is a worst-case scenario, isn't it?"

Uncle Carl raised an eyebrow but didn't speak. He shook her shoulder. "We're going to get you to the truck now, then to the hospital."

She opened her eyes, nodded, but did not speak. The light reflected off her watery eyes.

"Listen. I'm not going to lie. It's gonna be a bumpy ride."

She nodded.

"Josh is staying here."

Her eyes popped open and glared at Uncle Carl. "No."

"He'll be fine. He's got a plan. Ed should be home this evening if he left Vandby as soon as the storm ended."

She frowned. Then, with a sigh, she closed her eyes and nodded, a tear rolling down her cheek. Josh had expected a fight, but she was too weak.

It made sense for him to wait for his dad, though. She had to know that he could do this.

Uncle Carl leaned down and gathered her by the shoulders. "Josh is going to lift your feet. Easy now." They eased her onto the stretcher. She was lighter than Josh expected. Uncle Carl fastened the straps.

"Now, up on three."

Josh gripped the handles, and his mother gripped

the side with her good hand.

"One, two, three." She clenched her teeth as they lifted her off the floor. Uncle Carl took the stairs backward one at a time. Josh tightened his grip on the handles, moving with each step.

"Slow and easy, here." Uncle Carl lifted his end, and Josh lost his grip as he reached the top of the steps. She gasped.

Josh clenched his jaw and adjusted his hands on the stretcher, his eyes on her feet. He couldn't look at her face.

"You got her," Uncle Carl said, his voice low and steady.

Josh made it around the corner. They crunched through dining and living rooms strewn with glass, onto the porch, down the steps, and to the truck. Josh's hands were slick with sweat, but he gave Uncle Carl the okay nod.

Uncle Carl situated her head and shoulders on the back seat of the truck and ran around to the other door. He grabbed the handles, and Josh pushed her onto the back seat as Uncle Carl pulled her. She moaned, clamping her eyes shut. She lay with her knees bent so Josh could close the door.

Josh jogged around the truck. Her gray face startled him, and he stumbled against the truck. Uncle Carl put a hand on his shoulder to steady him.

Josh wiped his lips on his sleeve, then kissed her forehead. She reached up and clasped his hand.

"It'll be okay, Mom."

Uncle Carl jiggled his keys.

"I'll have the radio on, so if you hear anything—" Josh said.

"Ditto." Uncle Carl grabbed his hand and drew him into a hug, then held him at shoulders' length. "You'll need that solar circuit, right?"

Josh nodded. Uncle Carl climbed into the truck. It roared to life and bumped through the barn and down the driveway. Josh slid the barn doors closed and locked them. Then he turned and stumbled to the house, the front porch a blur.

He was on his own now.

Chapter Twelve

Emma

Emma wiped her hand across her brow. Jade wanted her in charge? Why did she spend all her time messaging friends and playing games? She could have checked out her surroundings occasionally.

She sniffed and tightened her grip on Jade's waist. Jade winced, and Emma slowed her pace. How would Jade make it across town? She owed this woman her life, so slow would be her new fast.

Broken glass crunched underfoot with each step, setting Emma's teeth on edge, like when Sarah ground her teeth in the car. It gave Emma a headache, but Emma couldn't stay mad at her.

Lilli stopped at the front door. It gapped a couple of inches. "I thought Mikey closed this."

Jade's body went stiff. She gazed into the street and swayed. Lilli steadied her.

Emma stepped forward. If she was the leader, she should go first. She stopped trying to make sense of the scene. Litter covered every inch of the sidewalk and street. Piles of debris had blown against cars and storefronts, and two men fought in the middle of it all. A fist seemed to wring her stomach, and she doubled over.

"It's mine."

"Give it."

One of the men drew a gun, and Emma took a step back into Lilli and Jade. A shot rang through her skull, a dull throb. The other man fell to the ground unhurt and cowered, letting go of the water they were fighting over. Emma stood, frozen, and the gunman disappeared around a corner, dropping bottles as he ran.

The cowering man pushed himself to a stand, grabbed some bottles that had fallen, and ran in the other direction.

"Might equals right?" Lilli said, her voice dry and low.

"Does everyone have a gun?" Emma's voice shook. She glanced at Lilli and Jade, who wore blank expressions as they backed into the shop. Emma followed, and Lilli closed the shop door. Emma pressed her hand to her chest to slow her heart.

"Did not see that one coming." Lilli chewed the pen to splinters. She leaned against the wall for support.

"We need to get out of this shop and away from here, now." Jade raised her hand to her scar buried beneath layers of sweater and coat. Lilli brushed dust off of a leather bench, and Jade sank onto it.

"Four days ago, Jim was sitting right here sketching that Celtic knot, remember? Seems like years ago." Jade's blank eyes roamed over the bench, to the T-shirt rack lying on its side, to the dragon figurines scattered across the floor.

"So, what's the plan?" Lines etched Lilli's eyes and her mouth.

"This will only get worse. We leave now or we'll be stuck here."

"Worse?" Emma sat at the far end of the bench.

Jade's dull eyes mesmerized her. Was this what shock looked like? Emma was here because she wanted to pass out flyers, do her part to save the planet, and now look at her. She was leading an expedition across Vandby, but she couldn't get beyond the shop door. Mom must be out of her mind. The door to the cellar stood open, and the cocoon-like safety beckoned her.

A wooden door with a broken window was the only thing standing between her and looters and people with guns. She stood and took a step toward the cellar. "Is leaving really our only option?" She took another step.

"Hold on there, Missy." Lilli grabbed Emma's coat sleeve. Emma struggled to get away, but Lilli held fast and looked her in the eyes. "Jinx is still down there, remember?"

Emma's eyes flew from Lilli, to Jade, to the cellar door. Another fight was breaking out in the market across the street. "What is happening?" Her head swiveled and she couldn't focus on any one thing.

"I know that look." Jade motioned to Emma. "Come here, darlin'."

Emma sank onto the bench, and with gentle fingers, Jade stroked Emma's stray hairs behind her ears. Emma wiped her nose on her sleeve, but only smeared tears and snot across her face. "What are we going to do?"

"We'll just figure it out as we go." Lilli shook her head. "Because we gotta leave, now."

Emma wiped her eyes. "You do see the glass half-full." Heat rose to Emma's cheeks. She'd never talked back to a grown-up who wasn't Mom. "What about the guns?"

Jade took Emma's face in her hands. "We got your back, Emma. We just need to keep a low profile and avoid people. Together we can do this."

Emma's shoulders tightened, and her head ached from holding back tears and failing.

"Safety in numbers." Lilli peered through the blinds, exposing the street.

Emma could make out an alley that ran between the buildings across the street, the green of Johnson Park at the other end a jumble of trees blown to the ground, their branches tangled and chaotic.

"Jade, if you can make it to that alley, we can cut across the park and make a plan when we reach the other side." Emma put her ponytail in her mouth then brushed it out. Had she just planned something that didn't suck?

"I can make it. No problem." Jade stood.

A vise grip twisted her stomach. "I have no idea how long this is going to take, guys. I don't even know how far—" She gritted her teeth. No one needed to see her cry.

"What's your address? Maybe I can guesstimate." Lilli's forehead was creased as she gazed at Jade, who pressed her hand on her injured leg.

"It's 1417 NE Wilson Street, in the Alphabet District."

"I've been to the Alphabet District, once. You're right. That's way across town." Jade stared through the blinds.

"I'd say it's probably two or three miles through city streets. Lots of restaurants and shops, and we have to get through the Market neighborhood, which might be a bit rough."

"Look on the bright side, hon. At least we don't have to cross the river."

"Well look whose glass is half-full." Lilli grinned at Jade and turned to Emma. "We can do this, Emma."

Emma rubbed her palm with the thumb of her other hand, a trick her grandmother taught her after her dad died. She pushed the clutter of thoughts from her mind and focused on the littered street before her. Sunshine glinted off glass shards and pop cans. She had lived her whole life in Vandby, but she'd never been on this street filled with tattoo shops and hair salons. The market across the street stood open, windows broken. Nobody had emerged in the past five minutes. The shelves must be picked clean by now.

The alley loomed dark and filled with shadows. Anyone could be hiding in there. She cleared her throat, stalling for time. "One block at a time, right?" She glanced at Jade who nodded.

"That's right. One block closer to home."

A car door slammed, and Emma spun around ready to run, or scream, or both. A kid Sarah's age ran from a car to an apartment building. Emma giggled, but every muscle remained tight.

Lilli peeked over her shoulder. She'd found a pencil somewhere. It hung from her lips. "The coast looks clear." Her dark eyes did not waver.

Emma took a final glance at the shop, her haven until guns happened. Was it safe anywhere now? Home? The rules were changing by the minute. She leaned out the door and scanned the street. All clear.

She couldn't stall another second. She took off at a sprint, the water bottles and apples in her backpack bouncing, throwing her off-balance. She ducked into the alley and pressed her back against the wall. She glanced back at the shop. The door was still shut.

Lilli gripped Jade, her gaze boring into Emma. How would Jade make it through the piles of wood, broken glass, plastic bags and bottles, metal roofing, lampshades?

The quiet unsettled her. The familiar engines revving, bus brakes squealing, jets flying overhead, people in conversation on the street—none of those noises filled the air.

Her heart battered against her ribs. She motioned to Lilli and Jade, but footsteps echoed in the street, coming fast. Emma held her hand up, and Lilli froze, shielding Jade in the doorway. Emma pressed into the shadows of the alley.

Two men ran by, bulging pillowcases slung over their shoulders. Emma clutched her backpack to her chest. She would not lose her food in the first five minutes of their journey.

The footsteps faded, and Emma scanned the street. The sky was so blue and bright, but what Emma needed was the comfort of darkness and shadows.

Lilli waved from the doorway.

Emma waved back then crossed her fingers.

Lilli and Jade hobbled across the street, a red spot blossoming on the bandage covering Jade's wound. They slumped against the wall beside Emma.

Lilli and Jade huffed and puffed. Emma let them catch their breath then, with a nod, she raced to the other end of the alley at the park side, scanned Johnson Street in both directions. All clear. She motioned for Lilli and Jade to follow. They hobbled, slower with the safety of shadows surrounding them. They'd already improved their three-legged-run.

The sun blazed on the park, and Emma covered her face with her hands. Where were the lawns, the benches, the statue of Captain Vancouver? Under that tangled mess of maple and Douglas fir? Root systems the size of bulldozers had lifted from the ground, exposing dark soil, the rich earthy aroma filling the air. What kind of storm did this? A badass storm. Emma leaned against the wall of the alley, rubbing her palm until the skin was raw.

Lilli placed a hand on her shoulder, and she jerked away. "Calm down, girl."

Jade bit her lip, her face a grimace of pain. Lilli gnawed on a pencil, her eyes glued on the park. They had expectations of her, of course, but was she capable? She had to be.

"Right." Emma focused on the chaos of trees, branches sticking out at all angles. In the tangle of evergreen foliage stood a sign.

"Look." Emma pointed to the tourist sign, its plaques pointing to The Wharf, The Market, Vandby U, and Founder Square. This was her streetcar route.

"We cross Johnson Park, go right until we hit Market." She stared at the chaos of trees. But how?

"Good plan." Lilli winked.

Emma pressed her hand to her temple. Her head might just crack wide open. She took a step, and then another, until she was running.

"You got this," Emma whispered. She crossed the street toward the branches.

"Hey, kid."

She stumbled and glanced to her right. A man stood in the middle of Johnson Street. His hand reaching for her, his eyes glued to her backpack. Did he want to help her?

No. She bolted for the park and tumbled over a tree trunk, her movements quick and stiff. She kept climbing farther into the park. How would Lilli and Jade get by him unseen? She sank into the branches and waited.

Her skin itched and her left calf cramped. Every rustle and crack made her neck muscles spasm. She hunkered.

"Blessed virgins."

Emma clapped a hand over her mouth. With the grace of two elephants in the bush, Lilli and Jade pushed through the tangle.

"You made it." She threw her arms around Lilli then Jade.

"That dude. What did he say to you?" Lilli drained half a water bottle before handing it to Jade who finished it. "He finally left, but I thought he was going to follow you in here."

"All he said was, 'Hey, kid.' " Emma's hands went clammy, and she sank onto a branch.

"Did you know him?"

"No." Did she know him? "I don't think so. Everyone looks like a zombie to me, so maybe?"

"We gotta move in case he comes back." Jade pushed herself up. "He didn't have food or water. I don't think we want to find out what he wanted."

Emma nodded. She glanced at Jade who gripped her thigh and hissed air through her teeth. Emma slipped under branches and climbed over trees, sweat trickling down her temple. How big was this park anyway? Every patch of lawn was a relief, but she preferred the cover of the branches. They hid them from people with guns, people who wanted their water and food.

She climbed over another trunk, and her thighs ached. She sat to wait for Lilli and Jade. The sun had moved across the sky. It would be dark soon, and this walk through the park was becoming her worst gym-class-obstacle-course nightmare. Closing her eyes, she leaned back against a tree trunk.

"Waiting for us?" Jade had found a branch-crutch.

Emma stood, a smile cracking her dry lips. "You hardly made a sound. And you're not helping her?" Emma looked from Jade to Lilli.

"So independent, our gal." Lilli hovered behind Jade, her pencil now a stub hanging out of her mouth.

Independence. That's what Emma had wanted, but independence was highly over-rated and came at a high price.

Emma nodded, too tired to speak. She pushed through yet another branch, stepping on something soft and lowered her eyes. She sprang back—purple hoodie. Was that an arm? She scrambled under a branch and over a tree trunk.

"What is it?" Lilli stood on a tree and gawked through the branches.

"Nothing," Emma blurted and rushed through more branches, scratching her hands and face. It was not a body. It was only a hoodie blown here by the storm.

She sank to the ground when she came to a patch of grass. She grabbed her water and drank, waiting for Lilli and Jade. The sun glowed even lower to the west.

"On a good day, that would have been a ten-minute stroll," Lilli said. "My favorite bench is right over there." She pointed into the branches.

"I think it took us over an hour based on the sun's position now." Jade leaned on her crutch, searching the sky. "It's going to take days to get to your house, not hours." Jade held her hand over her eyes, squinting at Emma, out of breath and sweaty.

"We have to keep moving." Emma left the little piece of exposed lawn and climbed through more branches.

****

Emma stepped onto Park Street, and every muscle in her body hurt. She perched on a tree trunk under the cover of branches and waited for Lilli and Jade. The rustling of branches and an occasional curse told her they were close.

She scoped out Park Street. Fallen trees blocked the road to the left, a familiar sight now. To the right, a giant maple tree had fallen across the tracks, and on the other side—a streetcar? Emma stopped and scratched her head.

The blue line? SUVs and sedans created a logjam of vehicles that blocked the other side of the streetcar. No way for it to move forward or backward. Emma had ridden that very streetcar to marches with Megan. Where was that girl now?

"Here we are." Lilli burst through the branches, a grin on her face.

"We're not out of the woods yet." Emma clamped a hand over her mouth, heat rising from her neck to her cheeks. Did that really come out of her mouth? Ugh.

"I guess someone had to say it." Lilli helped Jade over the last tree trunk, chuckling over her bad pun.

"Vandby is a city of trees." Jade rubbed her leg,

leaning on her crutch. Lilli reached for her hand, held it. "That's what drew us here."

"At least we're getting exercise. Sitting in that cellar was driving me bonkers." Lilli flexed her bicep, and Jade grunted.

"But does every block from Founder's Square to Emma's house have to have a pile of trees blocking our way?"

"Look on the bright side. We'll have plenty of cover to hide from looters," Lilli said.

"There you go again with that glass half-full crap. At least I have my gun." Jade patted the pocket of her bomber jacket.

Perspiration dripped down Emma's back, and she shivered. Of course, she brought the gun.

Chapter Thirteen

Emma

The birds all seemed to chirp at once, and Emma searched the trees, but the birds remained hidden in the branches.

"It's like they're celebrating their survival." Lilli kept pace with Jade as her crutch echoed off the pavement.

Emma stared at the trees lying across the street before her. Sunlight glinted off the reflective letters of a sign, its arrow pointing to the Market.

"We go that way a block then left onto Market Street." Emma scanned for movement of any kind then motioned for Lilli and Jade to follow. Jade leaned on her travel leg, as she called her crutch. She moved faster, but they were losing daylight. They'd never make it to her house before dark.

Emma stuck her clenched fists in her pockets. Alone, she could have run between the logjams and gotten farther, maybe even home. She kicked a stone. The sky dimmed, and shadows became more pronounced with each passing minute.

"We'll get there, Emm." Lilli gave her a thin smile but didn't wink. "There's safety in numbers. We only make three, but it's better than one."

Could Lilli read her mind? She hadn't said

anything about Jade going too slow, had she?

"It'll be dark soon. We should look for shelter." Jade hung on Lilli who swayed a bit.

Emma folded her arms. "I guess."

Her need to get home was a constant ache in her chest, but Lilli was right, and she would never leave Jade. Emma needed these women, and Jade wouldn't make it another block without a break. She trudged around three parked cars, a tree resting across them, and stopped.

"A Bomber Burger Shack." She wanted to leap up and down. Almost-sixteen-year-olds didn't jump up and down, though. She shook her head to clear it. "I worked here last summer."

The oldies were always blaring at Bomber Burger, and Emma murmured the words to her mom's favorite, "What does your love mean to me, baby? Ev-er-y-thing." Would Mom ever forgive her? She took a step.

Lilli grabbed Emma's hood. "Wait. Is it safe? The wind blew most of the roof off."

Emma glanced over her shoulder, and Lilli pointed to the roof. Jade leaned on her travel leg and rubbed her scar.

"Right. But we need to stop for the night, and I know this place. Let me check it out."

She jogged across the parking lot, peered inside, then opened the door. Lilli and Jade followed.

"Sybil? Gregory?" Emma waited for a response. It was cold, dark, and the odor of rancid grease filled her nostrils, so different from the tantalizing aroma of fries and burgers, the 80s music, and the strings of Christmas lights that lit Bomber Burger and gave it the party atmosphere that kept it filled with customers.

"Sybil and Gregory aren't here." Lilli spun a slow circle taking in every corner of the Bomber Burger's ceiling. "Looks sturdy enough inside."

Emma glanced at the ceiling. Gregory always said, "They don't build 'em like this anymore," and he'd pound on the wood wall. The ceiling wouldn't fall. Lilli was being paranoid. Emma paused. The door to the kitchen stood wide open.

Someone had been here. That door was never left open unless food was coming out. She peered inside at the deep-fat fryers and griddles.

"It's pretty damp, but at least we can lock the door." Lilli twisted the deadbolt. She scanned the ceiling again.

"Better than on the street." Jade coughed. "Stinks, though." Jade sank onto a booth and massaged her thigh.

"Not sure if breathing through my mouth is a better option." Lilli held her hand over her mouth. She plopped next to Jade.

"Ugh. I can taste it." Emma tried breathing through her dirty sleeve and sneezed. Her eyes adjusted to the dim interior. A window let in enough light to make out the grills and refrigerators in the kitchen. She snuck a peak at Lilli and Jade checking out the booths and tables in the dining area.

Emma opened a freezer and slammed it shut, stepping back, her hand covering her mouth. Thawed fish sticks. The stench clung to her nostrils, and she rubbed her nose. "No food that I can find." She walked into the dining area pretty sure the fish odor came with her.

"I could eat a horse." Jade hobbled to a booth near

the counter, slipped off her backpack, and sank with a grunt.

"I can take your order, if all you want is a PB&J." Lilli sank beside Jade and gave her a sandwich. "You should have two in your bag, Emma."

"PB&J? But I want a double bacon cheeseburger." Emma plunked down opposite Lilli and Jade and reached into her bag. She lifted a smashed sandwich and grinned at Jade.

"It's good to see you smile for once," Jade said and dangled a baggie from her fingers, jelly smeared on the plastic. "Poor sandwich."

Lilli bounced up and down on the bench. "These booths are comfy. I can sleep here."

"The door is locked. We should be safe," Jade said.

Emma swiped the greasy bench with a finger, rubbed the grime on her jeans. This was the booth where mom sat on Emma's first day. "Best table for watching you in action."

She'd stumbled through her orders somehow, like an ant under a magnifying glass, the heat getting hotter by the minute. Mom ordered fries and a cheeseburger dripping with grease, and she'd grin at her every time Emma walked by.

Emma's mouth watered as she chewed the dry peanut butter and jelly sandwich. The familiar spiral of booths was Sybil's idea, so that every booth had a view out the front window. Emma wasn't sure that was such a good idea now that looters wandered the streets.

She took another bite of the smashed sandwich. At least the jam made it moist. Her eyes drooped with each bite.

She wiped her mouth with her fingers and stuffed

the other half in the baggie. She was too tired to eat. She fluffed her backpack on the bench and lay back. It would have to do. She wedged into the backrest, the soft murmurs of Lilli and Jade lulling her to sleep.

A loud crack shook the building, and Emma shot to her feet as pieces of ceiling plaster and water crashed down around her.

****

Emma opened her eyes. She'd slept? She scanned the shelves, rows and rows of empty shelves. She sat on the cold tile floor and shook her head. It ached, and she raised a hand. That's right. Her mad dash to the storeroom had come with a price.

Jade sat on a stack of boxes. She bit her lip as Lilli changed her bandage. Emma rubbed the sleep from her eyes and pushed to a stand, her back stiff from the cold damp floor.

"That was a narrow escape, right?" Lilli wound the bandage around Jade's leg and fastened the end. "Hold still, hon. One more roll ought to do it."

"Good thing you knew about this room." Jade swung her gaze around the storeroom. She wiped her nose with the back of her hand and sniffed. "Still stinks, though."

"Why didn't I listen to Lilli? She said the roof looked bad." Emma shrugged.

"Water under the bridge, kid." Lilli grabbed more gauze wrap.

"Can I help?" She peered over Lilli's shoulder.

Dark red seeped from Jade's wound, and Emma's head started spinning. She clutched a shelf as Lilli unrolled the gauze strip and finished wrapping Jade's leg.

Emma clamped a hand over her mouth and rushed out the door into the alley behind the Bomber Burger. The fresh air cleared her head, and she sank onto the smoker's bench Gregory had built thirty years ago. She reached for her water and chugged half of it.

Jade limped out of the storeroom, her forehead creased and stared at Emma.

"What?" Emma rose from the bench brushing off her pants.

Jade handed her a piece of yellow paper. "Found it on the floor."

Emma stared at the scrap of paper, torn at the edges. "What's that?" She reached out her hand, and the curls in the handwriting gave her jolt—Mom's writing. She took the paper. Her hands trembled as she read:

Emma, sorry we fought. Come home. I love you, Mom.

Emma stared at Jade and Lilli. She scrunched the paper in her hand. "You read it?"

"How were we supposed to know it was for you?" Lilli took a step forward, chewing on a Burger Bomber pen.

"You fought with your mom?" Jade reached for Emma, but Emma jerked away.

She reread the short note.

"She's out here looking for you," Lilli said.

"We have to get you home, now." Jade adjusted her crutch.

Emma wanted to burst out of her skin, to race down Market Street. Did Mom go home after putting out notes? She balled the note in her fist. She didn't want independence. She wanted her momma.

"If we're going to get her home today, we need to get a move on." Lilli nodded to Jade.

"I can be fast." Jade swung her crutch at Lilli.

The birds sang in less frantic chirps this morning.

"We'll follow you." Lilli adjusted Jade's arm on her shoulder and chewed on her pen.

That's right. She was leading this trek. She scanned the crossroads of Market and 14th. Emma cleared her throat. "We stay on Market until we hit 16th."

"You should run ahead. Go find your mom. We'll catch up." Jade pulled a purple bandana from her jeans pocket and wiped her brow.

"No." Emma jammed her fists on her hips. "We stick together. Safety in numbers, remember?" Emma stepped over a branch and pushed through a tangle of branches, chewing on the tip of her ponytail. She wanted to run, but how much faster would she go?

Lilli and Jade hobbled behind her. Two blocks, and every inch was covered in scraps of plastic, downed trees, plastic bottles, glass. Why did it have to be so difficult?

Lilli stopped. "Do you smell something?"

"Smells like death." Jade had gone from drawl to monotone again, hunching her shoulders.

Lilli punched her shoulder, and Jade glanced at Emma. "Oh, sorry."

"Too late, hon. Be mindful." Lilli grabbed Jade's hand and stroked it.

Emma's gut twisted, and she pressed her hands over it. Who knew fear could hurt? That it could be a real thing in your belly that twisted and churned? Emma turned onto Market Street and stumbled over a branch. She stopped. Maples and cedars had fallen to

109

form a pile of trees that clogged the road. When would it end? The stench got stronger as they walked.

Emma tried to walk around the pile, but the pile blocked the entire road. She gazed to the top. It reached the second story of a brick building. "What a mess. Looks like we have to climb over this one, or walk around the block, which means triple more climbing."

"Let's stay on 16th." Lilli adjusted Jade's arm over her shoulder. "We can't go one extra step."

Emma nodded. She approached the pile and found one tree leaning like a ramp halfway to the top.

"Maybe I can see my house from up there."

Emma grabbed a branch. The tree seemed like a balance beam but at a steep angle. She climbed onto the trunk, pitch gumming her fingers. She placed one foot in front of the other, grabbing branches for support as she climbed. She stopped halfway. This was nothing like gymnastics. Her chest heaved with her efforts.

She glanced down at Lilli and Jade. Jade grinned at her and waved. Emma waved back, but her foot slipped. She screamed, falling to her hands and knees. How would Jade get up this pile? She stepped off the log and onto a branch the thickness of her thigh. It held, and she used the branches as hand holds as she climbed the pile.

"You're doing great," Lilli called.

Emma didn't answer. She wanted to shout, "No I'm not," but bit her lip instead. The mass of trees settled as she climbed, and each jerk stopped her cold, sweat breaking out on her upper lip.

"I'm coming down." She clung to a branch and glanced at Lilli and Jade.

"No. You got this." Lilli shifted from foot to foot.

"Easy for you to say," Emma muttered. She pushed

through a wall of branches, searching for footholds with her toes.

She glanced up for her next branch but saw only blue sky. Had she reached the top? Her throat was raw, and her arms hung like rubber bands. She rubbed blood back into them. A scuffle and growls came from the street, and she scanned the other side of the pile.

Several dogs growled and paced around a dumpster, the hair on their backs standing in ridges. They were fighting over garbage. She turned and began to climb down, her legs numb. She wanted to jump, but the ground was too far. She wanted to run, but she was fifteen feet off the ground.

"What is it?" Jade asked.

Emma couldn't speak. She counted five of them circling the dumpster tipped on its side. The contents joined the debris in the street, but the rotten food was worth fighting for, apparently.

"Emma," Lilli said. "Update, girl."

Emma's throat tightened. Was that Mr. Peterson's German shepherd? It started barking and growling at a Rottweiler, protecting a package of hamburger buns. That could not be Mr. Peterson's dog. Emma froze, her muscles tight. The shepherd's growl rumbled deep in its chest. Lilli appeared at Emma's side, and Jade rested her hand on Emma's shoulder.

"Feral dogs?" Jade kept her voice low. Her hands shook.

"That explains a lot." Lilli glanced from Emma to Jade.

"Feral?" Emma leaned on Lilli's shoulder, seeking the warmth of another human being. She couldn't let the dogs out of her sight. If she did, they might get her.

She swallowed hard and blinked.

"It means wild." Jade backed away from Emma's perch. "Happens when they get hungry."

Lilli reached for Jade. "It's okay, hon. They can't climb trees."

A Lab and two mutts circled a bag of carrots. Emma watched the German shepherd tumble one of the mutts and pin it on its back. It yelped. The growls and barks sent ice through her veins. This might be worse than humans with guns.

Lilli followed Jade to the far side of the logjam. Emma couldn't move a muscle. These dogs used to be someone's pets, licking faces and wagging tails, but now they wanted to kill each other. Why were they behaving like this? Nothing made sense anymore.

"We should have stayed at the shop." Jade's voice faltered.

"We couldn't stay there. Listen. We just need to go around the block." Lilli gave Emma a look.

Emma cleared her throat. "Yeah, we'll climb back the way we came. They won't even see us."

A screen door screeched, and Emma grabbed a branch for balance. A man in a plaid flannel bathrobe pushed through the screen, and it slammed shut behind him. He looked like Megan's dad, tall and slender with curly hair that stuck out from his head like wires. She had the urge to stand and ask if he had a running faucet, but something kept her silent. She stared at him as he walked into the street. What was he up to?

Lilli froze, her gaze on the man, but Jade cowered, her shaking hand rustling the branch she held. Emma reached for Jade, but the harsh voice of the man stopped her.

"Damn dogs. Shut your yaps." He swung a rifle to his shoulder.

She gasped. The shock wave blasted through her ears, the ringing a familiar pain.

The Rottweiler dropped and didn't move. The German shepherd and the other dogs scattered, and the man fired again and again. The third shot hit one of the mutts. It yipped and fell on its side. Emma ducked.

When she took her fingers from her ears and opened her eyes, the dogs had disappeared but for the two lying in the street.

The man yawned, dropped the muzzle of his rifle, and disappeared into the house. Emma stared at the porch. Lilli held Jade who clung to her.

"Oh my goddess, oh my goddess." Jade whispered. Her head spun left and right, like an ostrich searching for the dogs. "Where did they go? Did you see where they went?"

Emma brushed her hair out of her mouth. She had to quit that, or wash her hair, or both. She shook her head as though that might make the stars stop shooting across her eyelids every time she closed them.

Lilli whispered, "Emma? We gotta get off this pile before—you know," she nodded toward Jade.

"Right."

When had upstanding, rifle-toting citizens start shooting wild dogs in the street? She smoothed her hair and tightened her ponytail.

"We have to climb down the way we came and go around the block." She wiped her nose on her sleeve and began the climb down.

"No, no, no. You don't know where the dogs are." Jade's high whisper hissed in the silence.

"The dogs are gone, hon," Lilli said.

A rustling came from the bottom of the pile. Emma glanced down. It was the German shepherd sniffling at the path they'd climbed. "He's back."

Lilli grabbed Jade and dragged her to the other side of the pile. The German shepherd nosed the log they had used to climb to the top, panting as though it were laughing. It pushed through branches, climbing up the tree.

Chapter Fourteen

Josh

Josh read one section in the radio manual over and over, "Sending Code." Uncle Carl told him not to worry about it. Receiving was more important than sending. He shut the manual and dropped it on the desk. Papa never used the manual, neither did Dad, but Josh would depend on it. Why hadn't he memorized this stuff for the exam like Grandpa suggested? He could have aced that first one.

He swiveled in the chair. What if the radio cut out again? He could crank it, but electricity was easier, and that meant getting a solar circuit connected.

The radio began tapping out code. He tipped the chair over in his haste to grab paper and pencil. He jotted down the dots and dashes and used the chart. It began with CM, Uncle Carl's call sign.

At hospital. Sis on drip. Sleeping.

His body slumped with relief. Drip meant IV in Uncle Carl-speak. He grabbed the Morse code chart and wrote out his message, then translated it into dots and dashes and typed.

All good here. No Dad yet.

He ended with his dad's call sign, EW. If he got a fine from the FCC, he'd just pay it. He sat back in the chair and scrubbed his face with his hands. Would the electricity come on before dad got home? Would they send the National Guard? Uncle Carl had gotten through, but his radio was short range, Grandpa's was long. He placed a hand on the radio. It was warm to the touch, and he could picture Grandpa, last Christmas, sitting in this same chair sending messages late at night to his friend in Germany. Josh needed it to survive.

He gave the volume a final adjustment and opened the windows. The messages would rattle out loud enough to get his attention, and they repeated. He could write them down and translate them when he came in.

He climbed the steps and stood on the porch, scanning the yard. The sun warmed his face. Something glinted in the driveway. He kept the spot in his vision and hauled a solar panel from under the branches. He struggled to lift it without bending, carried it to the circuit frame where he found another panel tangled in the lower branches of a cedar tree.

Any tree still standing was a miracle as far as he was concerned. He reached between the branches and placed his hand on the bark, rough but warm. He cleared his throat and lifted this panel, placing it on the stack. Another panel lay right beside the frame flat on the ground covered with fir needles and scraps of plastic and paper.

This circuit held eight panels, and four were still in frames. Once repaired, he could switch from generator to solar power before the next storm, if the connections were solid. The generator worked, but it was noisy and attracted attention. He'd need it to keep the well pump, which meant a flushing toilet, water in the sink, and keep the radio running, which meant communication with the outside world.

He'd helped Grandpa install these panels, so fixing them wouldn't be a problem. He held one and checked it for dents and cracks. They all seemed to be in good shape, considering the wind had ripped them out of the frame. He brushed off the debris and fit them, one by one, into the mountings. He removed the pliers from his back pocket and began tightening screws and refastening wires.

He brushed off his hands and headed to the breaker box in the pantry for the true test. Shining the flashlight on the main switch, he flipped it. Green. He disconnected the generator, recording the gas level in his notepad, just in case he needed to switch back.

He jogged down the stairs and sat before the radio. The echo of his empty tummy as it growled was the only drumroll he was going to get. The radio dials blipped, and a message rolled in from Anchorage. It was a tally of fishing boats lost at sea.

His tummy rumbled again. A sandwich with his name on it was calling. He took the steps two at a time and headed to the kitchen. Three days without a proper meal, and his mouth watered for pizza. What were the chances? He grabbed the fridge handle and opened the door. A blast of putrid odors rolled out and enveloped him.

"Aww." He slammed the door. Too late, the smell of rotten salmon coated his nostrils.

Grandpa said without electricity the fridge would stay cold about four hours, the freezer about two days, and that was only if he didn't open it. All it took was three days of storm, and everything was rotten. No pizza. Plugging his nose, he cracked the fridge door open again. Tones of broccoli added to the bouquet of

117

fish. The catsup might be good. The lettuce had turned to slime. He'd prop the doors open and scrub it out, later. He shut the fridge and reached for the freezer door, eased it open a crack. Standing water with packages of chicken breasts and thawed beans floated in the bottom bin. What a waste.

He opened a cabinet, grabbed one of mom's shopping bags, and filled it with boxes of pasta, crackers, and canned soup to haul to the basement. He found bread, strawberry jam, and peanut butter in another one. Not the cheese he was craving, but the rotted food had dulled his appetite anyway.

He'd make a sandwich then tackle the fridge before the next storm hit.

A jug of purified water sat on the counter, and he grabbed a glass and poured, then drank big gulps. It left him full for the time being. He placed the water next to the bag.

He slapped together a sandwich and ate it in four bites. Mom would have said, "chew, but she wasn't here. His stomach growled again, and he rummaged through more cabinets, all the while taking inventory of the damage, four broken windows, one with a branch poking through, pine needles and glass covering the floor, the refrigerator full with rotten food, not too bad really.

He needed Dad to know that he could take care of the farm. Then maybe he'd consider taking it off the market. Besides, who would buy it now with all this damage. He took out the notepad and started a list.1. kitchen

He gazed at the blue sky outside, and it drew him like a magnet to the back porch. He scanned the open expanse, so unfamiliar with all the trees that had fallen. Dark clouds were gathering in the southern sky. Not so soon? The muscles in his neck grew stiff and cramped. He rubbed them as the clouds boiled on the horizon.

Had Dad headed for home? Would he get caught in the next storm? Vandby stood in the path between the storm and the farm, and Vandby U was two miles on the other side, so Dad would have seventeen miles to walk before another storm hit. He'd never make it.

The dark clouds loomed closer, and he combed his fingers through his hair. Frantic birdcalls filled the air. The storm was moving fast. He still needed to board the windows. A stack of plywood sat in the barn from Grandpa's sheep shed he'd never finished. He marched to the barn, loaded a tool belt with a hammer, a drill, and a fistful of fasteners.

He lifted a sheet of plywood and headed to the house. His arms cramped halfway. How had Grandpa unloaded that stack by himself? Leaning the plywood against the porch railing, he rubbed blood back into his aching arms. Grandpa had worked hard all his life, and it kept him in shape.

Josh began clearing away branches and glass then fastened the plywood over two living room windows. He used to help Grandpa do these chores. The weight of the plywood was nothing to the weight of his grief. He made two more trips to the barn and covered all the windows at the front of the house.

He checked the rest of the house. No broken windows on the north or east sides, thank heavens. The house should protect his solar panel circuit through the next storm, if luck was on his side, that is.

He collected his tools and headed back to the barn.

A rustling in the branches drew his attention.

"Dad?" Was he imagining things now? He scanned the yard and beyond. Dad was out there somewhere. If the roads were as clogged as the driveway, it would be the toughest commute he'd ever make without traffic.

He dragged a garbage can from the barn to the living room. The hardwood floors bore deep scratches in the polished wood. The storm had left its mark on everything.

A row of blue dishes rimmed the dining room wall above the windows, his great-grandmother's Danish plates. The winds had left them untouched. Josh stood mesmerized by each one. They told a story of family, home, and feasts during a time of candles before refrigeration. He could do this. People had survived very well without electricity. It would make life more difficult, though.

He threw branches outside and swept glass from the floors, his mind working through all the things that had happened over the last four days. Maybe his true calling was to be a carpenter not a doctor. Houses didn't cry when he fixed them. This house was solid. His grandparents had saved them with their carpentry skills.

He dragged the full garbage can to the barn. Bird song filled the air. A branch cracked and something else. Voices? Josh ducked inside the barn door.

Two men climbed through the trees and branches blocking the driveway. He leaned against the barn wall. Every muscle he owned tensed. Why hadn't he kept the hammer in his belt?

"If this…radio, maybe…Canada."

He could only make out a few words as they spoke,

but "radio" gave him a jolt. The men were headed to the house. Josh peered through a crack in the siding.

"I smell food, Bill, I'm telling you," said a man in grimy jeans and a sport jacket with a tear in the left elbow. His face was smeared with dirt.

Bill had silver sprinkled through his dark shaggy hair, and he was scoping out Josh's yard. His eyes seemed to glow from under black brows, his mouth hidden by a dark beard.

Bill stopped and held up a hand. "Hush, Chip."

Josh was paralyzed. Who were these men? They weren't farmers, not in those clothes.

Chip's shoulder-length hair hung in dirty blond strands. His beard was patchy, like he'd tried to shave but the razor was dull. Had the shaggy-haired man spotted the antenna? He'd want the radio.

Josh gritted his teeth. How could he get rid of them now? He didn't stand a chance if things got physical.

"What do you smell this time? Barbeque?" Bill's bootcut jeans were as dirty as Chip's.

Josh sank into a crouch. Why hadn't he gone with Uncle Carl? Why hadn't he taken weight training instead of racket sports? He backed deeper into the barn, his mind racing. He could sneak out the back and get to Uncle Carl's before the next storm, or he could stay, like he'd begged Uncle Carl, and confront these guys.

There was something about Bill that seemed familiar. Was it his beard? The men headed to the house, and Josh's belly did a flip. No, no, no. Not the house. Blood rushed from his head. Why had he swept up the glass? They'd be looking for the owners, for food, water, the radio.

They clomped up the porch steps and knocked. Knocking was a good sign, right? They didn't just break the door down. Chip stood on tiptoe to peer over the plywood covering the living room window.

"Someone's been cleaning." Bill scanned the yard.

"I don't smell food, though." Chip sniffed the air.

"That's because no one's cooking, moron. You've smelled food ever since we left Vandby." Bill jogged down the steps and headed around the house. Chip knocked again.

Vandby? If these guys had come all that way, Dad was probably right behind them. He reached in his pocket for the keys, empty. He hadn't locked the front door, but why would he? He was too worried about boarding up windows, not looters.

Bill returned to stand beside Chip in the driveway. Josh had to do something. Clearing his throat, he stepped out of the barn.

"Can I help you?" Josh kept his face a blank mask, clenched his shaking fingers into fists.

Both men spun around.

"It's a kid."

"Shut it, Chip." Bill's red cotton shirt was open at the neck showing a yellowed T-shirt. "Your dad here?" Bill looked Josh up and down.

He's sizing me up. Josh swallowed hard. "He's rounding up cows. They're spread from here to the next county." Josh clamped his mouth shut. He'd said too much.

Bill grinned. Nothing seemed to escape his scrutiny. "Your mom here?"

Josh's pulse jackhammered through his veins. He bit his bottom lip until it bled. "She'll be back soon.

Helping the neighbors, you know." He had to change the topic. "Where'd you guys come from?"

Josh stood and thrust out his chest, but Bill and Chip were taller, more muscular in the chest and arms. Josh stuffed his shaking hands in his pockets.

"We walked all the way from little, old Vandby." Bill rocked on his heels, his gaze taking in the barn, the yard, and the house, ending on Josh again.

Josh sniffed and wiped his nose. "That's a long way. You must be thirsty?" What was he saying? He'd just told them he had water. Next, they'd want food. Josh glanced at the house. He had to get a message to Uncle Carl, but Bill and Chip stood between him and the radio.

Chapter Fifteen

Emma

The shepherd climbed onto one tree trunk and then another, growling as it came. Emma pushed and Lilli pulled Jade until they reached the top of the pile. Who knew dogs could climb? Emma kept the dog in her sight. The pile shifted, and the shepherd lost its footing and slid back to the road. Emma glanced at Lilli, who had wrapped her arms around Jade.

"This pile isn't safe. We gotta get out of here." Lilli hugged Jade who had curled up under her. "Just give us a moment to untangle."

Dogs, wind, looters, Jade had cowered at them all, and she had the gun. The dog barked and growled, pacing the spot where the ramp log had shifted. It rose at a steeper angle, which kept the dog off.

She froze as the dog sniffed around the bottom of the pile. It tried the ramp again, but it rolled off after a couple steps.

The squeak of the screen door stopped the dog. The shepherd jerked its head in that direction, then lifted its nose and sniffed the air. Emma glanced at the screen door. It squeaked again, but it was just the wind. The dog turned and raced away.

"Thank all the goddesses," Lilli said, and Jade giggled.

Emma giggled, too, but she wasn't sure why. It wasn't funny. Jade's shoulders shook with laughter that turned to sobs, and the pile shifted again.

Emma clung to a branch. Why had she led them up this deathtrap? She wiped her eyes and cleared her throat. Lilli glanced at Emma with red eyes.

"It should be clear on the other side by now. I'll look." Emma began to climb. It was the least she could do for leading them into this mess. She climbed to the top and spotted the boutique where Mom bought Sarah's ballet slippers. The cross street was Jefferson. They'd gone two whole blocks since Market in the last hour, but it was two blocks closer to home. She scanned 16th Street for dogs, men in bathrobes with rifles, and looters.

"The coast looks clear. Let's go," she said.

Lilli helped Jade climb off the pile of trees, and Emma led them down 16th Street. Jade's movements grew more relaxed and graceful. Lilli pretended to take a selfie of them, the pile of trees in the background, and Jade laughed. The sound tinkled like snowdrops, and Emma sighed. They could do this.

"You know where we are now, right?" Jade's drawl was back.

"Jefferson and 16th. When we hit Bradley, we'll be in the alphabet district. All the streets there go A, B, C, all the way to W for Wils—" Emma stopped. Of course, they knew that. Jade stepped on a branch, and it broke with a crack. A chip of wood hit Emma's cheek.

"Oww." She put her hand to her cheek. Lifting her fingers, she stared at her blood then at Jade. Maybe they could do this?

"Sorry." Jade lifted a shaking hand to her mouth.

Emma's cheek throbbed. She searched the sky for the sun and found it farther to the west than she expected. She'd spent one night in Bomber Burger. She didn't want to spend another in some other greasy dive. They had to make it home before nightfall. Time dragged on with each step. It shouldn't be taking this long to get home, but all the piles of trees, feral dogs, men with rifles, and people fighting over water…

She kicked her way through sheets of roofing, metal panels, and tons of paper scraps. How had those dogs gone from pets to wild animals in just five days? A twig snapped, and she spun around.

Emma's foot slipped on the twisted metal of a wrought iron fence. Intertwined with tree branches and folded between the trunks of at least two fallen evergreens, the fence was twisted beyond repair. The filigree design was from a house that she passed every day on the way to school. The storm ruined everything.

She took a swig of water and held the bottle out for Lilli.

"Thanks, Emm." Lilli guzzled half then handed it to Jade.

"Closer?" Jade's face sagged with fatigue, her eyes sinking into her face.

"Closer." Emma stepped back. "Your leg?"

"Oh, that old thing? I hardly notice it anymore." Jade rubbed her hand on her thigh, smearing blood on her jeans.

Emma bit her lip. Jade was not fine. She was bleeding through her bandage again. "Maybe we should stop for a minute."

"This place is too open. We can't stop here, hon," Lilli said. "Dogs."

Could the dogs smell the blood? Emma shivered and made her way through the maze of evergreen boughs and wrought iron fencing, one step at a time. All she needed was a sprained ankle or a broken leg. Then she'd be worse off than Jade, tripping and cursing all the goddesses, most of whom Emma had never heard of before.

****

Lilli lifted Jade's leg helping her climb a log. Emma waited, her thighs aching. The journey had been twice as hard for Jade, but she never complained. She just looked like she was going to pass out all the time.

Pushing through more branches, Emma stepped into a yard filled with low shrubbery, no tall trees to topple. She stretched her arms to the sky then touched her toes, her muscles loosening as she stretched. She checked out the damage as she waited for Lilli and Jade.

The torn-up roofs, dented cars under trees, and telephone poles snapped in two had become an all too familiar backdrop to her walk home. The Gilford Street sign leaned against a fence. Inch by inch, she was getting closer to home. She rubbed the palm of one hand with the thumb of her other and tried to slow her heart rate.

Emma let the sun warm her face. "Please, no more storms." Emma pursed her lips and blew her plea to the universe with a kiss.

Lilli and Jade pushed their way through the branches and plopped on the grass. Emma welcomed their closeness, ignored the body odor. At least she had her saviors. She shivered. She never would have survived unconscious out in the storm.

A streetcar rolled to a stop on the next block, Hillman and 16th. It had a branch sticking out of a window, and other windows were broken or missing. Emma stared. This was a normal occurrence before the storm, but today it was like the Martians had landed.

"What the hell?" Lilli blurted and stood with her mouth open.

"Well, that's weird." Jade rose with Lilli's help. The streetcar stopped, and the doors screeched open.

Emma crouched, ready to run. Lilli was eyeing the doors like she wanted to hop on, but Emma wasn't so sure. This car appeared to be empty, but what about the others?

"Must be the new solar powered system. Cool." Lilli stood and brushed off her pants.

Emma reached for her phone out of habit. She wanted to snap a photo and send it to Mom to let her know she was on her way, but the black screen brought her back to reality, and she slipped it back into her pocket.

Lilli pointed at the solar panels on the roof of the streetcar. "Maybe we can charge our phones."

"No charger cord, right?" Jade gave Lilli a lopsided grin. "I didn't think of them."

"Damn." Lilli wiped her nose on her sleeve and nodded at the streetcar. "Emm, should we go for it?"

Emma took a step toward the streetcar. "Is this the Red Line?"

"Red Line. Yeah, that makes sense." Jade leaned on her crutch.

"The Red Line will take us two blocks from my house." Emma's voice got louder with each word. This was the break they needed, thanks to all the goddesses.

The streetcar doors stood open. Emma took off at a run. She leapt over a pile of insulation and aimed for the doors in the middle of the car. Tumbling through, she grabbed the metal handle then leaned her whole body on the door to hold it for Lilli and Jade.

She scanned the car. Empty. Emma was elated and disappointed at the same time. Who had she expected to meet? Lilli and Jade tumbled into the car, and Emma plopped down on a seat across from them. The door slid closed.

They sat hunched on benches, peering out the dirty windows as the streetcar carried them toward Emma's house. Emma closed her eyes. Could she imagine this was a normal day and pretend nothing had happened?

The streetcar stopped, and Emma opened her eyes. They were at Jamison Street, but the doors didn't open. Emma didn't think fast enough to push the button on the door. The streetcar jerked. She didn't want off. She wanted to go home. She was going home. The streetcar started rolling, but it was headed back the way they'd come.

No, no, no. Only two blocks? Emma sat and watched the landscape reverse. She couldn't speak. Lilli hadn't noticed the change of direction yet. She focused on Jade's leg, pressing a handkerchief to stop the blood. Jade sat her eyes clamped shut.

Lilli glanced out the window. Her head jerked up, and she stood. "Hey. We're going the wrong way."

"What?" Jade rose from the bench and pressed her hands on the metal frame of the broken window.

Emma's eyes ached as tears streaked her cheeks. "Sorry, guys," Emma said as the streetcar rolled toward town. It wobbled over branches and debris on the tracks. "I screwed up."

"You didn't know. Don't be so hard on yourself." Lilli sighed as Vandby Elementary School grew closer. Jade sat pressing the handkerchief to her wound.

A scream rose in Emma's throat, but she choked it back. Where had all the goddesses gone? Jade never should have put her in charge.

Jade wobbled as the car stopped at Hillman, again. The doors opened, and the sound of birds filled the air. Jade gasped, searching the street.

"No dogs, hon," Lilli embraced her and ran her hand over her hair.

Emma stared at the garbage bin on its side, the pile of trees they'd just climbed. She rubbed her face, unable to meet Lilli or Jade's gaze.

"We can just ride it back. It's two blocks we don't have to walk, right?" Lilli plopped down on the bench, drawing Jade with her, the decision made.

Emma sat back. Of course, they'd just ride it back then get off and continue the journey. No harm no foul, as Papa always said. She crossed her fingers. The doors closed, and the streetcar headed back toward Jamison Street.

"One pretty long ride for only two blocks." Lilli started chuckling, and Jade snorted. Emma watched as Lilli and Jade held each other and laughed.

"Its solar power keeps it running between logjams." Lilli wiped tears from her eyes.

Sending a silent thanks to all the goddesses, a surge of something filled Emma—happiness maybe? Relief? Yes, relief. It flowed through her veins the closer she got to home.

The streetcar creaked to a stop. The doors swished

open, startling a tall black dog. Jade screamed, and it ran away.

Emma stepped off and scanned the street. Two boys stood on the corner, and she froze. They were on the corner of Keller Street.

Lilli and Jade stepped off the streetcar, and it rattled away as one of the boys walked toward them. Emma looked from the boy to her friends and stepped out to intercept him.

"Hey, Emma?"

"Mark?" He'd been her neighbor since third grade, but still she tightened her ratty ponytail and smoothed her rumpled clothes. Mark didn't look much better. A yellow stain the shape of Ohio covered the front of his blue T-shirt.

"Have you guys been by my house? Is my mom home?"

"Heard she was super ticked. You'll probably get grounded for life." Mark shoved his hands in his pockets. "Did you just get off that streetcar?" He glanced from Emma to Lilli's boots, to Jade's bomber jacket, to the streetcar. His friend joined them. "Tom, it's Emma, my neighbor two doors down."

Tom lived out on Perimeter Road with his mom and sister. Since when were Mark and Tom friends? They never hung out at school. The storm had changed more than the roads and bus routes.

"Did you just get off that streetcar?" Tom asked.

"I just asked that, man." Mark shoved Tom's shoulder.

"Bless all the goddesses." Jade clanked her crutch on the sidewalk. "We don't have all day, guys. Is her mom home or not?"

Matt's hazel eyes had never seemed so bottomless as he scanned Emma's face. "She's probably home, waiting for this renegade." Mark nudged against Emma, and she was back in the halls of their school. Was he trying to memorize her face or just trying to find the girl he'd known before the storm? She wanted to him to look away and devour her with his eyes at the same time. Heat rose to her neck then to her cheeks.

"What are you guys doing out here?" Lilli chewed her pen as she adjusted Jade's bandage.

"We're walking to Cedarville with some friends. They said there's plenty of food and water, generators, you know, survivor stuff. You guys should come with us." He nodded to a group of people congregating on the corner of Jamison Street. They all wore backpacks stuffed full.

"Thanks, but I'm already in enough trouble with Mom." A chill shook her. When did Mom leave the note at the Bomber Burger, before or after the storm? What if she'd already left with Sarah?

"So, you're walking all the way to Cedarville? I guess it's not that far, maybe a twenty-five-minute drive on a good day, but with all this devastation and you're walking…"

Lilli's words didn't affect Mark, but then he'd always acted like nothing mattered, not even failing pre-calc. Tom, good influence that he was, shrugged and grinned.

Emma pushed her fingers into her cramped shoulder muscles. Mom would make that walk to Gran's if she had to, but would she leave without Emma? She might if it meant keeping Sarah safe and fed.

"Hey, we gotta go. Hang in there." Mark turned and left with Tom to join their group.

"Maybe I'll see you in Cedarville," she called after them. Mark waved his hand without turning around.

"What? Now you're going to Cedarville?" Lilli knelt by Jade, a fist on her hip.

Emma flinched and glanced at Lilli. "No. Well, maybe? We have to hurry."

"Getting a bad vibe from those guys?" Jade asked.

"More like an I'm-late-for-the-bus vibe."

Lilli tucked in the end of Jade's bandage, stood, and brushed off her knees. She bobbled the pen between her teeth. "I get it. Plan for the worst and hope for the best."

"That's my new motto." Emma raised an eyebrow at Jade and took a swig from her bottle as they walked. Jade's crutch tapped out each step she took, keeping a good pace.

"This is like a war zone." Lilli's words slipped out in a whisper. She wiped her brow with her bandana. "When the National Guard arrives, where will they begin?"

"I wish they'd get here already. I could use some pain meds."

"Don't worry, hon, we're almost to Emma's, right?"

Emma nodded and kept walking. At this rate, it would be dark before she got home.

Birds called back and forth. Their communication system still worked fine. She reached for her phone. The urge to pitch it into the branches almost winning. She gripped it in her hand, aching to hear Mom's voice.

****

Emma crouched behind a rhododendron and sipped from her bottle. Waiting for Lilli and Jade had become a national pastime. Shouldn't they have hit Quincy by now?

Lilli and Jade dropped beside her. Jade couldn't go one step farther than she had to, and the street signs had disappeared under trees or been blown away. Roofing, window screens, lawn chairs, and toppled trees made progress slow, and Jade seemed to stop more often since they'd seen Mark. Should she have gone with them? At least she knew Mark. What did she really know about Lilli and Jade besides the whole saving her life thing?

Without the trees, everything was so bright. Emma paused. Nothing was where it should be. Lilli and Jade passed her, but no one spoke as they plodded on. Birds sang, and the breeze blew through the branches—no planes, cars, buses, or loud music blaring.

This was her life without technology. "Off the grid," they'd called it at the marches. She'd never spent more than a day without her phone, and that was when she was in big trouble. What would Mom take now? She had no idea what the time was. Dad had a trick he used sometime, and she scanned the sky. The sun was a bright spot right above them, so it was close to noon.

Every muscle in Emma's body screamed to sit down. The bottoms of her feet pounded from hours of walking. Lilli and Jade leaned into one another, unable to stand straight. They could rest at her house before heading to Franklin.

Emma stumbled over a branch, like a sleepwalker, and raised her gaze. The letters of Sprague Street glowed from the sign in front of her like a topsy-turvy scarecrow pointing down the yellow brick road.

She stopped.

"What's up?" Lilli's head hung and she stared at the asphalt.

"It's only four blocks to Wilson Street."

"We're almost there?" Jade clanked her crutch on the pavement.

"Yes." Emma's vision clouded with tears. She wiped her eyes with her sleeve but didn't mention the fourteen blocks down Wilson from 16th to 30th.

"Thank all the goddesses." Jade sunk to the sidewalk.

"Give us ten, Emm?" Lilli searched Emma's face.

"Sure." Emma sank down on the curb. She would make it home before dinner if it was the last thing she did. *Please, goddesses, don't let it be my last thing.*

****

Emma's toes had grown numb by 24th street. She plodded to Mrs. Webster's white house. The front door stood open, and Mrs. W swept, the tinkle of glass reaching the street. Emma ran up the sidewalk.

"Mrs. W." Emma took the steps of her porch two at a time.

Mrs. Webster turned and dropped the dustpan. A smile spread across her wrinkled face. Warmth filled Emma for the first time in days. Mrs. W opened her arms, and Emma flew into them.

"Is that your mom?" Lilli called from the sidewalk.

Chapter Sixteen

Josh

Bill smiled, but his gray eyes glared at Josh. "Thirsty? That don't come close what we are, kid."

A knife hung from Bill's belt. Josh's shoulders stiffened at the name carved on the handle—Huntsman. Uncle Carl used a Huntsman to skin a deer.

He had to get them water and find a reason for them to leave.

Bill checked out the solar panels, the broken windows, and the garden plot behind the house. He'd had enough time to put the pieces together: food, water, and shelter, and Josh, the only thing standing in their way of this gold mine.

A chill ran the length of his spine. Why had he argued to stay? Uncle Carl had mentioned looters, but if he weren't here, these guys would be in the house already using the radio. His grandfather must be rolling over in his grave. Josh squared his shoulders.

"There's drinking water at the spigot by the barn."

"What about some grub?" Chip leered at Josh.

"Supplies are running low, but I can spare a couple sandwiches for the road."

"I'll take pastrami on rye." Chip hitched up his pants with boney fingers. His thin arms and legs, his lean face and greasy hair, everything about him screamed desperation.

"Pastrami? Who—" Josh blurted then grimaced.

"This is a farm. You got a generator. Must have the fridge nice and cold by now, right?" Bill glared at Josh and cracked the front door, peeked inside.

Josh's feet went numb. Now what? He had to stop Bill from going inside. He'd never get them out of the house once they got in. He bit the inside of his cheek.

"The food spoiled before I got the generator running. No meat." Just stick to the truth as much as possible. "Everything in the fridge ended up in the compost."

"Compost?" Chip's vacant eyes cast a dark look at Josh.

"Yeah, for the gar—" Josh began.

"Yeah, yeah. Blah, blah, blah." The edge in Bill's voice stopped Josh cold. "Give us whatever you got then."

"Peanut butter and jelly?"

"Perfect." Bill stepped back to let Josh by.

Josh balled his fists and strode into the house. They followed, and his insides dropped. He turned to face them, but he was no match for these guys.

"Man. What a mess," Chip stopped by the front door and scanned the Danish plates high on the wall.

How would he get rid of them? "I got water bottles. You can fill them at the barn."

They didn't move except to exchange a look. Josh backed down the hall into the kitchen. The basement door was closed. Did they notice it? His mind raced: where were the extra water bottles? He rummaged through the pantry by the back porch, found two water bottles. He fumbled one, and it clattered across the floor. *Get it together.*

Mumbling came from the two men in the next room. He stepped into the living room, and Bill cut the conversation midsentence. Josh picked up something about Canada and a guy named Mo with radio skills. He didn't want to find out.

"We'll get some water, but we'd like to eat here, rest up a bit before heading out if you don't mind." Bill glared at Josh. "Maybe your pa will get back so we can talk to him. Tell him what a great kid he has."

"Sure."

He rushed back to the kitchen. The sooner he got sandwiches made, the sooner they'd be gone. He hauled out the loaf of bread and opened the peanut butter, tearing the slices as he spread it. He put sandwiches in a paper bag, clutched the bag, his knees wobbling as he walked to the living room. With any luck, his legs wouldn't give out.

"There's a bench out by the barn by the water spigot." Why did they have to be so big, act so tough? He handed them the sandwiches.

"You aren't eating?" Chip asked.

Josh choked, his mouth bone dry. "I ate."

"Thanks, kid." Bill took the sandwich and stepped out onto the porch. The men opened the bag and divvied the sandwiches. They scarfed them where they stood, dropping the bag on the porch. Josh's chest tightened as they headed to the barn.

They disappeared around the corner, and Josh ran down the stairs to check the radio. No messages. Should he turn it off? If Bill and Chip heard the radio, he was screwed. They might hurt him or worse. Did he have time to get a message to Uncle Carl?

He turned the volume down in case Uncle Carl radioed then jogged up the stairs to the front door. He scanned the yard and the barn. Where were they? All the debris and fallen trees created a chaos that made Josh's head hurt.

He gazed at the southern sky. Dark clouds filled the horizon. Another storm? Now? How would he get these rid of these guys? They spoke in low tones letting water run onto the ground. Josh clenched his fists and headed over. How dare they waste—

A branch snapped, and Josh jumped. A third man appeared on the driveway. He waved to Bill and Chip by the spigot. Dressed in sweatpants and a bright orange vest, his buzz cut seemed tidy next to Chip's greasy hair. The man took a water bottle from Chip and drained it. Josh swallowed hard. A boulder-like heaviness sat in his tummy. He stood in the driveway, ready to run.

Chip smiled and led the man over to Josh. He had the manners of a used car salesman, cheesy smile, easy banter. "This is my brother, Dean. He needs a sandwich, too."

"Wha—" Josh clamped his mouth shut as Bill glared at him.

"That's twice, kid. It's like you don't want to help a fellow out."

Josh took a step back, but Bill reached out with both of his paw-like hands and grabbed Josh around the neck. Josh hung from his hands like a rag doll as Bill choked him. He gripped Bill's wrists to pry them loose, but they clasped his throat like a vise, cutting off air. Stars swam in his vision.

"Bill, he's just a kid." Dean took a step toward Bill,

who dropped his hands, his chest heaving from his effort.

"He knows the score, don't you, kid." Bill glared at Josh who choked and coughed as he backed toward the house.

The men followed him inside and closed the door behind them. This was it. *Home Alone*, only not a comedy. Josh's pulse pounded in his throat. Bill closed the gap between them, and Josh gagged on his body odor. Maybe if he fell to the floor, played dead, or should he take a swing? The front door burst open, and Bill stepped back.

Silhouetted in the doorway stood a tall, broad shouldered man, feet braced, his hair tied in a ponytail. Deputy Larson held a pistol with both hands and pointed it at Bill. A five-point star flashed on the breast pocket of his flannel shirt. "Hands up."

"God, Dean. You were followed." Bill's hand rose to his shoulders.

Josh raised his hands then dropped them to his side. The deputy's gaze never left Bill.

Chip reached into his back pocket.

"Look—" Josh called.

Larson glanced at Josh as Chip crouched and swung a knife in front of him. Larson shifted his aim.

"Drop your weapon."

But Chip raised the knife and took a step forward.

"Drop it."

Chip rushed forward, and Larson fired. He swung his gun to Bill and Dean. "On the ground, now."

Josh's ears rang with the repercussion. He couldn't move his feet.

Chip's knife clattered to the floor as he sprawled to

the floor on his back, a red splotch growing on his chest. Bill and Dean dropped to their knees, their hands spread on the floor before them. Josh stood frozen.

"Don't shoot. We're unarmed." Bill raised his head to look at the deputy.

"Bull," Larson growled.

"You can't just shoot a man." Dean held his shaking hands in front him as if in prayer.

"Did you warn that woman before you cracked her skull?" Deputy Larson kept his pistol pointed at Bill.

"Please, don't shoot." Bill lay face down, his gaze on the pistol.

Deputy Larson's words hit Josh like a hammer blow. So, Bill had killed someone, and Deputy Larson had followed them here? Had Bill spotted the antenna? He didn't act like he knew, but he needed to radio someone in Canada, right? Probably to get out of the US. Josh ran his fingers over the tender skin on his neck.

Dean reached out to Chip's body. "Bill did it. Not Chip. Why did you have to shoot him?"

A pool of blood formed around Chip. Josh's belly cramped. Chip bled on Mom's best wool carpet. This was a horror movie playing out in his own living room.

"Weapons. Now." The Deputy stepped closer to Bill and Dean.

Bill drew the Huntsman knife from the leather holder around his waist and a gun out of his boot. Dean grabbed a cell phone and a jackknife from his pocket. Larson waved the muzzle of the gun at him.

"Hey, man, it's all I got. I swear."

The Deputy kicked the weapons out of their reach and nodded to Josh. "Can you give me a hand here?

Take the cuffs from my belt."

A sharp pain filled Josh's chest. *Oh, God, I'm seventeen and having a heart attack.*

"Okay." His symptoms evaporated as instinct took over. Snapping the cuffs on Bill meant Larson was in charge, and these jerks were headed to Cedarville and jail. He let out a sigh. They'd be gone before the next storm hit.

Larson read them their Miranda rights then motioned for Bill and Dean to stand. Bill's moustache twitched and Dean sobbed. Larson never took his gun off Dean or Bill. "What's your name, son?"

"Josh."

"Josh, could you carry the weapons for me?"

"Oh. Sure." Josh scrambled to gather the weapons. Larson held the gun steady on the men.

"I didn't mean that lady no harm," Bill said.

"She died," Larson growled, and Josh stepped back.

"Died?" Dean's head swiveled from Bill to Larson and back.

Larson nodded his head toward Chip. "He's going too. Grab his feet."

Dean's face crumbled as he lifted Chip's shoulders off the floor, the cuffs holding his hands close hindering his efforts. "My own brother."

Bill clasped Chip by the feet, and they hobbled to the door.

Dean made it through the door when Bill dropped Chip's feet and rushed for Josh. Deputy Larson swung the pistol, hitting Bill in the back of the head. Josh grabbed the dining room table to steady himself.

"Don't test me," Deputy Larson said through

clenched teeth. He prodded Bill who lifted Chip's feet, his teeth clenched as they shuffled out the door.

Deputy Larson gave Josh a nod. "Lock the door after me."

Josh stumbled to the door and turned the deadbolt.

Chapter Seventeen

Emma

Emma absorbed Mrs. W's warmth as they stood in a bear hug. She'd made it. She was home.

A fresh breeze blew over her, coming through the front window. A branch the size of a small tree lay half in and half out of the house.

Mrs. W held Emma at arm's length as if to make sure it was really her. "I am so relieved. Is your mom with you?"

Emma went stiff. "She's not here?"

The one person she had struggled over trees and through no-man's-lands for wasn't here? "I found her note on my way home, but I thought—"

"Where—" Mrs. Webster began, but Emma didn't wait.

She dashed out the front door, flew down the steps, and leapt over Mrs. W's boxwood hedge. A fight could not be the last thing between them. Not like Dad.

"Emm?" Lilli called.

Emma ran past her and to the front door, yanked on the doorknob. Locked.

"No." She pounded on the door then reached into her backpack pocket, empty.

She pounded again. "Mom? Sarah?"

"Are we there yet?" Lilli shifted from foot to foot

on the sidewalk, her eyes shifting between Mrs. W, who stood on her porch, and Emma, who stood on hers.

"Yes, Lilli. We're there." Emma rubbed the back of her neck. Lilli deserved better than a flip remark.

She jogged down the porch steps, clutching her backpack. Where was Mom? Emma headed for the back door, passing Lilli.

"So—" Lilli threw her hands in the air. "Emma?"

She lifted the key from under a brick and reached for the lock, but the door was open a couple of inches. Someone was in the house? The hairs on Emma's neck stood on end. She pushed, and the hinges screeched.

"Mom? Sarah?"

Tiptoeing through the kitchen, she stopped at her reflection in the shiny floor. The whole room was untouched by the storm, but the dining room windows had all broken, dishes lay smashed where they fell on the wood floor, mail and magazines had blown everywhere. Mom's wedding crystal lay broken and scattered across the hallway.

Cuddles streaked through the dining room followed by a flash of black.

"Agh!" Emma leaped back. "Tigger, you dick."

The neighbor's black cat loved Cuddles' food, but not Cuddles. Sarah must have left the door open, per usual, and Tigger sneaked in. But where was Sarah? Had they left without her? They wouldn't do that, would they? She stuck the tip of her ponytail between her teeth and chewed.

She checked the den, the family room, the basement, the bedrooms upstairs. No one was here.

Emma entered the kitchen. Cuddles growled from the backyard. She stepped out the kitchen door. Cuddles stood on the branch of a weeping cherry. Tigger had disappeared. Emma held out her arms, and Cuddles stepped into them.

"I've got you." Emma ran her hand through the dusty fur, but Cuddles stiffened, bounded out of Emma's arms, and tore around the house.

Tigger shot out from under a bush, and the cats raced across the street and under Mrs. Macalister's porch. Emma chased after them, dropped to her knees, and gazed into the darkness. Her mind raced as fast as the blood through her veins. Nothing was the same, except for Sarah's cat.

"Cuddles." She clapped her hands hoping to lure her out.

Mrs. M hobbled onto her porch. Her wrinkled face and bent shoulders appeared over the railing.

"Emma? Look at your hair." Her voice quavered but still rang loud for all to hear. "Your mother is looking for you, young lady."

Why did Mrs. M always seem to be scolding her? Emma rose to her feet, and blood rushed to her head. She wobbled and grabbed the porch rail.

"That's what I've been trying to tell her." Mrs. W rushed across the lawn to steady Emma.

"Where's Sarah? Is she with Mom?" Emma leaned on Mrs. W's shoulder.

Mrs. M swatted the air. "Your mom left to find you the minute that storm ended."

"I watched Sarah while she looked. She'd go out and return so forlorn without you. A group left for Cedarville first thing this morning, so she sent Sarah with them." Mrs. W nodded to Mrs. M. "Said she'd follow as soon as she found you."

"She sent Sarah by herself?" None of this seemed real. Mom would never leave Sarah. Emma folded her arms and rocked herself, her eyes closed to the world.

"She's not alone. She's with Trudy Patterson. Aren't they best friends?" Mrs. M plopped onto her porch swing and rocked with a slow squeak. "Trudy's parents and a couple other folks have family just like you do in Cedarville. Sarah is going to your grandparents'."

"Right. Safety in numbers, you know." Mrs. W helped Emma to sit on a step. "We haven't seen your mom since they left."

"She's still downtown?" Emma put her head in her hands. "What have I done? I just wanted to…"

"You've done nothing wrong. Your mom will be home soon."

"She'll hate me if anything—"

"Your mom is so proud of you and your work saving the planet." Mrs. M rocked back and forth, pushing with her feet.

"But we fought before I left. She was so angry." Emma glanced at Mrs. M's face, but the old woman was smiling.

"You were standing up for what you believe in."

"But I didn't change anything. I was fighting to stop this storm from happening, but it happened anyway, and now I can't even find my mom?"

"You're strong, and your mother knows it." Mrs. W sat on the porch swing. "Right, Mrs. Macalister?"

"Right." Mrs. M smiled her slow smile. "You're young. You still have time to change the world."

Emma swung her arms around in a wide circle, shook her head. "Strong enough to change all this?"

Lilli cleared her throat. Mrs. M and Mrs. W turned to stare at the sidewalk.

Emma turned too. Her friends stood with ratty backpacks, tattoos, and spiked hair. Mrs. M and Mrs. W seemed unfazed.

"Oh my goddess. These are my friends Lilli and Jade." Emma waited for one of the old ladies to comment on Lilli's hair or Jade's tattoos.

Lilli and Jade waved. Jade staggered and leaned on her crutch.

Images of feral dogs, Jinx on the floor, people fighting over loaves of bread and water bottles filled her head. She couldn't stand to think of mom downtown in the middle of all that. Why had she put Megan before mom?

"Maybe we can catch the Pattersons?" Emma squinted from Lilli to Jade.

"Emma, you don't need to catch them. Just take your time and stick with your friends." Mrs. M pushed herself to a stand. She leaned on her cane, like Jade did her crutch, only Mrs. M's shoulders stooped, and her head wobbled.

"What about you?" Emma asked.

"Oh, I have Mrs. Webster."

"Yes, she does." Mrs. W put her arm around Mrs. M's shoulders and nodded. "Plus, Bill Salazar has an emergency radio, so we'll get the latest NOAA reports. We're in good company."

Mrs. M reached out to hold Emma's hands. "Besides, you have friends to travel with. You don't have to hurry."

Emma nodded. It had taken them almost two days to get from Founders Square home, and that was only about three miles, but Cedarville was a fifteen-mile trek.

The buzz of chainsaws filled the air, cutting branches and clearing trees. Some people were staying. The crisp scent of freshly cut wood teased her nostrils with hints of a normal November day.

Lilli and Jade fidgeted on Mrs. Macalister's sidewalk, stiff smiles, shoulders back.

Did Emma look like that, fir needles in her hair, hands black from pitch? Add tattoos and combat boots, and she could be their little sister. They had become sisters of the storm.

"We'll stick together," Lilli said. "We got this far, right? We can get her to Cedarville." Lilli wiped her nose. "My folks live up Highway 3. We'll follow 96 to the junction. Cedarville is just a few miles from there."

"You'll be with your mom by tomorrow, the next day at the latest." Jade rubbed the bandage on her leg, her pain etched in wrinkles around her eyes.

Emma smiled at Lilli then Jade. How could she tell them they were too slow? She'd already missed Sarah, and she didn't want to miss Mom too. "Maybe I'll just run ahead."

Mrs. Webster placed her hand on Emma's arm. "There you go, all in a rush. Slow down, girl." She gave Emma's arm a shake, but Emma jerked away.

"I have bandages in my bug-out bag," Mrs. W said. "That way Jade will be able to keep up. I know I said this already, but there is safety in numbers. Right?"

Emma nodded, tears rolling down her cheeks. She'd been rude, and she regretted her words. She glanced at Lilli who massaged Jade's back. Jade kept her head down. What was she thinking? Jade had gotten shot protecting herself. It wasn't murder.

She pushed down the urge to race after the Patterson family. Today was the day she was supposed to find Mom and sleep in her own bed. Instead, Sarah was gone, and Mom was out there with the looters and people with guns. She adjusted her pack on her shoulders.

"Okay. Safety in numbers, but I'm bringing Cuddles."

Emma stood on the bottom step of Mrs. M's porch her arms crossed. Mrs. M stared at her from the top step.

Mrs. W gave Emma her thin-lipped smile. "Leave Cuddles. She has nine lives, you know."

Emma couldn't stage a showdown with Mrs. M or Mrs. W. They only spoke the truth, but she didn't want the truth. She wanted her mom and Sarah here, and some sense of normal in her life.

Cuddles growled from under the porch, and Emma crawled on her hands and knees, searching the darkness. She sat up on her heels, turned to Lilli and Jade who fidgeted on the sidewalk whispering to each other. They needed to leave soon, but Emma wouldn't leave the only normal thing in her life right now.

"Here, kitty."

Something scuffled and growled. Gray fur and a black mask rushed past her and into Mrs. M's azaleas.

"Oh!" Emma flew onto her seat and crab-walked out of the way.

"Raccoon. Cuddles probably woke him up. He must have gotten caught out in the storm, like you." Mrs. M peered over the porch rail. "He's as confused by this topsy-turvy world as the rest of us.

"Come on, kiddo." Jade shifted her weight on her crutch, making it creak. "We only have about three hours of daylight left. We have to leave Cuddles."

Hanging her head, Emma nodded. Jade was right. Dark clouds were gathering in the distance, and they had to press on. Cuddles had at least seven more lives.

Lilli held up her half-empty water bottle, shaking it. "Is there any chance we could fill up before we go?"

Mrs. M nodded toward the side of the porch. "We never gave up our well when they built these new houses." She swept her arm in an arc. "There's a faucet behind the azaleas."

Lilli started. "Where the racoon ran?" She gathered Jade and Emma's empty bottles.

"There's another way under the porch there, so don't worry."

"I didn't know you had a well." Mrs. W smiled as she rubbed Mrs. M's back.

"My Henry installed an emergency generator ten years ago, his last project. I'll have water until I die." Mrs. M stood erect, but her gaze never left the azaleas.

Mrs. W placed her arm around Mrs. M, and they leaned into one another. Emma never saw Mrs. M downtown without her friend Mrs. W. Where was Megan? She stuck her hand in her pocket and ran her fingers over the smooth face of her phone. She'd never gone this long without a message from her.

"Thanks." Lilli ran water into the bottles as Jade shifted on her crutch.

"You'd better sit here on the step while I get my go-bag and bandage that leg." Mrs. W marched across the street and disappeared into her house.

Mrs. W had just bought Emma some time. "Here

kitty, kitty." This was it. She'd have to leave Cuddles if she didn't come out soon.

A rush of fur dashed from under the porch and into her arms. "Oh." A wave of relief washed over her. She stuck her nose in the cat's fur and nuzzled, ignoring the sting of her lips cracking. She must have smiled. Cuddles purred in her arms.

Holding a black gym bag, Mrs. W charged back to the porch and sat by Jade. A retired nurse, she cleaned and bandaged Jade's. She and Sarah had been patched up by Mrs. W's capable hands many times. Cuddles had dozed, and Emma daydreamed as the women talked storms and disaster preparedness.

Mrs. W brushed her hands together and placed a hand over the bandage. "You'll live," she announced and squirted sanitizer on her hands.

"Better?" Lilli held out a hand to Jade.

"Much." Jade rose to her feet.

"Thanks." Jade shook Mrs. W's hand, but Mrs. W pulled her into a hug.

"It's time then." Lilli handed Emma three dripping water bottles. Put these in your pack. Then she shrugged into her own.

"Well, I guess we're off. Over the river and through the woods." Emma passed Cuddles to Jade and loaded the water into her pack then took Cuddles, who appeared to have recovered from any trauma of being chased under the porch.

"Until we meet again, my girl." Mrs. M stood on her porch, Mrs. W's hand on her shoulder.

Emma nodded and fell in behind Lilli and Jade. She cradled Cuddles in her arms and cast one last glance over her shoulder at Mrs. M and Mrs. W. Would they be here when she got back, and when would that be? She brushed her tears on her shoulder and clung to Cuddles.

****

They trudged down Wilson to Perimeter Road, and Emma quit trying to put houses back together and trees where they belonged. The houses could be repaired, but the trees were gone forever. It would take a lifetime for them to grow that tall again. Would she be around then?

Jade held up a water bottle. "We scored with Mrs. M, but we'll need to find more tomorrow. Keep your eyes peeled for faucets, Emm."

"But Lilli gave me three bottles?"

"Remember Frieda, the Zumba instructor?" Lilli grinned at Jade.

"Crazy old Frieda. I'll never forget her or that panther tattoo I inked from her ankle to her thigh." Jade seemed to take larger steps since Mrs. W cleaned and wrapped her wound."

"'She'd preach water every time she came to the shop. 'Are you drinking your water? You need two-and-a-half quarts of water a day.' She carried gallons of water rolling around in the back of that Saab."

"Frieda was on to something." Jade gazed off into the distance, a grin on her face.

"My mom always warned us not to drink from the creek behind our house or we'd be sorry." Lilli shook her water bottle.

"You have a creek?" Jade's eyes twinkled.

"Yeah, I heard something about that." Emma didn't want to be sorry. "You packed some tablets to clean the water? Could I have a couple, just in case?"

"Purification tablets, yes, enough for six more

bottles. That should be enough to get us to Franklin and you to Cedarville. I'll give you some when we get to the junction." Jade rubbed the scar under her coat sleeve.

The junction. That's where they would leave her and go north, and she'd have to hike to Cedarville on her own. At least she had Cuddles, and besides, it wasn't far from the junction to her grandparents' farm.

Jade plodded down the road. With her backpack and her crutch, she could have been right out of one of Emma's history books. There was one photo with the caption, A Civil War Soldier Heading Home.

Was the storm their war, and now they were heading home? A tremor started at the nape of Emma's neck and ran down her back. Would life ever be the same?

"Mrs. M had a well. Other places will too." Lilli kept a steady pace, and Jade tapped along beside her. Emma walked beside Jade.

"Just think, Emma. You'll be at your grandparents by tomorrow." Jade nudged her with her shoulder.

"And Mom will be there." Emma nodded. Positive thinking was all she had right now. It had taken over two days to hike this far, and they weren't even out of Vandby yet.

The roof collapse in the Burger Bomber would give her nightmares, and so would the dogs. Emma hugged Cuddles to her chest, her warmth and deep purr calming.

Lilli led them around a corner and onto Perimeter Road. Devastation spread out before them all the way to the foothills, a tangled mass of downed trees and litter. What kind of storm did this? A speaker at one of her marches had talked about changing weather patterns and stronger storms in the future. Was it the future already?

"It's been four days. Where are the National Guard, the Red Cross, the police? That's not normal, is it?" Lilli asked.

"Mrs. W was filling us in on the latest info. One of your neighbors has a radio, and he heard the storm had wiped out the entire West Coast, from Alaska to Baja. It cut out power lines, cell towers, washed out roads, and not just on the coast but all the way inland to the Rockies." Jade's clipped report stopped Emma, and Lilli stood in the middle of the road scanning the landscape.

"What? The Rockies are hundreds of miles away." Emma twirled her ponytail in her fingers.

"I'm just the messenger. Updates were coming in from cities and towns up and down the coast. No one has electricity unless they have a generator."

"If it's that bad, it might explain why we haven't gotten help yet." Lilli grabbed the short stick she'd tucked behind her ear, flipped it between her fingers then popped it between her lips.

"That would also explain why Mom sent Sarah to Gran's. She lives in farm country. People have wells, food, and generators." Emma clutched Cuddles, but what she needed was her mom.

****

Cuddles settled into Emma's arms as they plodded down the middle of Perimeter Road to Highway 96. The rhythm of her steps wound through her brain like a melody. Cuddles stopped purring, and Emma clung to her. Barks and growls echoed on the distance.

"Lilli?" Jade tensed, and Lilli clamped her hand over Jade's mouth.

A pack of dogs raced around the corner and ran straight toward them. They were chasing a smaller dog that disappeared through a hole in a fence. The dogs, all much larger, milled about, sniffed at the hole, some dug.

One of them sniffed the air, spotted Cuddles, and growled. All the dogs stopped to sniff.

"Not Cuddles, you dicks." Cuddles' claws dug into Emma's arm, making her cry out, but Emma hung onto her fur. Cuddles twisted, and Emma lost her grip as the dogs rushed her.

"No!"

Cuddles leaped out of Emma's arms and ran. Emma watched, helpless, as Cuddles streaked down the road and around a fence, the pack of dogs after her. Their barks faded into the distance.

"No," Emma sobbed.

"Cuddles has skills," Lilli said, and Jade punched her. "What?"

Emma couldn't move. "What will I tell Sarah?"

"Tell her, Cuddles was alive the last time you saw her. Cats have nine lives, remember?" Jade cleared her throat and shook her head.

Emma swayed, her arms numb, hanging at her side. She missed Cuddles' purr against her chest.

"I think you needed Cuddles more than Cuddles needed you," Lilli said.

"Those dogs will never catch that cat." Jade's slow drawl soothed Emma's nerves. "Did you see her fly around that corner?"

Emma opened her mouth to speak, but her throat

had closed, and she coughed instead. She clung to Jade's words. The dogs were long gone, and only bird song filled the air. Emma fell in behind Lilli and Jade, and they trudged down the road.

Had "normal" vanished with Cuddles? Her head pounded with the effort of holding back her tears. Once they started falling, she wouldn't be able to stop them. She stumbled over boxes and branches, her vision blurred, her nose running.

"Jade has to rest, right hon?" Lilli helped Jade settle on a log, took Emma by the arm, and sat her between them. Jade handed her a tissue. Lilli leaned in on Emma's other side, and Emma closed her eyes. Just what she needed, a friend sandwich.

Emma cried. She cried until hiccups started. She cried until the tightness behind her eyes had been washed away. She cried until she couldn't breathe.

Lilli and Jade rocked her between them, and she dried her eyes. A metal baseball bat lay in the road before her.

"Where were you when I needed you?" She marched to the bat, grabbed it, and gave it a swing. "Next dog I see—"

"That's my, girl." Lilli grinned and helped Jade to her feet.

Emma rested the bat on her shoulder then, with a final glance behind her, Emma followed her friends down 27th. A stiff breeze lifted several strands of her dirty hair, and she looked to the sky. Dark clouds gathered in the south.

"No, no, no." Jade shaded her eyes and glared into the sky. "Not again."

Chapter Eighteen

Josh

Spots swam before Josh's eyes as he gulped air. Was he drowning? Larson marched Bill and Dean down the driveway his gun trained on them. Bill released one of Chip's feet, and Larson poked him with the gun. Bill snarled.

"Don't drop him." Dean adjusted Chip's shoulders.

"I didn't do that on purpose."

"Chip wouldn't be dead if you hadn't killed that lady."

"You ate the bread. We all ate the bread, remember?" Bill's jaw worked as though he were chewing leather.

"Deputy, you gotta believe me. I came to meet my brother. I don't even know this guy." Dean glared at Bill.

"I did read you your Miranda Rights, did I not? I'd appreciate you leaving your confessions for the judge." Larson held the pistol steady on Bill and Dean as they shuffled down the driveway.

Why was it taking so long? His skin crawled as he touched the spot on his neck where Bill had...

"You knew someone would be coming for you, Bill, storm or no storm." Larson disappeared behind the branches to his truck, glinting red through the tangle.

Josh rolled his tight shoulders and eased the door closed. He leaned against it. His gaze going to the spot where Chip had fallen, and his jaw clenched. Bill's voice filtered into the house. Would he never shut up? He turned the deadbolt with a click.

Blips of Morse code echoed from the basement, and he peered out the door window as Deputy Larson's truck engine roared to life. Finally.

He trotted down the steps as the message came through. At least they hadn't heard the radio, but they knew it was here.

The call-sign PH was all he could make out the first time, but the message repeated. He wrote as fast as he could then read:

Cedarville, WA: no utilities, some local services, hospital open.

Grande Center: apartment building collapse, forty-eight fatalities, dozens injured.

Alert: storm approaching. Expect high winds.

He slumped into the swivel chair. Forty-eight fatalities? Why couldn't he get good news for once? The room blurred as his eyes watered. Had mom made it to the hospital in one piece, and where was Uncle Carl now?

At least Deputy Larson showed up in time, and the farm was safe. *We prepared for this, so why all the screw-ups?* He gripped the arms of the chair, the walls seeming to close in on him.

He grabbed the Morse Code Key and wrote out his message, tuned the dial to the frequency Uncle Carl used. He listened. No incoming, so he tapped in:

Woolf farm. Looters apprehended. Dad still MIA.

He sent another message to the local frequency

without the bit about his dad. He balled his hands into fists then shook out his hands and coded his message. He checked each dot and dash he entered, and used his dad's call sign, EW.

If this helped another family avoid looters, or at least prepare for them, he had to do it. Bill's visit was his wake-up call. He would do whatever it took not to lose his connection to the outside world, even if he had to fight or all he got was bad news.

Grandpa always said, "You have to take the bad with the good."

The wind whistled around the house. This was El Primo, but how would they survive one storm after another?

He sprang from the chair and ran upstairs. He'd do one more check of the yard. His blood pounded in his ears.

Blood. That was the problem. He gazed at the stain where Chip had fallen. Bleach might take it out of the wood, but it would ruin the rug. He'd drag it to the barn.

He cracked the door. The branches on the apple tree waved as the winds picked up. He had to hurry. He rushed to the kitchen and grabbed twine from the pantry, then to the living room and stumbled. *Bill is gone. Larson took him into custody.*

He raised his hand to his throat where Bill's fingers had squeezed. Branches rustled against the house, but he opened the door to make sure.

It's only the wind.

He fumbled with the twine, his fingers slow and jerky, but he got the rug rolled and tied. The wind whipped through the branches now. A loud crack, and a branch flew across the yard. Pinecones hit the porch and sides of the house.

Nothing would stop him from getting this rug out of the house. He braced his shoulders and dragged the carpet to the front door. At least blood hadn't soaked through to the floor.

A gust hit the house, the wind a steady roar. He grabbed the house keys and locked the door. Gripping one end of the rug, he dragged it to the barn. It was like dragging a body. *Don't go there.*

The wind pushed against him, and the sting of fir needles made him squint. He had to get this done. Quick.

He dropped the rug by the barn door. The force of the wind blew branches and debris against the barn and house in bursts. A gust blew him to the house, and he scrambled up the porch steps. He fumbled to unlock the door, and it flew open. He used all his strength to press it closed. The wind roared as he slid the dead bolt. His ears pounded with the effort. He peered over the plywood on the living room window to see dark clouds billowing in the sky. Where could Dad be?

He raced to the kitchen, where the windows were not broken. Fir trees in the distance bent and swayed like tall grass. This was a repeat of the last storm.

The wind rumbled, and he dashed for the basement. Déjà vu. Dad had found shelter, right? Josh threw a piece of wood on the fire and sank into the chair, alone again.

Chapter Nineteen

Emma

Emma trudged past Oakville Furniture and Bath-Kitsch-N-Mor, smaller businesses like Lock-It Locksmith and TropiTan, and all the mattress and furniture warehouses. They went on for miles.

Mom called it strip-mall-hell. It had been fields and pastures. Now it was warehouses and parking lots that could hide people desperate for food and water.

She could use a pasture right now, grass with nowhere for looters to hide. Pallets and Styrofoam littered the streets, and large pieces of plastic hung from buildings like ghosts.

Emma plodded past a strip mall with a teriyaki place, and a nail salon.

"Follow the yellow brick road, or painted line, in this case. Will we meet the Scarecrow next?" Emma kicked a Styrofoam brick.

"*The Wizard of Oz,* right? I guess this is kind of like Oz, isn't it?" Lilli chewed on her stick as she plodded.

Jade hunched over and curled her fingers. "What a world, what a world," she cackled. "Wasn't it a hurricane that started all Dorothy's problems, my pretties?"

"I don't like where you're going with that," Emma

said. "But as long as we can get home by the end, I'll be fine."

"First time I've ever walked down the middle of a road in Vandby. Guess people can't drive with all the roads blocked." Lilli glanced over her shoulder. "Although, if someone did drive by, I might just chase them down and beg for a ride."

"At least we haven't seen any dogs." Jade said. She grabbed Lilli's hand.

"Yeah. Plus, we have sandwiches and water. Think positive, people." Lilli stopped in the middle of the road.

"Grab-n-Go?" She stared at the mini mart.

"Wait. I know that look. You think you're gonna find cigarettes in there?" The wrinkles on Jade's forehead deepened as Lilli jerked her hand from Jade's and moved like a sleepwalker toward the store.

"I'd settle for a pack of gum. I'm getting splinters in my teeth from these sticks."

"My mom never stopped at Grab-n-Go. She said Go-Go Juice was someone's science experiment and she wouldn't let us be guinea pigs." A shiver ran through her. Where was Mom now? All Emma wanted was to get home, like Dorothy. But where was home now? Anywhere Mom, of course.

"Keep your eyes peeled for cheese," Jade called, as Lilli disappeared into the store. "I got a craving."

"Cheese?" Emma rubbed the knot on her forehead. Where would she be without Lilli and Jade and their odd humor? They'd hit Highway 96 soon and then the junction to 3 where they'd go their separate ways.

She trailed Jade into the store. Empty candy bar wrappers and broken bags of rice, bits of hot dog buns and napkins lay strewn across the floor. The shelves were bare except for a package of lima beans and a couple jars of pimentos, no toilet paper, no hand sanitizer, no chocolate. Emma noticed a Starry Cluster wrapper. Sarah's favorite. Another a twinge of guilt hit her chest. Was Sarah safe? She had to be.

She shadowed Jade the length of an aisle, the crunch of glass under Jade's shoes like fingernails on a chalkboard. She regretted every decision she'd made since leaving home, starting with the march. Because of her, Mom was downtown, and Sarah was on her way to Gran's house, alone.

She wiped her eyes on her sleeve. She squinted as she scanned the aisles. The floor crunched with potato chips. What a waste. The refrigerator doors hung open, and the furry-tongued smell of sour milk hung in the air. Emma walked to the pop aisle—stripped bare.

"No cheese, no cigarettes, no gum, only frickin' lima beans." Lilli held up a plastic bag. "I'm out of here."

Emma took an apple out of her bag and took a bite, the juice running over her lips. She sucked it in.

"You're making that apple look like a gourmet dessert." Jade nudged Lilli, and Lilli handed her an apple from her bag.

"Yum. Health food." Lilli rolled her eyes and took a bite. "Hmm. Not bad." She strolled out of the store into the sunshine, Jade limping after.

Emma stopped at the end of an aisle full of cleaning products. She had to find at least one piece of chocolate, right? Would she ever taste chocolate again? She got on her hands and knees to look under a rack. *Am I this desperate, really?*

"I thought I heard voices,"

Emma jerked to her feet.

A man in torn pants, bloodstained and dirty, limped around shelves at the back of the store, something following him.

A dog.

With rigid movements, Emma slipped the apple in her pocket and clutched her water bottle behind her back. She crunched over the broken glass and potato chips, moving toward the front door.

"Give me your water." He reached out a hand. The dog growled.

Why was his dog growling at her? Emma didn't stop. She clenched her fingers around the bottle and backed to the door. The dog growled again, and she clenched her jaw. She searched the shelves for a can of something to throw. Why didn't he control his dog? He wasn't getting her water.

She spotted an exit sign at the end of the aisle, a closer door. She sprang for it, pulling down empty display shelves as she ran, her pulse pounding in her ears. She shot out the door and dragged a dumpster in front of it. Then raced to Lilli and Jade. Jade turned and smiled, but her face fell.

"Run," Emma gasped.

"What?" Lilli frowned at the store.

"A man with a dog." Emma pressed both hands to her chest.

"Dog?" Lilli grabbed Jade's arm and draped it over her shoulder. "Quick. Around that building."

Emma glanced back. The man was pushing against the door, but the dog had squeezed outside. It stood watching his master. "Get 'em." His voice echoed down the street, but the dog didn't move.

"Thank all the goddesses, this one's not feral, yet." Jade did an awkward hop-run.

"Get back here." The man hobbled after them, but the dog stayed by his side.

Emma grabbed Jade's other arm. The dog's barks followed them. They rounded the building and rushed onto Perimeter Road as the dog's barks grew distant.

Jade shot a wide-eyed glance over her shoulder. "He's not coming?"

"He was hurt, but he saw my water." Emma adjusted Jade's arm over her shoulder.

"We found water. So can he." Lilli helped Jade along until they hit a tangle of trees blocking the road.

****

Emma waited on the other side of the pile, hiding in the branches of a maple tree. Lilli swatted Jade in the face with a branch, and she grunted. Jade plopped onto the trunk of a tree, holding her face, a welt forming. She didn't yell or say anything, just slumped her shoulders and held her face.

Emma grasped her water bottle. Clean water meant life, and it had become more precious than gold. She handed her bottle to Jade who gazed at the setting sun, a frown wrinkling her brow.

"We need to find shelter, ladies, and we'll need more water by tomorrow." Lilli held up her bottle, shaking it for emphasis. "We should hit a stream before we reach the junction, or is it after the junction?" Lilli adjusted Jade's arm over her shoulder, but Jade kept her eyes on the sky. Emma followed Jade's gaze to the dark clouds boiling in the distance. The wind kicked up dust and debris.

"Not again," Lilli said, her voice low. "I thought we'd get to the junction tonight."

"I won't make it that far. We need to look for shelter." Jade sagged against Lilli, and both stumbled.

Jade ran her hand through her hair. "Katrina was over in a matter of hours. It was the aftermath of water that lingered, but this storm…" Jade shook her head. "This isn't normal."

Emma gripped her tummy as it tied in a knot. Taking her phone from her pocket, she stared at the dead screen. "Useless piece of crap." She slipped it back in her pocket, unable to chuck it in the bushes. She led Lilli and Jade around an appliance warehouse. They clung to the side of the building for cover. Something brushed her calf, and she jumped and glanced down.

"A water spigot." She tried it, and water gushed out.

"Thank all the goddesses," Lilli cried. She laughed as the water splashed onto the asphalt.

Emma drank until she'd emptied her bottle then topped it off again.

Lilli handed Emma bottles, and Emma filled them. It took way more water to trek across town than she imagined. How much more would it take to hike to Cedarville?

"The goddesses are on our side after all." Jade's eyes brimmed with tears, and Emma's throat closed.

"I would have walked right past that spigot." Lilli tipped her bottle to Emma and drank then refilled it.

"Me too, if I hadn't run into it." She rubbed her leg. "That'll leave a bruise."

Lilli chuckled. "A well-earned bruise."

"The water problem is solved. Now we need

shelter. Keep your eyes peeled, cuz we're losing daylight." Jade wrapped her arm around Lilli's shoulder.

They stepped around the corner of the warehouse, and a stiff wind hit Emma in the face. A field spread before her.

"We must be out of the city limits." Lilli turned to Emma, her face a blank. She dropped her gaze.

"What?" Emma couldn't take one more surprise.

"We're closer to the junction than I thought."

Bile rose in Emma's throat like a tide she couldn't push back. A storm was coming, and she'd be on her own soon?

"We won't get to the junction today. The sun's going down, and we need to find someplace before these winds get any worse." Jade ran her hand up and down her wounded leg, and Lilli grabbed her hand.

Emma pointed across the pasture. "Over there. A cement building."

Lilli nodded and tightened her grip on Jade's arm.

The wind flattened the grass as Emma trudged into it. Dark clouds raced across the sky, and the temperature dropped as the winds pressed against her. Jade was right, the sun was setting, and hiking in the dark was not an option, not in another storm. She pushed against the wind, willing her legs to go faster.

"Hurry," she called over her shoulder, but the wind carried her voice away.

She pushed her feet forward, one after the other. It was like treading through waist deep water. She could make out the cement walls. The building looked solid. TPC, TelePortal Communications was stenciled on one wall.

Emma put her head down and marched on. A flash of lightning lit the sky, and thunder boomed overhead. The hair on the back of her neck stood on end. She pushed through the roaring wind and collapsed against the building, protected from the gusts. Her thighs burned, sweat ran between her shoulder blades. Where were Lilli and Jade?

She peered across the field. Jade stumbled as Lilli dragged her along, but they still had the length of a football field to cross. Emma bit her lip as Jade stumbled again.

This wasn't helping. She grabbed the doorknob and pushed, but it didn't budge. She tugged, and it popped opened an inch. Kicking debris out of the way with her toe, she opened it enough to squeeze inside. The roof had collapsed, and part of it leaned against an inside wall. It would provide some shelter.

She poked her head out the door. Lilli waved. Emma grabbed the section of roof and shook. It was wedged in tight. She reached in and grabbed a stack of wet papers and threw them out the door. The ones on the bottom were dry. She spread them out to cover the space and was finishing as Lilli and Jade pushed through the door.

They scrambled under the roof, and rain began to fall in cold wet splats.

"Thank all the goddesses." Jade crawled in next to the wall and sneezed.

"It's not the cellar, but we'll be mostly dry and warm if we huddle together." Lilli spooned Jade.

Why did she have to mention the shop? Emma crawled under the shelter curled into a ball where the roof met the floor, a tight squeeze, but at least they all fit, and Lilli radiated warmth.

She zipped her jacket up to her chin and pulled on her hoodie. Lilli snorted, and Jade's breath was regular and deep. Asleep already? Would sleep come for her? She adjusted her backpack under her head, her muscles cramping and twitching.

The rain pounded on the roof, and the wind blew over and around their shelter. Tears rolled down her face, and she held a hand over her mouth. She'd earned a good cry, right?

She wiped her eyes and took a sip from her water bottle. *We'll be fine, right? We have to be.*

The sharp snap of branches popped like firecrackers each time one broke off, and each thump that shook the ground meant another tree had fallen. How could Lilli and Jade sleep through this? Emma shivered and closed her eyes.

Chapter Twenty

Emma

Sunlight glared off the wet walls, waking Emma. It was silent. She crawled from under the shelter and brushed off fir needles and debris, checked for spiders. Every movement she made was a painful reminder that she should have worked harder in gym class.

She stepped over the roofing to the door and pushed. It did not budge. She pressed with her shoulder, and with a pop, it opened an inch. Fir needles, leaves, paper, and branches had blown against the door, trapping her inside, but not for long. She leaned on the door, pushing until she could squeeze through. She squinted in what she thought might be the direction of the road.

Most of the trees that surrounded the building had toppled over, leaving the sky open and wide. The remaining trees stood like something from a Dr. Seuss book, toothpicks with feather-like branches sticking out here and there.

"Do you see the stream?" Jade's muffled voice came from under the metal roof.

"No," Emma whispered. Each storm downed more trees, tore off more roofs, and blew debris into smaller pieces until nothing was in its proper place or resembled what it had once been.

"Something wrong, hon?" Jade's voice came muffled from under the shelter.

"You have to see this for yourself." Emma couldn't find the words to describe the landscape.

There was a scuffle and slapping. "No, you don't want a cigarette," Jade said.

"Well, you'd better stop scratching that damned scar or you're going to scratch all my hard work off." Lilli said.

Arguing again. Emma kept her mouth shut. She'd miss even their bickering when they were gone, which would be too soon.

Lilli poked her head out of the door. "Crap." She shielded her eyes with her hand. "The National Guard will never get through all of this."

Jade pushed her way out and stared into the distance, silent and still.

"Can you make it, hon?" Lilli took Jade's hand to help her out the door.

"How can it get worse? If I wasn't seeing it with my own eyes…" Jade's soft drawl had a calming effect on Emma, even if the words were harsh.

Emma took a step and winced. Her thighs would be sore for a month after all the walking and climbing.

Lilli cleared her throat and pointed. "The junction sign might be down, but it's still pointing us in the right direction."

Emma followed Lilli's finger to a spot in the branches. No. Not yet.

"We made it. This is the junction." Lilli's impish grin gave Emma a start. We follow the 3 north. You'll take 96 east."

Emma couldn't be alone. The earth started to spin.

172

Lilli pointed to another sign that read: CEDARVILLE 7 MILES.

"Seven miles." Emma sank to the ground. "That's a little farther than I thought."

"Couldn't we go with her just a little way?" Jade raised her eyebrows at Lilli, who stood with her hands on her hips.

Emma wanted to grab Jade and kiss her, but she didn't. She could barely hold back her sob.

"Jade, your leg. I can't let you go one extra inch." Emma chewed her lip, fighting to hold in her tears. "Besides, Gran and Papa live this side of Cedarville, so it's closer."

"Emma's right, hon. You need all your strength to get to my house." Lilli adjusted her pack on her shoulders.

"Look. There's Prickly Bear Peak." Emma indicated a rocky bluff. The familiar landmark eased her mind. "I can see it from my grandparents' back porch, so I'm not that far."

"See, hon?" Lilli rubbed Jade's arm. Jade frowned. "Emma's almost home, okay?"

"Yeah." Emma stood as straight as she could.

"We'll need to find that stream or lake or some kind of water if we're going to make it the rest of the way." Jade's transparent excuse to stay warmed Emma. Jade sniffed and rubbed her leg. She didn't look up or agree with Lilli.

Emma had to give Jade a nudge to go, even if she did have to factor in getting lost on her own, and it might take her until tomorrow to get to Gran's, but she didn't mention that.

Emma pushed her shoulders back and held out her

hand. "Thanks for saving me from the storm, Lilli."

Lilli stared at her hand then slapped it away and hugged her. "I knew you were a survivor the minute I saw you."

"Can't we eat breakfast together, or something, before we head out?" Jade asked.

"That's a good idea. Yeah." Lilli slipped her backpack off.

Emma wobbled, her relief overwhelming her. She'd have her friends for a couple more minutes. She spotted the perfect log, and Lilli helped pull away the broken branches and brush off the bark.

She sat between Lilli and Jade, the morning sunshine warming her back. Lilli spread peanut butter on crackers, and Jade passed them to Emma. She nibbled on one. She'd need her strength.

"You know, this whole getting-back-to-nature thing is nice, but we wouldn't be out here if the storm hadn't forced us." Jade spit saltine crumbs as she spoke.

"I'd be in school right now." Emma couldn't fathom school, her friends, the crowded halls, Megan.

"I bet you ace all your classes, don't you?" Lilli grinned at Emma.

"I wish." Emma licked peanut butter from her fingers and took a swig of water.

Lilli helped Jade to stand, and they adjusted packs and stowed water bottles. "Well, this is it. Here's looking at you, kid." Lilli drew Emma into another bear hug.

Emma couldn't breathe. Was this really happening? Was this where they left her? She opened her mouth and closed it, afraid she'd ask them to go with her, afraid they'd say yes.

Lilli pushed away first, clearing her throat, wiping her eyes with her sleeve.

"Jade," Emma croaked.

Jade embraced Emma then held at shoulders' length, as if trying to memorize her face.

"Well…" Emma couldn't finish her sentence, the words, like peanut butter, stuck to the roof of her mouth.

"You got your apples? How about the water purification tablets?" Jade brushed Emma's hair behind her ears. "That will last you until you get home."

Emma nodded.

"No talking to strangers." Jade tapped her walking stick on the pavement. "Mrs. M said it best. Until we meet again, my girl." Jade clasped Emma in one last hug, and Emma clung to her.

Jade, who feared dogs, looters, storms, even the wind, made sure Emma would be okay. She stumbled a step when Jade released her, and Lilli took Jade's hand and gave Emma a final wave. Emma tightened the straps on her backpack and watched the two women as they hobbled into the tangle of downed trees blocking Highway 3.

Bird song filled the air as Emma turned to the east. Her vision blurred, and the trees turned to green blobs in a fuzzy landscape. She was heading into farm country. Maybe the cleared pastures and fields would make her journey easier.

With a pause, Emma glanced at the spot where Lilli and Jade had disappeared. They were gone. She turned and pushed through the branches looking for the yellow line of Highway 96.

"I'll be home soon."

****

The sun inched across the sky, and she longed for shade. Sweat ran down her back. Her throat itched with thirst. She had never worked this hard or spent this much time outdoors or away from Mom. Except after the accident. Dad.

She wanted her mom. Where was she? She scanned the devastated landscape. Was that a man? She squinted at the shape—a stump. She didn't want to see anyone or anything—no people. Maybe a cat.

"Cuddles." She wiped her nose on her sleeve. "She has at least seven more lives, right? And now I'm talking to myself."

What did it matter? She was alone.

Emma searched the sky for the sun, found only a bright spot behind the clouds. It hung farther to the west than she expected, and her bowels tightened. She wasn't going to make it home today. Being technology free, unplugged, "off the grid" wasn't so bad, though. The sun was setting. What more did she need to know?

She wasn't prepared. No extra clothes, sleeping bag, extra water, but she'd survived. She sniffed her underarm. Yeah, not prepared.

She left the road in search of shelter for the night, keeping the sun to her right. If a farmhouse suddenly appeared that would help. She stopped in the middle of an enclosure of trees.

"This will do." She sat on a boulder and took out her water, half full. She pulled out an apple and sank her teeth into it, savoring the juice. Her arms ached, and her head was pounding. Dehydration? Probably. She rubbed her temples, hoping to relieve some of the pressure.

She wouldn't reach Gran's until tomorrow. Prickly Bear Peak seemed taller, so she was getting close. Everything took so much longer than she calculated, and now she was stuck sleeping outside, alone.

"Mom," she whispered, willing away her sore throat. She gazed at the tall trees in the east. She blinked as she slipped off her pack and snuggled into the branches. She let her tears fall. "I will bend in the storm just like they do. I will not break."

****

A mist hung over the trees, and birds sang their morning song. The sun slanted over Prickly Bear Peak. Gran and Papa's wasn't far now. She sat, wiped the sleep from her eyes, the pressure in her sinuses pounding. *Ugh. A head cold? Really?*

She shivered as she drank the last drops from her water bottle. She'd have to start moving to get warm. That stream Lilli mentioned must be close. She munched on a saltine then grabbed the apple from her pocket and sank her teeth into it. The apple juice soothed her dry throat, but she'd need water soon. She bushwhacked her way to the road and searched until she found the sign: CEDARVILLE 5 MILES. Easy-peasy. She'd be there before lunch.

Crawling through the branches and fallen trees was like the worst gym class ever. Where were Lilli and Jade right now? She missed them and all their complaining to the goddesses.

A chipmunk scolded her from a fallen tree. It must have held its nest. Emma glanced up at it and shrugged her shoulders.

"Dude, I did not do this."

The chipmunk flicked its tail and jabbered.

Laughter bubbled to her lips, but she pushed it down. This wasn't funny. It was tragic.

A crow swooped through the clearing, cawing a warning. Great. All of mother nature was against her. Perspiration dampened the back of her shirt, but her throat remained dry, and her head pounded as though it would burst. Where was that stream? Thirst pushed her on, and she clung to branches to keep from falling.

She paused and closed her eyes. A breeze hummed over the landscape, but no roar of jets, no cars on 96, no technology of any kind, just the chattering chipmunk, the caw of the crows, and the gurgle of water.

Gurgle of water?

She scrambled over trees and peered under the branches. Several Douglas firs had fallen across a bridge, knocking it off its foundation. It no longer reached the other side. White water ran through the logs and rushed over the concrete and asphalt.

Rapids. Lilli had called this a stream. This was a raging river. She reached for her water bottle. She'd fill first then figure out how to get across.

She climbed along the bank, over trees and through branches. The rushing water taunted her, her throat raw and tight.

She could taste the water, and her parched throat drove her. She wobbled on a log. A dizzy spell dropped her to her knees. Was she going to die of thirst right next to water? She never understood the meaning of irony, but this sure seemed ironic.

She walked along the river's edge to a wider spot where the gurgle turned to a murmur. She scrambled onto a stack of trees that crossed the river like a bridge. She lifted a branch, and the glint of sunlight off water blinded her. If she could just reach…

She lowered herself to a large tree trunk and reached through the branches. The water caught the bottle, tugging it from her grip. She gasped and clutched it.

Dipping it again, she let it fill then drank until water ran down her chin and neck, drenching her chest. Wiping her chin, she sat back and tipped the bottle, emptying it.

She straddled the log and bounced. It seemed sturdy enough, and it ran from shore to shore. Maybe she could cross here? Pushing herself to a stand, she put one foot in front of the other. Her weight sagged the tree until it hit the fast-moving current. The drag of the tree as it hit the rapids created a rotation, like a bucking horse.

She fell to her knees then clasped the tree, slipping off the log. She swung her leg up and scooted back. The log rose from the water, but she was dizzy and disoriented from the motion. Stuffy sinuses didn't help.

She sat back and scanned the river. It was wider in this spot. *Pay attention, Emma.* She inched backward, grasping the tree until her fingers bled around the nails. The apples flopped around in her backpack and threw her off balance. She slipped where the bark had sloughed off.

She scooted backward until she was on solid ground. Then bent at the waist, letting the blood rush back to her head. What if she had slipped? But she didn't.

She clamped her eyes shut, her heart beating as though she'd sprinted the hundred-yard dash, five times. She held up her empty bottle. She had to find a better spot, one where the water was exposed.

She filled her bottle, sniffed it. Who was she kidding? Her stuffy head made it impossible to detect anything.

Jade's water purification tablets—oh no.

She should have used them. What was she thinking? Where were they? She checked her pack pockets. How bad could it be? Putting the bottle to her lips, she downed it.

The river narrowed, and water rushed under a logjam. She tried several logs until she found a big one that didn't sag. Brown foam created a scummy froth that floated in a whirlpool under the logjam. She watched the brown pillow of foam as it swirled under the logs.

"That's not good." Why hadn't she used the purification tablets?

She hauled herself onto the large tree, and, holding her arms out to balance, she sang, "Over the river and through the woods…"

Chapter Twenty-One

Emma

The sun blazed through the branches, burning the top of Emma's head as she climbed over and around tree after tree. The winds had toppled the forest, and it left her exposed to full sun. *Why does everything have to suck right now?*

How far had she gone, two miles? And the sun was setting already? Tears sprang to her eyes as her sinuses pounded, and a cough rasped her throat. "No."

She sank to the forest floor and pulled the branches around her, making a nest.

She woke shivering. She'd dreamt she was sleeping at her grandmother's house in a real bed, a down comforter tucked around her. She staggered to her feet and walked around the trees. If she had to climb another one, she was going to scream. Her head spun, and she couldn't take another step. She'd stopped to rest, but it had turned into a nap. She had to get to Gran and Papa's.

She stumbled to another stack of trees but couldn't lift her leg to climb. Why were they all sixty feet tall? They were strung out for miles. She should be at Gran's by now. Was she even going in the right direction anymore?

She let her eyes droop. An indentation beneath the

stack of trees created a little cave of sorts. She crawled in and curled into a ball.

****

She woke shivering. Every muscle ached. Forcing her arms and legs to move, she crawled out of her shelter, stretched her arms over her head, but the trees swirled. She lost her balance and dropped like a stone. Her bowels cramped, her tongue stuck to the roof of her mouth, and her arms and legs hung like lead weights. Why was this happening?

Sweat beaded on her upper lip and her brow as she dropped to her knees. A wave of heat surged through her then nausea hit. Her middle gurgled, and she clutched her belly, vomiting apple and all the precious water. The smell cut through her congestion, and she gagged and vomited again.

Weightlessness replaced the churning heaviness in her gut. She wiped her mouth with the back of her hand. Where were Lilli and Jade now? Were they sick too? Her eyes refused to focus, no matter how hard she squinted. Where was the sun?

Her head spun faster, and she lay back, focused on the rise and fall of her chest, which moved in quick bursts.

"No." Tears blurred her already fuzzy vision. Her head pounded, and she sank into the branches. She would not reach Gran's before nightfall. Jade would never have let her drink that water, not without the purification tablets. What did Emma know about surviving? Nothing. She was going to get herself killed.

Her insides churned, and she turned her eyes to the sky once more, a brilliant shade of blue, and no clouds as far as she could see.

"Thank the goddesses."

****

She woke to the smell of rotten eggs. Lifting her cheek, she put her fingers to her face and let them fall. Her own vomit dripped onto the branches. At least it was daylight. The last time she opened her eyes it was to a starry sky. She slept, but for how long—four hours or twenty-four hours? The branches rustled, and she raised her head off the ground but dropped it back again.

Please. Let it be a chipmunk.

"What was I thinking?" she asked the sky. "Why did I drink? Maybe this is the flu."

The branches rustled again, and she stiffened. Her gut gurgled, and a wave of nausea stronger than all the others took hold of her. She rolled onto her hands and knees and dry heaved until her throat burned, then collapsed.

****

She became aware of darkness, of stars blinking in the black veil overhead. "Dark-thirty." Where was Mom? Cedarville? Two days without Lilli and Jade and she still wasn't there. She might not ever make it.

She lay on her back, gazing at the sky as frosty air brushed her cheeks. A shooting star blazed overhead. She made a wish that Mom would appear, hold her, and tell her everything would be all right. But nothing happened.

"My phone is broken. The weather is broken. Come on, stars."

Another star shot across the sky.

****

She woke to daylight, but what day?

183

She lay on her back and giggled. "Over the river…" Was she delirious now?

Blue sky filled her vision, and sunshine filtered down to her nest. At least another storm hadn't hit. Her throat ached with thirst, though. She held her throbbing head and sent out a plea to all the goddesses. *Help me.*

She rolled over and pushed onto an elbow, but the world spun, and she fell back. The smell of her soiled clothes overpowered her. She retched, but nothing came up.

"Water," she moaned.

No one was coming for her. She would never see her mom. She pressed her face in both hands as tears squeezed out of her closed eyes. Her shoulders shook with her sobs. Would she die here, so close to Gran and Papa's? Wild animals, or maybe even someone's pet dog, would eat her.

"Stop it." She wiped her eyes and sniffed. "You have to do this."

She sat gathering her strength. "Now, get up, Emma. No one's going to save you. You have to save yourself."

Rolling onto her side, she pushed to a sit and rested against a log. Her pulse pounded in her temples. Wobbly and weak, she grabbed broken branches to stand. All this misery from water? She tottered but held herself upright clinging to a log. Apparently, the goddesses were on vacation.

Her chest ached from coughing, and the dizzy spell settled into a woozy head. Putting one foot in front of the other, she came to a log but couldn't climb over it. She walked to the thick end until she'd reached the jagged tree stump. The break formed steps.

With slow, measured movements, she climbed onto the log. She scanned the distant pasture with blurred vision. Was that a movement? She blinked, focused. It was a man. She lifted her hand to wave but teetered on the log.

"There are no more chances, Emma. Make something happen."

With a grunt, she stood on the highest spot of the log. The man was lifting something large and shiny from under a pile of branches. A black mirror? She called, but her words seemed to fall straight to the ground. She coughed until she bent at the waist. Maybe he'd hear her coughing.

A whistle. That's what she needed. How many times had Mom suggested that, and she had scoffed? But even if she had a whistle, did she have enough energy to blow it?

"Help." Her hoarse voice crackled in her ears. A dizzy spell hit, and she tilted. She gripped a branch sticking off the tree and stared at the boy, willed him to see her.

"Help." She waved her arm. Why wasn't her jacket bright red or yellow, not this drab gray? She had to do this for Mom. She tore a bushy twig from the branch and waved it like a flag. She swung it over her head. She swirled it in a circle. How long could she keep this up? Not long.

The guy stopped what he was doing and turned his face toward her. Had he seen her?

The man dropped the shiny, black thing, and her brain buzzed. He raced across the field in her direction, and she sank onto the log.

"Thank all the goddesses and the stars."

Chapter Twenty-Two

Josh

The clock read 6:58 am. He leapt out of bed, the silence creating a vacuum. No storm meant he had to work as fast as he could. He threw a coat over his rumpled shirt, grabbed a granola bar, a water bottle, and a backpack then headed to the barn. He had to find enough solar panels and create a reserve stack in case any panels were destroyed. He might even enlarge the circuit.

He grabbed the hacksaw, garden shears for clearing branches, a drill motor, and some screwdriver bits then put them back. Without electricity he couldn't charge the battery. It was useless. He grabbed a plus and minus screwdriver and a hammer and threw in some rags.

He hiked through the long grass to the back pasture, knee high in grass. Trees lay across the fence in several places. Dad wouldn't be able to sell the farm with all this damage, right?

He trudged through the open field, stepping over branches, pieces of plastic, scraps of cardboard, and an old horse blanket tangled in the long grass. The striped red and yellow umbrella from the patio lay upside down in the grass, looking festive and surreal.

He spotted a panel under the umbrella covered with fir needles, strips of plastic, and sheets of insulation.

Fallen trees on the adjoining property created a chaotic wall of trunks and branches, a garbage stopper or fortress wall. Josh couldn't decide.

He wiped pine needles and debris off the panel and leaned it against a water bucket lying on its side. He found another panel, then another, each one buried under branches and debris. He added a fourth panel to the stack then stood to stretch his back. He tugged a bandana from his pocket and wiped his brow, but a movement in the distance stopped him. Shielding his eyes, he peered into the distance. Someone stood on a log, matted hair framing a white face, and clothes hanging like rags. A girl? She swung a branch in short strokes over her head, her arms flapping. Her thin voice floated across the field, but he couldn't make out the words. Then she disappeared.

She'd fallen. He dropped the solar panel and grabbed his water bottle. He leaped over branches and debris, climbing over tree trunks. He scrambled over the fence, focusing on the spot she'd fallen. Time was against her if she was dehydrated or sick, and she was probably both. He searched the logs lying on the ground. If she'd fallen behind one, he could lose her.

He climbed onto a log and spotted her. She lay like a broken doll in the salal. He dropped to her side and bent to check her pulse. The bouquet of rotten eggs mixed with the tang of vomit and crushed fir needles flooded his nostrils. It mingled with the solid aroma of moist dirt churned by uplifted roots.

He gagged. Heat rose to his cheeks. Her eyes were closed, so maybe she hadn't witnessed his reaction. He held his breath and checked for broken bones. She was in one piece, thank goodness.

He lifted her head and held his water bottle to her lips. She sipped, her tongue clicking against the top of her mouth. Dehydration.

"You found me. Thank the goddesses." She tried to sit but groaned, falling back.

The goddesses? Josh scratched his head. "You're sick. I can help you, but we must get to my house. It's not far." He tried to help her stand, but her legs collapsed. He eased her onto the ground, her stench thick in the air.

"I was so thirsty." She clutched her middle, her face bright red.

"No. You—"

"Drank from the river."

"Oh." He frowned. Who drank from the river? Didn't she know?

"Jade gave me purification tablets."

He frowned. "You had purifica—" He shook his head.

She didn't open her eyes. She wouldn't be sick if she'd used them. She seemed to understand that now. Who was she? He climbed a log to decide the best route home. She could barely walk let alone climb, so it had to be log free.

Where had she come from? Logs obstructed any trail she might have taken. He glanced at her thin form sprawled in the salal. She'd never make it to the house on foot.

The rushing water of the river mingled with bird song. He ran his fingers through his hair. Sunrays slanted through the few trees still standing, but he only had about twenty minutes of daylight to move her to the house. She tried to sit, and a putrid smell rose. Did he try to clean her up here? How did he make that happen?

"We need to go." His mouth had gone dry.

She shook her head. "No. Not like this." She rolled over, and the stench hit him full force. She knelt on hands and knees then rose.

"Let me help," he said, his voice cracking.

"No." Her cheeks glowed pink. "Go." She waved him away with one hand while struggling to remove one of her shoes.

He turned his head and swallowed a lungful of air. He slipped off her shoes then backed away, his cheeks burning. "I'll be back. I have to get my tools."

She nodded. He climbed over the log and jogged back across the pasture. Did she know how sick she was? Could he really help her? He gathered the hammer and other tools, stuffed them in his pack, and walked back to the girl. She'd need time to do whatever she was going to do, and he'd make sure she got it.

He leaned over the log to where she lay, the odors still strong. She'd piled her soiled clothes under the log and covered herself with a button-down sweater, but she hadn't moved far from where he'd found her. He climbed down to her, and she watched his every move. He dipped his finger in his water bottle then ran it over her chapped lips, winced when her skin caught on his finger. She licked the water off as he lifted her head and held the bottle to sip. With his thumb and forefinger, he took the skin on her arm between them and pinched, not hard, but her skin stayed pinched. Dehydration, page 52.

"We've got to get you to my house and start you on Rejuvelyte. Hopefully you can keep it down."

The girl nodded, then strained to sit. He put a hand

on her backpack and felt a lump. "Is that an apple?"

"Mine." She glared at him.

"Okay." He held his hands up.

How had she gotten here alone? She was here now, and he had to move her to the house. He couldn't carry her. Helping her walk that distance wasn't an option.

Maybe a stretcher would work. He rummaged through the branches and sticks and found two straight ones the length of a broom handle. He sawed them to an even length. He took off his hoodie, laid the poles lengthwise inside his hoodie, and zipped it. He took the other coat out of his pack and did the same. He lifted the poles to test the tautness of the coats. They would support her, and her weight would keep them taut.

He knelt beside her. "It won't be the most comfortable ride, but it's the fastest way to get you to my house."

She stared at him, her eyes blazing.

"I can't leave you here. This stretcher should work. We just have to get you on it."

She had tied the sweater sleeves over her legs and zipped her hoodie, pulling it down over her hips. Her apples bulged in the backpack lying across her legs. *She might not be prepared, but she's brave.*

He held his breath as he helped her to stand and guided her to the stretcher. She lay on the makeshift stretcher, small and thin. It sent a chill through him.

What if I hadn't seen her?

He'd mix some R first thing and heat some bone broth. He placed her shoes next to her feet still in gray socks.

"Ready?" He threw the saw in the backpack and shrugged into it.

She nodded her eyes closed. A sheen of sweat glistened on her forehead. He lifted the poles, and the stretcher tipped. The girl yelped.

"Sorry. Sorry." Heat rose to his cheeks. "I didn't think you'd need a seatbelt."

She grunted, and he glanced at her. Her lips rose at the corners. Was that a smile? With slow determination, he dragged the stretcher around logs and to the fence, cut a hole in the wire, towed her through, and hauled her across the pasture. He avoided the larger piles of branches and roofing.

She moaned when they passed the umbrella, and he glanced over his shoulder. Was that a laugh? Her eyes were closed, and she clutched her sweater over her legs.

He hauled the stretcher to the back door and set the poles on the steps to keep her head off the ground. She didn't stir. Was she still alive? He checked her pulse and found a steady beat at her wrist. She opened her eyes.

"We're here." Now for the hard part.

She tried to sit but fell back.

"Wait a minute. You might want to…"

He waved his hand at the sweater over her legs, and she nodded. He turned around and stared at the clouds and the remaining treetops in the distance. He wiped his sweaty hands on his jeans and glanced over his shoulder. She had adjusted the sweater to cover her legs.

"Ready." He glanced at her, but she was focused on retying the sweater and buttoning as many buttons as she could reach. She nodded.

He lifted her shoulders and helped her stand on wobbly legs then, with her arm around his shoulder, he walked her up the porch steps and through the kitchen. They shuffled down the hall to the basement door.

"The steps are steep, so we'll go slow." He stood with her at the top as she stared into the darkness. He flipped the light switch, and a shudder shook her frame. He adjusted her arm over his shoulder, and they made the slow descent, one step at a time.

He helped her to the couch. "I'll get you a drink." He mixed a pitcher of Rejuvelyte and carried a glass to the couch.

"Here." He held it to her lips. She drank several gulps.

Kneeling beside her, he placed his fingers on her forehead. Fever, page 80. He held the glass to her lips again and noticed that her skin was wrinkled, and her eyes seemed to sink into her skull. He'd found her just in time, or had she found him?

"Take little sips, in case you can't keep it down."

"Keep it down?"

"You could vomit this too, which would exacerbate your dehydration. Then we'd have another set of problems."

"Exacer-what?"

"You'll get worse, and—"

"I'm *not* going to die." She glared at him.

Grandpa was the first dead person he'd ever seen, but that had been in a funeral parlor, and he'd expected it, sort of. Chip was a total surprise—that scene still made him nauseous, but he couldn't let this girl die.

"Of course not." He looked into her dark eyes. She needed a shower, but she was too weak. "I'll get you a washcloth and some clean clothes."

What was he thinking? She needed a woman

helping her, not him. He rushed to the bathroom and ran a cloth under the faucet. At least she'd get warm water, thanks to Grandpa.

He handed her the washcloth. "Can you manage?"

She nodded, and he headed upstairs to the spare room. He grabbed a box marked "Donate," and carried it into the basement. He sorted through and found a T-shirt he'd worn in the seventh grade. He held it up. It would be huge on her, but it would have to do. He found a pair of gray sweatpants from sixth grade. Why had his mom kept this stuff? Thank heavens she did. He carried the clothes to her, but she'd fallen asleep, her face scrubbed pink. That was good, right? Sleep was good.

The dark bruises under her eyes and her pinched face told him she needed to be in a hospital on a saline drip, but she was here, and he was all she had for now.

He needed fresh air. The girl snored in soft huffs, and Josh crept up the basement stairs. Why was he tiptoeing? He plopped on the top step of the front porch. The excitement of getting her home and settling her on the couch left him restless. He stared at the barn, solid and squat across the driveway, a sheet of metal roofing curled in one place, missing in another.

Why had he brought this girl home? She would have died if he'd left her. He sighed and dropped his head in his hand. Now he'd have less time to work on the solar panels, but he would have more time to listen for radio messages. He stood and paced the porch. When would help arrive? When would power be restored?

Bird song and the rustle of branches eased his restless mind. Doctor. Would he be any good at it, really?

The sky was a brilliant blue behind the white clouds billowing in from the southwest—the calm before the next storm. Beautiful, but the wind picked up, and he turned and made his way down the stairs.

She lay so still on the couch, so sick. Sick Girl, that's who she was, but she must have a name. He couldn't call her Sick Girl all the time. He studied her pale face. At least her snoring had stopped. He pressed the back of his fingers to her forehead, still warm but not hot.

Where was she from? Where were her parents? Who was she?

He needed answers that would have to wait. He poured out a fresh glass of R. It didn't seem like enough, but it was the best he could do. He prodded her shoulder gently with his fingertips until her eyelashes fluttered, but she kept her eyes closed.

"You have to drink." Holding the glass of R to her lips, he waited until she had choked down a tablespoonful.

She seemed weaker now than when he'd found her. He tucked the blanket around her legs. Gravitating toward his violin, he lifted the case and opened it, held the instrument. Its weight alone comforted him. It had filled the hole in his chest after Grandpa's funeral. He'd play for hours, disappearing into each note that strung into a melody. The simple act of running his hand over the smooth wood eased the tension from his shoulders.

Sick Girl moaned from the couch, and he stopped, placing the violin in the case. He grabbed a bucket and set it beside the couch. Then he pressed the glass to her lips again, but she shook her head.

"Hey, you're dehydrated. You'll die if you don't drink." Had he said the wrong thing? Her eyelids had fluttered at the word "die." He raised her head and put the glass to her mouth. She moaned. Hard flakes of skin were cracking from her lips. He reached a finger to touch them but drew it back.

He grabbed the dirty washcloth from the end table and threw it by the washer on the far side of the room then grabbed a clean cloth from the bathroom. He turned on the faucet. It barked out air, and he turned it off.

Not the water, please? He turned it on again. It spurted, then a steady stream rushed out. A loud clunk followed by another, and another made Josh cringe.

The next storm had arrived. At least he had water. He scrubbed his hand then rinsed the rag under warm water, carried it to the couch. What would he do without running water? What were other people doing? He grabbed the glass of R, wet his finger, dabbed it over her chapped lips, then picked up the rag and took one of her hands. She let him rub more dirt from her knuckles and wrists. Her nails, broken and chipped, had small flakes of pink polish, a reminder of better days.

He held the glass to her lips. She tried to swallow but frowned. He waited until she took a sip. These little movements seemed like monumental tasks for her. She opened her eyes and glared at him. They were golden brown, like sunlight glinting off the pond out back. Beautiful. He stared. She closed them.

He reached for his grandmother's timer, turned the dial to thirty minutes. It ticked away as he ran his fingers through his hair. He caught a sour whiff. He needed a shower, too. He'd wait. She'd need a drink in ten minutes.

He threw some wood on the fire then opened his violin case. He lifted the instrument, polished it with a cloth, then fit his chin in the holder and ran the bow over the strings.

The whine of the strings echoed through the basement, and he cringed, glancing at Sick Girl. That was way too loud. He scanned the room. Maybe it was quieter in the storage room?

He placed his hand on a wood wall panel by the desk. The black handle was the only giveaway. He pulled, and it popped open. He stepped into the storage room and glanced at the door halfway up the wall that led into the root cellar. He had access to carrots and potatoes, but also an emergency escape route. He grabbed a candle and lit a match. Jars of applesauce and raspberry jelly glistened on the shelves.

He placed his candle on one of the jars and sat on a stool. Sound was muffled in the small space. Josh finished tuning as the timer rang. He pushed through the door. She didn't move, but her pink lips seemed less chapped each time she drank. He reset the timer for thirty minutes and returned to the storage room, back to his violin and peace.

The candle flickered in the darkness as the root cellar door clanked from the high winds blowing overhead. Then the storage room door slammed. He stood tipping the stool with a clatter. The wind created a draft.

He tugged on the handle: It held fast. The wood must have swollen in the storm. He yanked again. The door didn't budge. Bracing his feet on the cement floor, he jerked, and it popped open.

He poked his head around the door. Sick Girl's chest rose and fell in even measures. The walls seemed to press in on him. The timer, the girl, the winds, it was too much. He ran up the steps and to the front door. He fumbled with the deadbolt and turned the knob. It blew out of his hand in a blast of wind. A twirl of paper, plastic, and wood chips twirled across the floor.

He scanned the yard, but a gust blew branches and more debris against him. He squinted at the sky, thunderheads racing across the sky. He was trapped.

He shook his fist at the clouds. "Screw you, wind. Screw you, storm. Damn it."

A plastic bottle flew up and hit him between the eyes. He fell. Was that a sign? No cursing at storms? The timer rang, and he balled his fists.

Would the circuit survive storm number three? It had to. He closed the door and locked it, jogged down the steps, and reset the timer. He scrubbed his hands and face. It helped. He had to stay sharp.

He placed his fingers on the girl's neck, a pulse beat strong. He lifted her head a bit, pressed the glass to her lips. She sipped. He let her rest for a couple breaths then offered her the glass again. She swallowed hard and coughed.

Placing the glass on the coffee table, he turned to the radio. He dialed in a local channel, and the messages came streaming in, one after another. He grabbed a pencil and paper:

Juneau, Alaska: Snowstorm, high winds.
Prince George, BC: High winds.
Bella Coola, BC: Flooding.
Bellingham, Washington: People heading for storm shelters.

The winds blustered around the house. At this rate, he wouldn't have to clean at all. The wind would just blow everything away.

He switched to transmit and dialed in Uncle Carl's frequency. Then he coded:

Woolf Farm: All's well. Rescued girl. Dehydrated and vomiting.

He tapped in the last bit of code, and the timer rang. Had he just sent out gibberish? Grandpa had always said not to worry about transmitting. In an emergency, an experienced radio operator would get the gist. Mistakes were expected.

Would he get a response from Uncle Carl? He could use one about now. He needed to know Mom was okay, that Uncle Carl was coming back. Then the radio clattered.

Still at hospital. Sis sleeping. Hydrate the girl. I'll be there ASAP.

He slumped in the chair. The final letters were music to his ears—*ASAP*. He headed to the couch where Sick Girl lay. He willed her to get better. What was her name? He couldn't call her Sick Girl forever. She moaned again, and his belly tightened.

"You can do this, Josh. If you don't…"

He lifted her head, and she sipped and smacked her lips. Then she put her hand to the glass. He helped her, and she took a full swallow. She opened her eyes.

"Good job." He nodded and grinned.

She grunted.

"I'm Josh. What's your name?"

She stared at him, dark shadows around her eyes. He poured more R in the glass and held it for her. She drank then cleared her throat.

"Ehhhh—" she croaked through chapped lips.

He held up his hand. "You don't have to speak." Her hoarse voice made his throat hurt with sympathy pains.

"Emmmm—" She frowned at him with her fierce brown eyes and coughed.

"Shhh." He placed a hand on her shoulder.

"Emm-ah," she mumbled.

A coughing fit doubled her over. He held the glass to her lips, and she sipped then fell back against the pillow.

"Emma." He sat back in his chair. Sick Girl had a name. "Hmm."

She smiled but didn't open her eyes.

Chapter Twenty-Three

Josh

The third storm hit with the same gale force winds of the first one. More trees toppled, more debris struck the house in clunks and whacks. How long would this one last? Uncle Carl had left with Mom over two days ago. It seemed like weeks. He rubbed his temples and yawned. At least his hair was clean. The shower refreshed him, but still he yawned. How could doing nothing be so exhausting?

He rummaged through a drawer in the kitchen and found a container of green play-putty. He pressed it through his fingers and pulled it until it snapped, pacing the floor, and keeping watch over Emma. She lay on her side, deep regular snores filling the air. She must still have some congestion. He sat at the kitchen table, rolling the putty under his palm.

Emma. He knew her name, but that was it. She could be related to Bill, for all he knew. No. She couldn't be. He pulled the putty and wadded it into a ball. Would he treat her any different if she was?

He pressed the putty against the table. She came from Vandby, and so did Bill. What was taking Dad so long? Why hadn't he sent word? Didn't they have a radio on campus? Dad.

Please be safe, old man. You're the only old man I

have now.

The wind seemed to swirl around the house like a demon. It was happening just like Dad said. One storm after another with no time to press restart, to catch a breath, to get away.

He'd play his violin, to let the music flow through him. He pushed the door, but it was stuck again. Maybe if he rubbed the edges and frame with bar soap. He gave another push, and the door opened. He stumbled on something.

He bent to retrieve a wedge of wood. Grandma's doorstop. That's right, she pushed this under the door to keep it from slamming. How'd he forget that? He rubbed his eyes. Because he was exhausted, that's how.

He propped the door open with the piece of wood then held out the candle to find his violin. Did he throw it? Light reflected off his violin, and he lifted it from the dust.

Crap. A scuffmark marred the shiny finish. He rubbed it with his thumb. A little oil would fix it. But where was the bow? He spotted it by the door.

He sat on the stool and put the violin to his chin. He played until the fluid notes eased the tension from his neck and shoulders. He played until the timer rang. Then placing his bow and violin on a shelf, he reset the timer, and poured a glass of R.

Emma's cheeks were flushed, but her lips were still chapped. He hated to disturb her, but she needed the liquids as much as sleep. He lifted her head, her hair dirty but silky, her ponytail wrapping around his wrist.

She snorted and cracked her eyelids as she drank the entire glass. He eased her head back on the pillow, and her breathing grew deep and regular again. The smell of rotten eggs still clung to her. Maybe she'd be strong enough to shower—soon?

He stirred the fire and set another piece of wood on top then headed back to his violin. He ran through the chords, adjusting the pegs, but his mind wouldn't settle. Emma on the log waving a branch, her almost falling off the stretcher, her light arm around his shoulders, it all plagued him. Was he doing enough?

He reached his hand to his neck where Bill had choked him until he gasped for air. The image of Chip falling to the rug, the red stain on his shirt. He couldn't stop the images racing one after another. People were getting desperate.

He rolled his shoulders then lifted the bow. The sweet notes of Pachelbel's "Canon in D Major" filled the space, and soon he was lost in the melody, the ringing of the timer the only distraction.

He emerged from the storage room and found Emma pushing herself on her elbows, trying to say something. He rushed to her side and raised the glass, but she shook her head.

"Toilet," she murmured.

"Oh." He jerked away, sloshing R onto the blanket. The bathroom, built in the 1960s, didn't even have a fan, and she needed to use it?

He shook his head, heat rising from his neck to his cheeks. He jostled the glass as he set it on the coffee table.

"You don't have one?"

He nodded. At some point, she'd put on the sweats, and as she stood, they hung from her thin hips. Was her face flushed? Was it from fever or embarrassment? It didn't matter. He was certain his face was redder.

He held her elbow and guided her around the couch and to the bathroom. She bent at the waist, her tummy gurgling, her mouth twisting in a grimace. She gave him what he took to be an apology glance, and her cheeks turned brighter red. If she didn't have an accident before they reached the bathroom, it would be a minor miracle.

She put her hand on his chest at the bathroom door. "Don't go on any hikes or anything," she whispered.

He slumped against the wall. At least she didn't need help to use the toilet, and she had a sense of humor. That was a bonus. After several minutes, he began pacing the floor, the wind howling outside covering any sounds coming from the bathroom. He plopped on a kitchen chair, staring at the bathroom door. Had she passed out? The toilet flushed, and he sagged back in the chair with relief.

"Okay." She stepped through the door.

He rushed to her side and draped her arm over his shoulder. The smell hit him, and he coughed. He hustled her to the couch then rushed back to the bathroom without inhaling.

Where was the air freshener? Plugging his nose, he pulled it from the cabinet under the sink and sprayed the toilet, then the room, then slammed the door. He rushed to the kitchen sink and scrubbed his hands. He must have been mumbling the whole time because when he turned, her shoulders were shaking. Was she laughing?

"That bad?" She held her middle and began coughing.

"Worse."

"I'd clean it up if I could stand for more than a

second without falling."

"It's okay. I know." He'd have to work on his bedside manners but still… She coughed harder, and he handed her a tissue. She blew her nose and reached for the glass

"Drink up." He scratched his head. What was so funny? He'd never understand girls, especially this one.

She gulped it down and handed him an empty glass, her cheeks glowing pink. She scrunched under the blankets and closed her eyes. He sat by her side until her chest rose and fell in a steady rhythm as she settled into sleep.

The fire snapped, and he rose and threw on more wood. He was alone again, but he was doing something right. She seemed to be getting better, and he wasn't really alone. His muscles ached, and his eyelids grew heavy. He glanced at Emma then dropped into an overstuffed chair, the storm raging above them.

****

Even through the crashes of the storm, Emma slept, but so did Josh. He started setting the timer for an hour. He rose like a zombie from his half-sleep and gave her R. She'd snort in little huffs and buzzes. Was that part of her recovery? He wasn't sure, but he would sleep as much as she did tomorrow.

He groaned and glanced at the clock, 7:04 am. "Ugh."

He stretched his cramped muscles, the wind clattering against the siding. He'd have to check for loose boards. He craved fresh air and natural light. Rubbing sleep from his eyes, he grabbed the poker and stirred the embers then threw on kindling. The fire caught, and he placed a larger piece of wood on top.

Something was different. He scratched his head.

"Oh."

It was silent.

He jogged up the stairs and out the front door, stood on the porch, reveling in the clear dawn sky. The sky overhead glowed blue and clear, but dark clouds hovered on the western horizon. The storms came so fast, like Dad's prediction for El Primo. Trees swayed in the distance, like bobbleheads nodding in the winds that grew stronger every passing second.

He locked the front door and clambered down the stairs in time to shut off the timer. Emma lifted the glass and drank without help this time, her complexion glowing. She set the empty glass on the table and rolled over, covering her head with the blanket. She didn't utter one word.

He grunted. Her ability to sleep would be legendary if these storms ever ended and they got out of here to tell somebody. He cracked the door to the storage room, raised his violin to his chin, and stroked the bow over the strings, tuning each string, then started in on Pachelbel. Music filled the small space, and the tightness in his neck released, his back straightened. He swayed to the rhythm, until the timer rang. He was beginning to resent his grandmother's old windup timer. It took him from the soothing melody, set his teeth on edge. He wanted to throw it in the fireplace. Leaning the violin by the door, he stepped through.

"Beautiful." Emma held the glass he'd left for her to her lips and sipped.

"What?" He shook his head. Did she find it beautiful that she could drink on her own, or was it the R?

"The music."

"Oh." He ran his fingers through his hair. Was she serious? He sat in the chair by the fireplace.

"What's it called?" Her eyes reflected the low flames from the cozy fire. She sank back on the pillows. Wisps of her hair had escaped her ponytail and created a halo around her head. The silkiness made him long to touch it. He cleared his throat and stared at his hands folded in his lap.

"Pachelbel's 'Canon in D Major.'" Heat rose to his cheeks. How could she like his scratchy playing? He was pretty sure classical music was not on her playlist.

"It's my mom's favorite," he murmured. *Really, Josh, your mom?* At least she hadn't laughed at him.

"Beautiful." She smiled, and her eyes closed as she drifted into sleep once again.

"Huh." A chuckle escaped, and he sat back in the chair. She was attractive, sick and dirty as she was, and he couldn't seem to redirect his gaze, as though she were a sunrise, unique and colorful. He stood to check the shower.

He might need a cold one.

****

She slept for ninety minutes. Each time the buzzer rang, he poked his head out of the storage room to make sure she drank then refilled her glass. She drank without his help now. On the fourth ring, he found Emma pushing her legs off the couch. She sat back, perspiration on her upper lip from the small effort.

"Hey, you're not strong enough to get up." He rushed across the room to her. Her full lips pouted, no longer chapped. He stopped. He'd almost touched her. He should have taken that cold shower.

"I feel better." She laid her head against the couch, her face losing color.

"I'll get the bucket."

"I don't need the bucket." Her soft voice came to him like a caress, and he sank into the stuffed chair.

"I need answers."

"Oh. Okay." He clasped the armrests.

She stared at the fire, the only light in the room, but she never glanced at him. Did she even know he was here? It gave him an excuse to keep his eyes on her while she spoke.

"Where am I, and how did I get here?"

Oh, man. Did she remember taking off her filthy pants in the woods? Her eyes met his, and his mind whirred. He cleared his throat. "Uh, well, you are at Woolf Farm. It's my family's farm. I'm Josh. Woolf." Did he hold his hand out for her to shake? He crossed his arms over his chest.

"Okay," she murmured. She tucked her legs under the covers and slid onto the pillow, pulling the blanket to her chin.

He sank back like a stone until her breathing became soft and regular. That went well, short and sweet, which was about his limit. She would have more questions next time, though, and he gripped the armrests.

****

He set the timer for two hours, but now he just poked his head out of the storage room and, when she needed another glass of R, he'd get it. Other than that, she drank then dropped back into sleep.

Sleep would heal her, he kept telling himself, but still he sometimes sat and willed her to open her eyes as the storm destroyed the world outside. He needed answers too, like who was she?

He sank into the chair. Was that really what he wanted, though, to stick his foot in his mouth again?

****

He lifted his head from the armrest and rubbed his eyes. He'd fallen asleep. He sat up. "What?"

Sitting on the couch, she sipped from her glass. "I asked if you were asleep. I guess you were." She grinned.

He ran his fingers through his hair. Did she wake him up? Why?

"Oh. Yeah." He ran his fingers over the soft stubble on his chin. "You look better. R really works."

"You look like you could use some R and a comb." She held out her glass. "What is this stuff anyway?"

He ran his hand over his hair. "Rejuvelyte? Oh. A mix of electrolytes and vitamins for hydration. Helps when you exercise or if you're sick." He sat back. She gazed at him, and he looked away first. Maybe he'd pretend she was his patient, then he wouldn't stick his foot in his mouth. "How did you get so far off the road?"

Her mouth worked like she was searching for words. "I have a problem with directions, and my phone died, so I didn't have Maps." She paused then gazed at him, her eyes tearing. "When I got home, my mom was gone, out looking for me, I guess. And I lost Cuddles." She slumped over, her shoulders shaking, her head in her hands.

He sat stunned, trying to process her progression from okay to not okay. He didn't know what to say. Nothing she said made sense, but he gathered she'd come from Vandby and missed her mom. That part he got.

He glanced around the basement and then at her. He sat in a comfy chair by a warm fire in his own home. He got messages from Uncle Carl, and he could hike to his uncle's house if things got too bad.

"I'm sorry."

She didn't respond, and he rushed to her side. He checked her pulse, but she was only asleep. Why did she still sleep so much?

****

Emma rustled on the couch, and he stepped out of the storage room to check. She lay on her side, her hair covering her face. He tossed a couple pieces of wood on the fire then closed the screen.

"It's so cozy down here." She had rolled over, and the firelight glinted off her dark eyes. Her face was no longer angular and pinched. Had she been watching him? He couldn't move or speak.

She scowled at the flames. "You saved me. Thanks for that." She glanced at him as she sat. "I was so unprepared for this, and you are prepared for everything."

"Oh. Um." That was the last thing he expected her to say. He shuffled his feet and cleared his throat. "We try. My family, I mean, but it seems like no matter how prepared you are, you're never prepared enough." Her eyes never left his face. "Lots of people out here have generators, wells, gardens. The power usually goes out twice, sometimes three times, a year. We're on the outskirts of the grid, you know?"

"What was your name again?"

"Josh. Woolf." He waited. She moved from topic

to topic so fast he couldn't keep up.

"Do you know Dr. Woolf? I heard him speak at one of the climate marches."

"Oh." He glanced at her, taking in her small form, her slender hands. "Yeah. He's my dad. How do you know him?"

"Your dad? Wow. I'm such a fan. He came to our Youth for the Planet March one time to talk about changing weather patterns and monster storms."

"That sounds like him."

"So why isn't he here? Why did he leave if he knew this was going to happen?"

That last question stung, and he swallowed hard. "He didn't know...when it would happen, I mean. So, I guess he got caught off guard, like everyone else."

She gave him a thin smile, and he continued.

"He was at a conference this weekend, but hopefully he's on his way home." He clamped his mouth shut. How much did she want to know?

"El Primo." She nodded. "That's right. Why didn't the government do something? This didn't need to happen." She balled her hands into fists and shook them as she talked. She sank into the pillows and blew her bangs out of her face. "I can't believe he named it," she said, then closed her eyes.

He rubbed his face in his hands. What had he gotten himself into?

Chapter Twenty-Four

Josh

Josh perched on the stool in the dark storage room, the violin at his chin. Time was measured by storms now, and this was number four. The rich melody filled the space, calming him.

The timer went off, and he peeked his head through the door. She shrugged and gave him her apology-grimace. His shoulders tightened.

"Right." He shuffled across the room to help her.

Two weeks ago, if anyone had told him he'd be helping a girl he didn't know go to the toilet, he'd have laughed in his face.

He waited for her to finish, heat burning his cheeks. Still, he hovered outside the door, just in case. She emerged, and he took her arm, but she pushed past him and walked to the couch on her own.

She sat down and tightened her ponytail. "Does the shower work?"

"Um…well…yeah. If the circuit holds. Do y—"

"Yes. I do, and any food?" She scanned the kitchen cabinets.

"Umm." He opened a cabinet and grabbed several packets of soup. "Chicken noodle, vegetable, or tomato?"

"Oh, tomato. Got any cheese?"

"Cheese? Uh, no cheese. I have peanut butter and jelly."

"You cook, and I'll shower." She stood and headed to the bathroom.

"Clean clothes? You want some?"

She nodded and disappeared into the bathroom. He rummaged through the box and found another clean T-shirt and pair of sweats.

He knocked on the door. "They're on the floor."

She popped her hand out, scooped the clothes into her arms, and shut the door, whiffs of steam escaping.

He resisted the urge to peek and grinned. He'd done it, healed her. After Mom, he wasn't sure.

Well, this time he was doing something right.

****

She was on her fourth spoonful of soup, but he'd finished his entire bowl. He sat and munched on crackers, crumbs falling on his chest.

The lights flickered and went out. Emma's head jerked up.

"Great. I'll light some candles."

"Listen." She held a finger to her lips.

"The wind?" He rose from his chair.

"It's so quiet."

"I should go check the solar panels and see what happened before the sun goes down."

He took her bowl and set it in the sink then stirred the fire and added more wood. The flames brightened the room in a warm glow. She'd eaten the whole bowl, which was one less thing to worry about. Now he had to sort out the solar circuit.

He put on his jacket, and she frowned at him. He slipped on his shoes. "Don't you want lights?" She didn't respond.

"I won't be long." He climbed the stairs and pushed on the door, but it didn't open. He pushed harder, and sunlight burst through the crack, catching him off guard. Humidity was affecting every door in the house, it seemed.

He leaned all his weight against the door. Debris must have collected, blocking it. He poked his finger at the bottom of the crack and encountered debris packed against the door. Pressing the door, he used his foot to kick away the fir needles and debris.

It gave way, and he stumbled into the hall. He left the basement door open to let the brisk breeze blow in. So far, the front door had held against the winds and looters. Climbing over pillows of insulation, pinecones, paper, and torn curtains, he staggered into the living room. Light filtered in through holes in the walls. Those were new.

He stepped onto the porch. Bugger's blue paint peeked from under a fir tree, roofing caught in the fence, branches covering the ground. The winds had been off the charts, like Dad had said they would. It was a miracle the circuit had held together as long as it did. He rubbed the cramp in his neck.

A piece of green metal roofing from the barn tilted against the fence. The barn would need a new roof soon. Josh gazed beyond the barn to the sun sitting low in the western sky. He squinted, taking in the billowing clouds against a blue sky and golden horizon.

"Beautiful." He stood with his hands balled in his pockets. Did Emma like sunsets?

With slow, deliberate steps, he climbed over debris to the solar panel circuits. Two had been twisted out of the frame, but the metal wasn't broken. The breeze blew his hair back, and clouds gathered to the southwest. The scent of fir trees on the soft breeze caressed him. Clouds streaked across the sky. Did he have enough daylight to repair the circuit?

He climbed the steps to the back porch and checked the gas level in the generator. He still needed the radio, so he hit the start button. It roared to life. He hit the transfer switch in the breaker box and made his way into the basement.

"What was that noise? Is another storm coming?" Emma slumped on the couch. The edge of impatience in her voice cut through the air. She must be feeling better if she was getting cranky.

"It's just the generator," he said. "I don't want to miss any radio messages." He flipped the switch, and the radio came on. "No storm yet. I should be able to fix the circuit in a matter of minutes, but—"

"I better go with you." She pushed herself up.

"Wait. Um, but I just got the lights back on."

"I'm going."

He scratched his head. "Are you strong enough?"

She pushed the covers to her knees, and he held up a hand, but she didn't stop.

He reached for her. "Wait. I can't watch you and work on—"

"I don't care. I've been on this couch long enough." She swung her legs off the couch.

"What? I mean, what if you have t—?" His face grew warm.

"I'm fine." She turned red, but the thin line of her lips kept him quiet.

Why did the wrong thing always fly from his

mouth? He put a hand to his cheek. He was probably as red as she was.

Emma wobbled, and he reached for her arm.

"You have to stay—"

"I'm not staying inside."

"Okay, listen, I'll help you up the steps and onto the front porch, but you will sit there while I work on the panels. Deal?" He glared at her, but her face was so serious, he almost laughed.

"Deal." She hitched up the sweats.

He held her elbow, and they took the stairs one at a time. She did seem stronger, but she sank onto the top step. She scanned the barn and driveway with a grin that made him want to laugh again. Grandpa said it was the little things in life, and Josh was pretty sure he meant moments like this.

"I don't remember how I got here," she said.

"You don't? Well, the back door was closer, so—"

"Even if it wasn't to this door, shouldn't I remember something?"

"You were pretty sick."

The grin never left her face. She didn't seem to mind not remembering. He shrugged. Girls.

"The panels are on the other side of the house, so remember our deal?"

She nodded. He jogged to the pantry and flipped off the switch on the breaker box, grabbed his pack filled with tools and fasteners and the duct tape, the universal fix-all. He'd tape those panels in if he had to.

Grandpa would have had every inch of the circuit checked and repaired already. Josh would have too if Emma wasn't so sick. He grinned. Grandpa would like her.

He charged out the back door and around the corner to the solar panels. The kitchen porch and yard were protected by the house, but turning the corner, branches and insulation and a small tree blocked his path. Did each storm have to leave so much destruction and more work? He could barely keep up.

He removed branches from the first panel separated from the frame and swinging loose. He repositioned it and replaced fasteners, securing the connections, then went to the next one.

He stretched his back as sunrays burst through the clouds and shadows from the trees still standing spread across the yard and house. It really was the little things in life that kept him going. He wiped his hands on his jeans and grabbed his tool belt.

He walked around to the porch but stopped. Where was she? He scanned the driveway, the barn, and across the pasture. No girl. Did she fall behind a pile of something?

"Emma?" he called. Mom had been healthy when she fell down the stairs. He raced into the house and peered into the basement. No Emma, thank God.

He ran back outside. "Emma!"

"I'm in here."

Her voice came from the barn. He marched across the yard and slipped through the giant door that was hanging off one of its hinges. Emma stood in the middle of dad's weather instruments and equipment at back of the barn.

"I thought we had a deal?" His eyes adjusted, and he could make out her face. A slow burn consumed him.

"I didn't go far." She rummaged through Dad's

equipment, lifting one thing, examining it, then lifting something else.

"What are you're doing?"

"Helping."

"How is this helping? And don't touch that." He balled his fists and marched across the barn.

She opened the stall door and stepped into the paddock. She opened the weather station door, a small metal box on stilt-like legs. "What's this?" she asked, pointing.

"It's an anemometer. It measures wind direction and speeds. Inside are some other instruments: a thermometer, barometer, and—"

"What's this?" She picked something up and waved it at him.

Dad's sling psychrometer? "Careful. That's fragile." He grabbed for it as she held it like a toothbrush. "How did you get all the way out here? You could hardly do the steps by yourself."

She closed the weather station door and tripped as she walked into the barn. He flinched. The sweatpants hung off her thin waist and bagged around her ankles. She blinked at him, small and frail. She spun his grandfather's rusty weathervane with one finger, and he clenched his fists.

"You should be—"

"What is all this stuff?" She brushed her hands on her sweatpants. "It looks old."

"Some of it is old." He glared at her, but she didn't notice. "That is my dad's weather station." He pointed outside. "We gather weather readings even when the electricity goes out. Low-tech."

"So, he can read storms?" She stared from one

piece of equipment to another.

"Yes. He gets humidity readings and wind speeds, stuff like that." Maybe she'd tire herself out, and he could get her back inside before the next storm. She was feeling better, and this is what he got, a nosy girl poking through Dad's things.

"This reads air pressure." He pointed to the barometer. "The weather patterns are changing, but some people don't believe it."

"I bet they do now." Was she in control now, and how had that happened?

"Maybe. Or they'll call this an act of God now that it's too late."

She scanned the walls of the hayloft above them. "Is that a fishing net?"

"No, a cargo net. We use it for strapping down hay in the back of the truck." Emma wobbled, and he reached out and took her arm.

"Thanks." She grinned at him. "Maybe I should go in now."

"You think?" At least he'd get her inside without a fight. "You've probably done the equivalent of a marathon for someone in your condition."

She chuckled and held his arm in a light grip. They made their way one step at a time into the basement as the radio transmitted a message. He settled Emma on the couch, grabbed a pencil, but recited the message aloud:

At hospital. Sis feverish. Truck won't start.

"You understood that?"

"I guess I did." He bit his cheek. Fever meant Mom wasn't getting better, and if the truck didn't start, no one was coming? Why couldn't she be fine? The radio clattered in the background repeating the message.

"What if we there's another storm?" Emma asked.

"Not if, when, and when it comes, we'll deal with it." He handed her a glass, and she held it.

"How?"

"You need to drink, or you'll relapse." What was with all the questions?

"I want to help."

What could she do? He rubbed his temples, clamping his eyes shut. He couldn't take any more. He backed to the stairs and ran. He stopped beyond the barn, leaned on Bugger's bumper, wiping his eyes. A branch punctured the front of the car. Good thing the engine was in the back.

He rolled his shoulders. She wanted to help, and that was a good thing, right? Did all girls ask so many questions?

Branches rustled, and he jerked his head around, the hair on the back of his neck prickling. Was that a flash of red? Bill wore red, but Larson had him in custody.

He jogged back to the house, glancing over his shoulder several times. The flash of red had to be garbage. It was something from the barn or Highway 96 blown in by the storm. He closed the front door and locked it, crossed to the basement door, and locked it too, then rushed downstairs. Messages came in one after another, and he turned the volume low.

"Where'd you go? Messages are coming nonstop." Emma scrunched her forehead. "What's wrong?"

"Shhh." He grabbed a pencil and paper, ignoring the icy fingers of fear. He swallowed hard. "They're warnings."

"I still can't believe you can und—"

"Shhh."

She clamped a hand over her mouth.

"People are running out of food and water. Communities are creating relief centers."

"Who says?"

"Emergency radio operators. They keep communications open, share info." He clenched his jaw, trying to decide if he should tell her the part about the people getting killed for water and food or that the smell of food attracted looters, or about the patch of red he'd seen by the barn.

He had to be honest with her, though, for both of their safety.

"I saw something out by the barn."

"What?" Her mouth dropped open.

A crash upstairs startled Josh. Footsteps sounded on the floor above them, and Emma shut her mouth.

"Shhh!" He scrambled to the top of the stairs and pressed his ear to the door. One pair of shoes crunched over glass shards, but whose?

Josh's pulse pounded in his ears. Was it Uncle Carl? He would have called out. Bill and Dean? How did they get away from Larson?

The radio.

He sank onto the top stair, his legs numb.

"Who is it?" Emma sat forward, her hands on each side of her face.

"Maybe it's upstairs, Bill."

Josh shivered. Bill was back, but he didn't recognize the other voice.

"Shhh." He rushed down the stairs to her side. "Whoever it is, we can't let them know we're down here."

"But we have to do something."

He met her gaze. Her white fingers clutched the blankets. A clunk came from upstairs. They were going through drawers.

"We need a plan," he whispered. He scanned the room, but his brain wouldn't stop whirring. He gazed into the flickering fire.

"What plan?" she asked. Her voice shook.

How had Bill escaped? "Those guys killed someone. We have to get out of here." He sat beside her and held her hand. "You are still sick, so it won't be easy."

"Look. If we need to plan, I'm helping."

"I don't hear them anymore." He scanned the ceiling. He stood and paced the floor, pictured them climbing the steps to the bedrooms, his mother's jewelry.

"What about that little room where you play your violin. We could hide in there, right?"

"The storage room? That will work." He sank onto a kitchen chair. "Actually, it's how we're going to get out of here. We'll pack some bags and head to your grandparents' farm."

"What?"

"Keep your voice down," he whispered. He glanced at the ceiling and then at Emma. "Your grandparents live about two miles from here. Let's hope they are home because the hospital is another three. That's five miles. I don't think you're strong enough for that yet."

Emma sat with her hands folded in her lap, her lips quivering.

"This is going to take more energy than you have right now, but we can't stay. If we leave now, we might make it before another storm hits." He flinched when she gasped.

"Another storm? We just had a storm." Her face grew pale and waxy. "When will this be over?"

"Those guys will break the door down to get into the basement when the storm hits."

As if on cue, a crash followed by a muffled shout and another set of footsteps crunched across the floor.

"We'd better hurry." Emma whispered.

"Fir—"

"What first?"

"You need warmer clothes." He rushed to the donation box, grabbed a jacket, and threw it to her. He carried the box to the couch and set it between them. Emma opened the lid and held up another sweatshirt and a hat. She put the sweatshirt on, and he poured R into bottles and threw protein bars and crackers in his pack and pulled on his coat.

"What now?" She slipped into the jacket and zipped it.

He opened the door to the storage room. "Follow me. This will get us outside." He pointed to the root cellar door halfway up the wall. The footsteps crunched through the living room. They were coming.

"Okay?" She leaned back to check out the door and swayed.

He grasped her arm, helped her inside the storage room, grabbed the backpacks, and shut the door behind them. He turned on his flashlight, pointed the beam of light at the stepladder that led to the root cellar door.

"We might see spiders or earwigs."

"Yuk." She shivered.

"Just don't scream."

Emma climbed, one rung at a time. He climbed behind her and reached over her shoulder to unlatch the door. His body pressed against hers, and she turned her face to his. He could feel her breath against his cheek, and he climbed down two rungs, touched his cheek where her breath had caressed him.

"Just crawl up, and you're in the root cellar. I'm right behind you." Real smooth, Josh. Is she more dangerous than Bill?

She climbed to the top and stopped. "What is a root cellar, anyways? Looks like a grocery store." She'd gone from scared to curious in two seconds.

"It's cold storage for our carrots, beets potatoes, apples and pears, all the stuff we grow." He patted a crate full of carrots covered with sand. Boxes and bins were stacked on one side of the root cellar, and garden tools hung on the other. It had an order and organization that only Grandpa could give it. He pointed to a red door with a rounded top and a half-circle window.

"Like Bilbo's door." She turned to him and grinned.

"Gran's idea. Now, keep your voice down." He stepped toward the door.

Emma grabbed her middle and doubled over. "Oh."

"Gas?" He clamped a hand over his mouth. Did he say that out loud?

Emma's cheeks turned pink then white.

"Are you okay?" He couldn't believe he'd said that either. Of course, she wasn't okay, but if it was Bill... Bill would never meet Emma, if Josh could help it.

"We can always come back if I can't make it, right?" She scanned the root cellar.

"Uh. Sure. That's not the best option, but…"

He put a hand on her shaking shoulder. She was running on adrenaline, but that wouldn't last for long. "It could take an hour to get to your grandparents'." He paused. "Maybe two."

She wiped her nose on her sleeve. "Then we need to be gone already, because with my luck it will take five."

He opened the door and looked at his watch. "It's 6:12 am. It won't be light for an hour, so stay close, and be quiet. If we can make it to the road without being seen, we'll be in the clear."

"Okay."

Her belly rumbled, and she glanced at him and leaned forward. He reached for her, but she turned her head and retched out the door.

Chapter Twenty-Five

Emma

Emma wiped her mouth with the back of her hand. She pushed her shoulders back, stood her full five-feet-four-inches, and placed a hand on her midriff. She spit out the door. No. That wasn't embarrassing at all. Josh patted her back. "I'm fine. I'm fine."

What did that even mean? She wanted to be fine, but she might never be fine again. People were in the house. They had to leave, end of story.

Josh raised an eyebrow at her.

She cocked her eyebrow back. "I'm as ready as I'm ever going to be, okay?"

Josh's frown made her want to punch him, and she flinched at her reaction. Who was she turning into? They couldn't stay. He'd said so himself. She stared at her hands unable to meet his eyes. Her gurgling bowels had settled to a low simmer. She gave him an I'm-okay grin. He nodded.

"It's downhill to the road. If we keep to the left, we'll be hidden by the berries." Josh pointed into the darkness, but all she could make out was a row of scraggly vines hanging over a cedar fence.

"We'll use the vines as cover until we hit a pile of trees near the road. Once we're through the pile, we'll be at the end of the driveway and out of hearing from the house." He glanced at her. She nodded. "We'll follow Highway 96 to your grandparents'."

"I took 96 from Cedarville. I guess it makes sense that your farm is off 96?"

He nodded.

"Huh. I wasn't that lost after all." She shrugged into her pack, the fog in her head lifting. She could do this. She was doing this. She would be at Gran and Papa's today. The hair on the back of her neck tingled.

"Um. Ladies first?" He bowed to her.

"No. Age before beauty." Blood rushed to her face. That was the stupidest thing she'd ever said to a boy, but she couldn't lead, not in her condition. She pressed a hand against her middle.

"Okay, but try to keep up. We have two miles to cover."

In the predawn light, she was able to make out the shapes of trees beyond the barn. She crept behind Josh to the fence with the berry vines draped over it. The thorns had caught debris from the winds, creating better cover for them.

He held up his hand. She froze. Voices arguing came from the house. Josh grabbed her arm, and she dropped into a crouch beside him. He held a finger to his lips. She peered through the tangle. Two men stood on the porch, one pointing right at her.

"I heard voices right there."

She ducked. Was it possible for her heart to pound out of her chest? She gazed behind them to the root cellar then peered through the vines toward the house. The door opened, and another man with red hair came out. She couldn't breathe as she waited for the men to find her.

Josh crouched even lower. "That's Bill and Dean. I don't know the guy with red hair."

Josh did not take his eyes from the porch. In the growing light, his face had turned white. A shiver ran from the back of her neck to her tailbone. Her leg cramped. She gripped it, sat, and straightened it.

She put a hand on his shoulder. "What's going on?"

Josh pointed. "Dean."

Dean walked down the steps. He pointed a flashlight right where they were crouched. The light bounced as he fumbled it.

"I'm telling you, I heard voices," Dean said. "I swear it."

"Well, I don't hear nothing. No more false alarms, you hear me, you coward. We're trying to send that message."

Josh pointed. His finger shook. "Bill."

Bill stomped back into the house, leaving Dean in the driveway holding the flashlight. He ran up the steps and turned off the light. If he was the watchman, he sucked. Josh touched her shoulder and motioned to the downed trees at the end of the driveway.

"Do you think you can run?" he whispered.

She nodded, massaging her leg.

"Stay close."

Crouching low, Josh ran along the fence and into the tangled mess of downed trees toward 96. He eased through the branches. She rushed behind him, but a branch swung back hitting her in the face.

"Ow." She fell to her knees, holding a hand to her cheek. They'd only gone one hundred feet, and she wanted to cry.

She clenched her jaw. *Get up, Emma.* She scrambled herself through the branches one by one, straddling trees as she swung her body over yet another log.

Trees looked so organized standing upright, but on the ground, they were a nightmare of branches and trunks. Sweat made her shirt damp, and her legs quivered with each movement.

Josh waited on the other side of a large log, and she grabbed his arm for support. The wavering flashlight beam was no longer visible.

"I need a drink." She wanted a nap, but a stop for a drink would have to do.

Josh grabbed a bottle from her pack and one from his. They sat in silence, drinking R.

"You okay?" R dripped down his chin, and he wiped it on his sleeve. His chest rose and fell as fast as hers, which was a small comfort to her. This was hard for him, too.

"Yeah. I'm fine." If she could keep that promise, she would make it to Gran's house.

The sky grew lighter with each step, and the rough contours of the bark and the needles on the fir trees come into focus. Her feet swam in the boots. The bottoms tingled and grew numb as she trudged down 96.

She gazed at the tops of the Cedarville firs. "Why didn't they fall?"

"I have no idea. Strong root systems most likely."

She'd driven with Gran through the tall column every time they went to Cedarville, but the effect of walking through the column was breathtaking. They stood like sentinels in the early dawn, swaying in the rising winds.

"How many storms have we had now? I've lost track." She ran the back of her hand over her forehead.

"This is day eight, so four? The first one was the worst."

"So next one will be lucky number five?"

As if on cue, the wind whistled through the branches. Not now. Another storm would ruin her day. The breeze grew stronger. Her gut clenched.

"What if the storm hits before we get there?" She regretted the words the minute they flew from her mouth.

"Don't say that. You'll jinx us." He scanned the clouds rolling in.

Heat rose to her cheeks. He hadn't seemed like a superstitious kind of guy, but then again, she didn't know him. A branch cracked off a nearby tree and sailed over their heads to land in a field. She held her stomach, leaning against a log, waiting for it to quit rolling.

"You okay?" Josh looked at the sky, a furrow wrinkling his brow.

"I'll make it. Just needed a breather. How much farther?"

"We're getting closer. This took longer than I thought it would." He grinned at her. "How'd you make it all the way from Vandby?"

She shrugged. She forgot the hat on the couch, and the wind blew her hair in her face. The sun sat low in the sky, and dark clouds were visible, rolling in from the southwest. Her jaw clenched, and Josh frowned. They had to keep moving. She pushed herself off the log, the standing trees swaying like graceful silhouettes all around them.

"Come on." He glanced at his watch. "It's almost nine. I'd want to get you to your family before noon so I can go on to Cedarville." He jogged to the next downed tree, slowing to climb through the branches.

She followed, but she was breathless after two trees. She lifted her head as Josh disappeared into yet another tangle of trees. The wind grew stronger, pressing against her back. It was like déjà vu.

She tumbled across one more log, struggling to keep up. He ran back for her and grabbed her hand. She tried to smile, but he didn't notice as he hauled her across a pasture, dodging branches and metal roofing. It seemed effortless for him, and she let him drag her along.

He came to a dirt road, dropped her hand, and jumped a ditch. She followed and blessed all the goddesses for pavement once again. Josh stopped, shielding his eyes as he scanned the area. She gazed into the mess of branches and trees.

Were they getting close? Nothing looked familiar. The wind whipped her hair, stinging her eyes until the landscape blurred. Josh gripped her hand again, and she raced with him through a parking lot filled with snowplows and piles of sand.

She willed her feet to run faster, but Josh dropped her hand and ran ahead. She tried to keep up, but he ran too fast. She couldn't even catch her breath. Why had she told him she could do this? She couldn't do this, not on her best day. The wind gusted as if to mock her, pushing her down.

How far had they run? It seemed like ten miles. How many hours had passed since they'd left Josh's?

Her chest ached, and coughing rasped her throat. The wind raced through the trees, blowing fir needles in her face. Josh ran toward a house in the distance.

"Josh," she called, but he kept running. Storm number five wasn't lucky at all, and how was it that she was outside getting blown around? Again. Her gut tightened, and she doubled over.

Josh turned, and his mouth opened, but his words did not reach her. He held out his hand and she forced her legs to keep moving until she could grab his hand.

"The wind." Her tummy rolled. She clenched her jaw.

"We're almost there." Taking her arm, he helped her over trees and through branches.

A crack broke the air, and she grabbed Josh's arm as a branch flew overhead. The trees thumped as they blew into one another. Josh held her hand, and she raced behind him. She tripped over a stump, and he helped her to her feet. All she could do was grip his hand and clutch her middle as they slogged on.

She stumbled over a fence and into a yard. A house stood across a grassy expanse, a swing creaking from a rusty swing set.

"This is Gran and Papa's place?"

The wind howled, drowning out her words. She scanned the lawn, Papa's pride and joy littered with garbage right up to the rhododendrons by the house. She stared at the yellow chicken coop, a tree lying through the middle of it. Where were the chickens? Josh held her hand, towing her to the house.

All the windows were either cracked or broken, and the front door stood open. Glass, pinecones, and fir needles covered the hardwood floor.

"Gran?" she called. Her voice echoed, but no one answered. "Where are they?" She scanned the living room. What had she expected, Papa sitting in his chair reading the paper?

She tiptoed over the broken glass, following Josh through the living room to the kitchen. He turned on his flashlight and opened the basement door, but she stopped at the top of the steps.

A cold chill ran through her. Another dead end with no Mom. Her feet were numb, and her hands tingled.

Dust motes floated in front of Josh's flashlight beam. He took a step, and the wood creaked. She clenched her teeth.

A white streak exploded out of the blackness and slammed into her leg, disappearing out the front door.

"Agh!"

"Cat." He glanced at her then disappeared into the darkness.

"Poor Frosty."

She stared into the black hole of the basement. Her Papa had teased her about spiders hiding in every corner, so she'd never gone down these stairs, ever. She shuddered and followed Josh.

Papa had cut back on gardening, so Gran no longer canned the vegetables, especially after her dad died, so their basement was the opposite of Josh's, no rugs, no furniture, no jars of carrots or pickles shining on the shelves. Papa's tool bench and table saw sat against one wall, gathering dust. A mismatched washer and dryer stood on the wall opposite the stairs.

The damp and cold sank into her bones, and she shivered under her sweat-drenched shirt. She rubbed her arms and stamped her feet, but her intestines gurgled, and she bent at the waist. Had Josh heard? She needed to figure out the bathroom situation, and quick.

"What's that?" She pointed at a big metal box, hoping it might be a toilet of some kind.

"Furnace." Josh patted the metal.

She struggled to stay upright. "Hmm. And that?" She pointed at another large barrel-shaped object. Please goddesses, let it be a toilet.

"Water heater." Josh frowned at her. "Don't you have these things in your house?"

"I avoid basements at all costs. Spiders."

"Oh. Um. You did well in the root cellar then."

"I closed my eyes." She waited for him to laugh at her, but he didn't. The wind toppled a tree with a thump. Between spiders and trees falling, she might have an accident or a nervous breakdown.

"Where do you think they went?" She rubbed her hands together for warmth, shuffling her feet.

"The hospital." Josh offered. "Are you okay?"

"Sure." She raised her shoulders raising the collar of the coat to hide most of her face. "Why the hospital?"

"One of the messages said seniors and sick people could shelter there."

"Gran just had cataract surgery." She bit her lip. Why hadn't she listened to Mom? The room began to spin.

Grabbing her bottle of R from the side pocket of her pack, she emptied it in two chugs. She shook her empty. Josh pointed at her bag, and she took out a full one. The wind whistled through the open front door and through the house. Josh lit a candle, protecting the wick as it waved in the drafty basement.

"It's in full force now." Josh peered out of one of the dirty windows that let in dim light.

"How long do you think this one will last?" Her belly gurgled again.

"Uh. I don't know. None of them have been the same. The shortest was only a couple of hours." He glanced at his watch. "11:17 am. I hope this one's short. We need all the daylight we can get if we have to walk to the hospital."

"The hospital is three miles, right?" Her tummy rolled, and she clutched it with both hands as she scanned the basement for a bucket. She'd never make it three miles.

She needed medicine to stop the diarrhea. She needed Mom. Josh stared at her.

"You don't look so good. My house is only two. I think we should go back." He glanced at her. "It will be easier for you."

"What? That's a horrible idea. I didn't come all this way to go back." She clutched her middle. Why did she drink from the river? She wiped her nose on her sleeve. "Bill's there, remember? It makes more sense to go to the hospital. Don't you want to see your mom?" Her tummy started to roll in earnest, and she broke into a sweat, tears rolling down her face.

"You're going to be sick." His brow furrowed, and his eyes bore into her. "Here, lie down."

"On the cement?" Sick was an understatement. Couldn't he tell she needed a toilet? How did she tell him?

He pulled out a blanket and grabbed some cardboard boxes Papa had broken down for recycling.

He laid the cardboard out then helped her onto it and covered her with the blanket.

"Thanks." Her tummy rumbled, and she tucked her knees to her chest. Her intestines groaned, and she glanced at Josh, his cheeks bright red.

"I'll try to find a bucket or something, just in case." He spun from her and paced the basement, peering behind the furnace and the washing machine.

"Yeah, just in case." How humiliating. Her middle rolled again, and she closed her eyes. She would have spent her Saturday watching *Frozen* with Sarah for the millionth time. She should be with Sarah and Mom wherever they are.

She doubled over, her hand on her cramping abdomen. "Where's that bucket?"

"Found one." Josh emerged from the other side of the washing machine tipping a white plastic bucket upside down and beating the bottom. Lint and dryer sheets fell to the floor. He placed it next to her and backed away. She glanced inside, the rust stains and green mold visible even in the dim light.

"A little privacy?" Her cheeks grew hot.

"Oh. Uh. Yeah." Josh pointed to a dark corner and went to inspect it.

She flipped on her flashlight, spotted a tarp. "Hey. We can make a wall."

Josh lifted a corner of the tarp. "Or not."

The aroma of cat urine hit her like a stink bomb. She pinched her nostrils. Josh held the flashlight, scanning the basement, stopped on a cardboard box with "DRYER" printed on the side. He dragged it over to her.

"Use this for a partition." He turned away and

switched off the light.

Her abdomen cramped, and her legs wobbled as she rushed behind the makeshift wall with the bucket.

"I'll just apologize now."

She could hear him humming to himself. The wind roared outside, which helped, but Josh had nowhere to go, no way to escape the odors.

Weak with cramps, she cursed all the goddesses. Josh had done nothing but help her. Why couldn't she help him by being stronger? Who was she kidding? She couldn't do any of this.

"If I had my violin, I could play something loud enough to—you know."

"Yeah, I do know. What would you play, 'Ode d' Poo'?"

He chuckled.

A loud crash and whump shook the ground close to the house. Would any trees be left?

"That one was big." Josh sloughed his pack off then his coat.

Was he talking about her or the tree? Her tummy settled. She grabbed her flashlight and scanned the floor, revealing a square piece of plywood. She covered the bucket.

"Well, that wasn't humiliating at all." She panned her light over the makeshift bed. "Any hand sanitizer?"

"In your pack."

She wiped her hands three times. Her eyelids grew heavy, and she crawled under the blanket, the wind howling around the house.

They couldn't go anywhere until this storm blew over. "Maybe after I sleep I'll feel well enough to make it to the hospital."

Josh sat on a stack of cardboard and leaned against the wall. He grunted.

He hates me now. Her vision blurred, and questions filled her mind. Did Gran and Papa make it to the hospital? Did her mom?

She closed her eyes.

****

She bolted upright to Josh shaking her shoulder. He stepped back. She took in her unfamiliar surroundings then searched Josh's face. He stood above her but avoided eye contact, and her bucket episode crashed through her brain like a bad dream. Would she ever live this down? And he was cute. Dang. She wiped the drool from her mouth. "What's up?"

"The storm's over."

"Oh." She sat up and rubbed her eyes. "How long was I out?"

"Four hours." He stuffed his blanket in his bag. "It's almost 2:00 now, so we'll only have a couple hours of daylight."

She guzzled R, trying to shake the heaviness from her head.

"If we hurry, we'll get to the farm before dark." He adjusted his pack on his shoulders.

"What? No. Can't we discu—"

"We planned on your grandparents being home. It's three miles to the hospital from here, all uphill. You'll never make it before dark, and we can't hike in the dark, and we can't stay here with no running water or toilet. We'll have to—"

"Hide in the root cellar." She sniffed.

She hung her head. No argument would change his mind, but he was right. She'd never make it three miles, not before dark. She hated being sick.

She stuffed the blanket in her pack. "At least it's downhill all the way."

Chapter Twenty-Six

Emma

Emma took one step at a time, with Josh holding her elbow. She blinked at the bright sky but couldn't speak. Dark clouds raced above them. He gave her a grim smile, then set out the way they'd come. She trudged behind him, her brain in a fog. She had slept, but it was a restless, dreamless sleep that had left her more zombie-like than refreshed.

He stopped, and she sank to the ground. Rubbing her forehead, she gazed at him. He had that frown again. She dropped her eyes, unable to lift her chin. What was she doing out here, and why did he always have that frown? Was she sicker than he let on?

"This fell out of your pocket. I wasn't snooping." He held the note in his fingers.

She slumped against a tree. Was that why he was angry? "I found it on my way home."

"Sorry we fought?"

"Like I said, I snuck out because Mom didn't want me to go out in the storm." She couldn't meet his eyes. Without her, he would already be at his uncle's or the hospital not rushing for shelter between storms. Without him, she would be dead.

"I screwed up." She let her head hang. This would forever be her fault. Is this what happened when you disobeyed your mom? When a storm destroyed the world?

He frowned. "You wha—"

"I snuck out and got caught in the storm." She squirmed under his harsh gaze.

"Why wou—"

"I had flyers for the march. I promised Megan." Each time she explained her reason, it seemed more ridiculous. Mom had asked her how she would survive in the storm, and she'd been so sure, so certain that she'd be fine. It was no big deal.

But she wasn't fine, and it was a big deal, and because of her, neither was he.

"Flyers?"

"For the Youth for the Planet March." She rubbed her face with her hands.

"Wait. Wasn't the last one—"

"Cancelled." She clamped her eyes shut to stop the pressure building behind them.

"So, you're saying you walked all the way from Foun—"

"Founders Square, yes. Why all the questions?" She folded over her chest and huffed. What was this, a trial?

"Oh," he said. "Uh, so you ran away?"

"No. It's not like that." She stared at her dirty hands, her eyes losing focus. She looked up. "Mom hates storms because dad had an accident in one. She always overreacts, so I never listen, but this time I should have. Are you happy now?"

"Did he get hurt, your dad?"

"He died." She buried her hands in her face. She could never bring Dad back, and now she might have lost Mom and Sarah.

"I'm sorry." He stood, hands in his pockets.

She sniffed and wiped her eyes, the heaviness in her chest a steady ache.

"We have to keep moving or we'll get caught out here in the dark." He gripped her hand and helped her to her feet.

Was he still angry? Did it matter? She leaned forward and fell into a steady tromp.

The return hike was downhill, but Emma's thighs ached. She stumbled as she plodded behind him. She ducked as he held a branch for her, and in front of her stood a cedar fence, but not the one in his yard. She groaned, and he pointed to the rail on the fence. He sat beside her as the wind blew her fly away hair into her face. At least it was clean. She turned to him.

"You must have been to the marches?" she asked. "Your dad came." She glanced at the Cedarville firs, several now lying on the ground. Her sentinels were falling. The severity of what had happened over the last week left her numb.

"Dad led the team of researchers who predicted this pattern of storms, but none of them knew when it would hit, my dad included. It was a constant battle with politicians calling his team wackos, doing junk science, spreading fake news." He paused to take a shaky breath.

She blinked. "So, who ignored your dad? The governor? The president?"

"You've been to the marches. You've seen the signs. Lots of people still don't believe. But lots of people do, and some were prepared." He stared at his boots and hung his head.

She shuddered, looking away. "I wasn't prepared—not for packs of dogs, looters, no cell service, electricity, or light rail." She glanced at him then turned to the trees in the distance.

"I thought I was prepared, too, but I wasn't prepared at all, not for this—no 911, no phones, roads blocked." His words tumbled from his mouth.

"That's not true. You are really prepared." She turned to face him.

He didn't respond. She wiped her nose on her sleeve.

"We crawled over piles of trees from Founder's Square to my house, through branches just like this." She swung her arm to the trees and debris piled around them. "The stink of the garbage, rotting food..."

She clenched her jaw, and tears coursed down her cheeks. "I left Lilli and Jade two days ago then drank from the river, and I guess you know the rest. That's how prepared I was."

He reached out his hand, and she grasped it, the warmth of him seeping into her. It shocked her, but she didn't let go.

"I don't know who could have prepared for this." He helped her to her feet. Once again, she would not make it to family today. Would she ever see them again?

She ached from missing them. Jade's words ran through her brain as she followed Josh. "Until we meet again." Then Lilli's, "Are we there yet?"

She tried to mimic Josh's ambling gait. He confused her. Was he angry with her? Fatigue kept the edge on her nerves, and if she sat down one more time, she'd fall asleep.

He steered her through a pile of trees, and with a jolt she followed him down the row of berries by his garden. They were home. She stumbled and rubbed her temples, and her vision cleared. The red barn came into view. He glanced over his shoulder but didn't stop. The porch came into view, and he crouched. Bill, Dean, and the guy with red hair stood there.

The dark clouds gathering in the distance blocked the sun, and the wind lifted strands of her hair tickling her face. Another storm? She shivered as she squatted by his side. The men on the porch were arguing, but she couldn't make out their words. She rested her hand on his shoulder and leaned closer to hear them. He glanced at her, and she pulled her hand away, unsettled by his warmth.

He focused on the men. All she needed now was for her belly to rumble. She braced herself for his next move. If the men caught them before they got to the root cellar…she had to keep up, that was all.

Bill and Red-hair-guy disappeared into the house.

"Dean's still on lookout. The guy with red hair must be Mo. Bill mentioned a radio expert the last time he was here."

She nodded. He held a finger to his lips. "Let's go before they come back."

Her knees shook with each step. He opened the root cellar door, and she tumbled in behind him. She glanced at him as he sat beside her.

"Until we meet again, root cellar." She slapped a hand over her mouth. Where did that come from?

A small smile formed on his lips. "What?"

She raised her chin and kept her gaze focused on the bins of carrots and potatoes. If she met his eyes, would she cry? Maybe.

Her face burned, and she fumbled with her backpack straps. "It's something my neighbor, Mrs. M, said before I left. I probably won't see her again."

"Why?"

"I don't know. She's so old." She sat up and turned to Josh. "What day is it?"

He shook his head, his face blank. "Wednesday, I think?"

She leaned against the wall. "My birthday was Thursday. The march was Saturday, and today is Wednesday? I've been sixteen for a week, and I want cake. I haven't had my cake yet." She pounded the floor with her fist. She did want cake, could taste Mom's sour cream chocolate frosting.

"Cake? Huh." He combed his fingers through his hair. "Happy birthday?"

She hung her head. Was Thursday the day she drank from the river? Of course, it was. Happy birthday.

"I have applesauce, but that's the best I can do."

He glanced at the door that led to the storage room. Was chat-time over?

"When things have settled down, I'm going to hold you to that applesauce." She nudged his shoulder, and he nudged her back. Her insides fluttered. Butterflies? Hmm.

"We need to make a plan." He knelt on one knee.

She nodded, biting her lip. She'd wanted to help, and she'd fly to the moon, if that's what he needed, but how much help would she be in her condition?

"We'll climb into the storage room, and I'll push open the door a crack while you check for Bill or anyone in the basement. Then I'll ease it closed. It will be quick, so stay sharp." He sloughed off his pack and opened the half door. "No talking. Ready?"

"Now? I mean, I don't thi—"

"Of course, now. You can do this."

She shrugged off her pack.

"If no one's there, I can send a message to my uncle. He'll send Larson and come and get us. If someone is there, I close the door and we wait."

She nodded.

He raised his eyebrows at her, climbed into the storage room, then held his hand up to her. She took his hand, and he held her steady. She climbed down, his warm breath tickling her neck.

He turned out the flashlight. She crouched by the door. The darkness disoriented her, and she wobbled, but he held her by her shoulder, and the shelves wedged her upright.

He eased the door open. She peered through the crack. Blue socks and dirty jeans, it was the red-haired guy. The fire crackled, and the radio clattered away. She tapped his hand, and he eased the door shut. He helped her stand and followed her into the root cellar.

She pressed her hands to her temples. Was her head going to explode? "The guy with the red hair was sending a message." Blood pounded in her ears.

"I heard. It was directions on how to get here," he whispered. "Stay here. I'm going outside to check something."

He placed a warm hand on her shoulder, but she shivered. He disappeared out the door, and she chewed her lip, tasted blood. She brushed her hand over her hair. Spider? Probably not. She crouched in the dark room. When would he come back?

Footsteps coming fast approached the door, and she picked up a piece of wood from the floor. The door opened, and he shook his head, dark circles under his eyes, frown lines creasing his forehead. She dropped the wood with a clatter. She rushed to him, and he embraced her then dropped his arms and took a step back. She cleared her throat, avoiding eye contact. *We make quite a pair.*

"What's going on?" she asked.

"Bill and Dean are arguing. Bill wants to wait for a reply, but Dean's freaking out. He thinks the law is coming. His words, not mine, but Bill is the boss, which means they might be here for a while."

"The law?" Her belly gurgled.

Again? Her face burned as she held her middle.

"Deputy Larson had Bill and Dean in custody. Somehow, they escaped, obviously, or they wouldn't be here." He paced the small space. "We need that radio."

"So, what do we do?" Her heart battered her ribs.

"We check again. Ready?"

"No."

Her hands shook as he took her by the elbow and helped her down the stairs. She sat next to the door, and he opened it a crack.

Bill's voice thundered down the stairs. "Mo, Larson's back."

"What?" Mo leapt from the chair and ran up the stairs.

She fell back. "Mo is gone."

He took her arm, and she stood. He opened the door and rushed to the radio. "What a stroke of luck."

"What are they doing?" Emma stared at the ceiling

as the men rummaged through the house, footsteps clomping from room to room. The radio beeped to life, transmitting then repeating the message. He scratched notes on his tablet.

"It's from Uncle Carl." He swiveled to face her. "He wants to know who's using this radio, and if we're okay. Apparently, that guy sent all his messages to Uncle Carl." He rubbed his chin and chuckled. "He's no expert. What a relief."

"That's a relief." She leaned against the desk. "Bill won't get any backup."

Josh didn't respond. He sat, focused on the radio, and tapped in his message. The response was almost instant, and he plopped back in the chair.

"What?"

"He's already on his way."

"Maybe Uncle Carl could give me a ride to Cedarville?"

A loud crash shook the floor above.

She jumped. "What are they doing?"

He stared at the ceiling. "They're trying to get into the gun safe. Larson confiscated all of Bill's weapons."

The footsteps ran out the front door.

He jogged up the steps and peeked into the dining room then motioned to her. "Come on."

"What? No." She scurried after him, grabbing a flashlight and gripping it like a weapon.

He raced to the front door and skidded to a stop. She caught up to him and peered over his shoulder. The sun peeked through the clouds, and she squinted into the yard as Mo and Dean ran into the barn. A tall guy in a cowboy hat chased them, his pistol in his hands.

"I didn't see Bill." He started running, motioned

for her to follow, and skirted the yard. He stopped under the apple tree behind a pile of broken branches.

"Stop," echoed from the barn.

She rushed to follow him, blood pounding in her ears. She huddled by the trunk of the tree, clutching Josh's coat sleeve.

A shot rang out, and Larson fell on his stomach into the barn, the soles of his boots splayed at odd angles. He lay still as death.

Chapter Twenty-Seven

Josh

Josh stared at Larson's boots, willing him to move. He struggled to get air into his lungs. Had Bill killed Larson? He pressed his hands to his chest, his heart racing. Emma clung to his sleeve, and he dropped his hands.

He glanced at her. "Ah…"

"What's wrong? Do you have asthma?" She scowled, the skin under her eyes purple and shriveled.

"What? No."

Dehydration. Of course. Yet she had the energy to worry about him?

She sagged against the tree trunk. She needed fluids or she'd relapse.

His bag with R in it was in the house, but he needed to get to the barn and help Larson before Bill got the upper hand.

"There's a spigot by the barn. Can you make it that far?"

She nodded. He took her arm, and they scurried around piles of branches to the side of the barn. He peered into the side door as she crouched behind him. He struggled to breathe, as Bill's harsh voice echoed to the rafters.

"Now." He ran halfway down the side of the barn

to a side door and the faucet. He gave the spigot a half twist. She drank then he did, and he shut it off.

"Was that a gun? Did they shoot the deputy?"

"Yeah." He counted to ten backward, pressing on his chest. He closed his eyes, and Emma placed her hand on his shoulder. He nodded.

"Do we have a plan?" She held his gaze, her eyes bottomless.

A plan, right. He glanced at the sky, the cirrus clouds rushing to the east. No storms coming, so what was the plan?

"We need to help him. He might die." She pointed inside the barn.

He took her hand and held it in both of his. "He won't die. Follow me." He pushed the door open and pointed at the ladder right inside. "To the hayloft."

He helped her to stand, and they slipped through the door. He peered into the storage room then held his finger to his lips and waved for her to climb. A clank and some rustling came from the storage room. He followed her up, rung after rung.

Someone pushed the big center aisle doors open wider, and the interior grew brighter. Dean walked out of the storage room with a coil of tow rope.

Josh shielded Emma with his body. He could feel her warmth, the scent of her hair an exotic perfume. Dean rushed past without a glance.

"Stay down," Bill growled.

"This is your plan? Shoot the deputy?" Larson said, and chuckled.

"He's alive." Emma's voice was a sigh.

Josh slumped against the ladder in relief.

But how could Larson laugh at a time like this?

Was that part of his training? Show no fear? Josh shuddered. Bill stood over Larson, pointing the gun at him. Dean waved the tow rope. They couldn't tie Larson with tow rope. The knot would never hold.

"That's the best rope you could find?" Bill took a couple steps toward Dean.

Josh froze. If Bill glance up, it was all over, but Bill didn't look up. Larson rolled to his side clutching his shoulder, blood seeping through his fingers. Bill rushed at him and kicked him in the side. Larson grunted.

"You'll never get away this time." Larson spat out blood.

"You're the one shot and lying on the ground." Bill's words came out like a soft caress, like a snake slithering through the grass.

Josh's hand slipped. He grabbed at the ladder rung. Emma tensed in front of him.

"Sorry. Slow and steady, now." The words were for him as much as Emma. His fingers tingled from gripping the ladder. She climbed onto the hayloft and crawled away from the edge. Josh eased over the top and lay on the hayloft floor. He glanced over the edge. Bill towered over Larson.

"Here, hold this." Bill handed the gun to Mo. "I'll tie him."

"Uh, Bill," Mo said, holding the muzzle pointing at the ground.

"Hold it up, stupid." Bill raised the gun until it pointed at Larson.

"What's happening?" she whispered.

Josh squinted at Emma. "At least Larson's alive, but he's hurt."

Mo shifted from foot to foot, the gun aimed at the ground again. Josh leaned farther over the ledge, and hay drifted to the floor. Dean and Bill were fumbling with the heavy rope and didn't notice. Josh rolled away from the edge.

He crawled to her side. "They're tying Larson with tow rope." He clamped a hand over his mouth to stop his laughter.

"Why is that funny?" she asked.

He nodded. "It's too thick to hold a knot. Larson will slip right out of it." He rolled back to the edge.

"Let's just shoot him." Bill threw the rope across the floor.

"Wait. What?" Mo turned and pointed the gun at Bill's chest.

"Watch it," Bill said, grabbing for the pistol, but Mo clutched it away.

Josh stood and reached for the cargo net hanging on the wall. It fell to the floor. He clenched his teeth and peered down at the men, but none of them seemed to notice him. He motioned to Emma, and she grabbed a corner. Together they untangled it and laid it out flat. He nodded at her, but her pale complexion gave him a start. She held the net in her tiny hands. Would she go flying off with the net?

She shook her head as though reading his mind, her jaw clenched. He pointed at a spot on the edge of the loft, and she took her position. They each held a side of the cargo net, their arms spread wide. He checked below one last time. Larson lay sprawled on the floor gripping his shoulder. Mo stood holding the gun, with Bill and Dean to his left in a half-circle around Larson.

A shadow cast across Larson. Josh glanced at the

barn door as another man stepped into the barn. Josh leaned into the shadows, and Emma did too.

"Oh no," she whispered, her thin voice falling flat. She rushed to him, and he held her close.

"What's going on here?" the strange man said.

Dad's voice hit Josh like a splash of fresh water. Emma's knees buckled, and he crushed her to him. He pointed and whispered, "My dad."

She nodded, her mouth a perfect O.

He gazed into her eyes. She nodded and she moved away to take her position. She gripped the net, her knuckles white. Josh scanned the scene again. Larson lay at Mo and Bill's feet. Dean stood behind Bill, right beneath them. It was time.

He glanced at Emma, her lips pressed together. He made a swinging motion with his arms then he held up three fingers. She nodded.

They swung the net back and forth, back and forth, back then released. The net sailed through the air, and he froze. It floated out in an arc, unfurling as it fell, imprisoning Mo, Bill, and Dean.

"What the—" Bill hit the ground with a thud, taking Mo and Dean with him.

"We did it." She wobbled near the edge, and he grabbed her hoodie and hugged her to him. He inhaled the musty smell of her and smiled into her hair.

Mo pushed his hands against Dean, and Bill thrashed next to him. Larson grunted to his feet. His shirt was torn at the shoulder, but the bleeding had stopped.

"He was faking. He must have seen us and kept Mo, Bill, and Dean occupied so we could toss the net." He grinned at Emma, and she leaned into him.

Larson tugged a corner of the net to secure the criminals. He twisted the gun from Mo's grasp as Bill grabbed for it, but Dean's struggles twisted the net tighter.

"This ain't fair." Bill growled. "I know my rights."

"So, you have a right to shoot me then threaten to kill me?" Larson put a hand over his wounded shoulder. "The judge will love that."

He helped her climb down the ladder then walked out of the shadows. "Dad?"

"Son?" Dad smothered him in a bear hug then held him by the shoulders. "Are you okay?" He scanned the barn. "Where's Mom?"

"Uh." Josh sniffed. His throat tightened, but he choked the words out. "She's at the hospital."

Chapter Twenty-Eight

Emma

Emma leaned against the ladder. Dr. Woolf hugged Josh. His speech had persuaded her to help solve the climate problem and disobey Mom, and there he stood—with Josh. She put her hand over her chest. Was it worth it? Did it matter anymore?

She stared at them. They had the same strong jaw and dimpled chin, the striking hazel eyes. She cleared her throat and took a step toward them, but something about Josh's slumped shoulders stopped her. He was telling his dad about his mom. She turned away, her head spinning.

Dean and Mo pushed and twisted the net.

"Damn you, Bill. I wish I'd never met you." Mo kicked at him, but his foot was trapped.

"Bill was Chip's friend, not mine, Officer." Dean raised clasped hands to Larson. "I'll tell you anything you need to know."

"Yes, you will, but begging isn't going to help you now." Larson kept the gun trained on Bill, who mumbled nonstop under his breath.

She hadn't expected the net to be so heavy, and now it held three grown men on the ground. Her throat tightened as Bill struggled to sit but fell back against Dean. She would have laughed, but it took all her energy to stand upright.

"You're going back in the holding cell." Larson said. "No storm to save you this time."

She took a step and leaned against the wall. What was wrong with her legs?

"How'd they escape?" Josh asked.

"A tree fell in front of the truck, and a branch got lodged in the bumper. I hate to admit it, but I forgot to lock the back doors. This one knocked me out cold." He pointed the gun at Bill.

She took a step, but her stomach rumbled, and she stopped.

"And Chip?" Josh asked.

"He made it to the coroner." Larson glanced at Josh. "Wilbur's working by generator, the whole hospital is. I'm out here trying to keep yahoos like these from stealing food and ki…"

Larson clenched his jaw and wiped his brow. "They won't be hurting anyone else. I'm just sorry they came back here."

"Nothing my son couldn't handle. He's a chip off his grandfather's block." Dr. Woolf gazed at his son.

Josh raised his eyebrows and shrugged.

Emma opened her mouth to speak. She shuffled forward, but the world spun as she fell.

Chapter Twenty-Nine

Josh

Josh held Emma's wrist, took her pulse, but couldn't focus. What kind of doctor would he be? He let all his patients get worse. But she didn't seem sicker. This was exhaustion.

"How is she?" Dad placed a hand on Josh's back. He was exhausted, too. "Did her eyes just flutter?"

She groaned and tried to sit. "Josh?"

He glanced at his dad then leaned down to her. "You scared me." He helped her to sit, her shoulder blades rigid against his hand. "You need some R, or you'll relapse."

"R, right." She opened her eyes. "Where's Bill?"

He held her hand. "Larson has him. He's still under the net with Dean and Mo."

She closed her eyes and let him caress her hand. He'd only known her four days, but it seemed like she'd always been part of his life. A warmth grew in his middle and spread to his chest.

"Larson said he'd give us a ride to the hospital. It's crawling with people, so your family is probably there."

Josh scanned her face. Was she blushing? He squeezed her hand, glanced at Larson, who never took the gun off the men. Dad held one end of the net, keeping it taut.

She gave a slight smile, the bruises under her eyes still dark. Dad walked over, placed a hand on Josh's shoulder, a frown creasing his forehead. His concern filled Josh with a different kind of warmth.

"So, this is Emma." Dr. Woolf held out a hand, and she shook it.

"Pleasure to meet you, Dr. Woolf. I'm a huge fan." Her face turned scarlet, but her gaze didn't waver.

Josh grinned at his dad. "She's full of herself, Dad, so watch out."

What was he thinking, letting her trailblaze four miles? Anyone with eyes could see she wasn't strong enough. He glared at Bill. This was his fault, her dehydration and exhaustion. Bill.

He glanced down and met her steady gaze. What did she see? He squeezed her hand. She seemed to be sizing him up, but her smile softened her scrutiny.

"Hey, Ed."

Dad rose and left them.

Throwing the net had been the easy part. Her pinched face and cool, thin hands were torture. She needed to get to the hospital. He clenched his teeth.

"Help me up." Emma grunted with the effort to sit, then to her feet. She leaned on him, light as a bird, and the connection seemed so natural to him.

Larson and his dad had the men handcuffed.

"Settle down." Dr. Woolf grabbed the cuffs holding Bill.

Bill tried to shake him off but fell. Dean and Mo landed on top of him. "Tarnation."

"Pfft. Not so tough now," Emma whispered.

Larson stood over Bill. "What is wrong with you? You're caught. Never underestimate my deputies." He winked at Emma.

"Deputies?" Emma's jaw dropped, and she tilted her head, her brows furrowed.

Josh shrugged and grinned.

Dad's laughter rolled from him like music. It filled Josh with a calm he had missed, even more than his violin, even more than Grandpa. Maybe grief wasn't forever.

"We better get this circus on the road." Larson gave the net a tug, and Bill grunted.

Chapter Thirty

Emma

Larson drove over branches, around trees, and through pastures. Emma grabbed Josh's arm, his warmth seeping into her, and she melted into the seat beside him. She nursed her bottle of R between catnaps as Larson and Josh's dad talked in the front seat. The constant drone of Bill, Dean, and Mo cursing and arguing as they bounced around in the truck bed blended with the whine of the engine.

The trek to Gran and Papa's farm, then back to Josh's, then the netting incident in the barn left her whole body aching.

Questions rushed through her mind: Would Mom be at the hospital? Why were Josh's hands so warm? How could she apologize to Mom? The song "Over the River and Through the Woods" ran through her dreams like a loop.

She bolted upright in the seat and gazed at her surroundings. Bill and company still complained from the back, but the truck had stopped. Larson carried a chainsaw to a tree. Josh and Dr. Woolf carried the sections he cut to make way for the truck.

She sank back in the seat, the buzz of the chainsaw playing like heavy metal through her dreams. She woke again. Josh had opened the door. He helped his dad winch a car off the road. She quit counting all the stops, thankful she didn't have to climb over all these trees. She closed her eyes and mumbled thanks to the goddesses.

****

She pushed herself from Josh's shoulder and smoothed her hair. The truck had stopped. Josh watched her, grinning. She wiped her face. "What?"

"We made it. We're at the hospital." He caressed her shoulder with a warm hand.

A tingle ran from her shoulders to her toes. The turn signal blinked. A gray stone building sprawled in front of her, filling the whole block. She counted five storeys, as Larson turned the corner and parked. Did the patients have to climb stairs now?

"All out for the hospital." Larson hopped out and walked to the bed of the truck. Dr. Woolf opened her door and took her hand. She stepped down. He took her elbow and walked her to the sidewalk. The crow's feet around his eyes mellowed his rugged features.

She threw her arms him, and he raised his arms in surprise then wrapped them around her patting her back.

Not too long ago, she'd feared every stranger she met, but these men gave her faith that there were still good guys in the world. Lilli and Jade did too, and of course, Josh.

"I think I need to go to the hospital." Bill poked his head over the side of the truck. "My whole body's numb."

"Quit crying, you big baby." Larson scowled. He turned to Josh and his dad, grinning. "Thanks again. I couldn't have caught these bad guys without your help.

You and Emma make a good team." He shook her hand first. She nodded, stunned. He shook Josh's hand.

"Emma?"

She spun around. A woman stood near the glass doors to the hospital, running her fingers through her hair. She wore dirty jeans, a wrinkled flannel shirt, and no makeup. She was beautiful.

"Mom?"

Emma rushed into her mother's open arms, the hospital blurring. "Mom." She clung to her, "I thought you were…" Tears flowed, and her shoulders shook as she cried.

"I'm here, baby. I'm right here."

She hiccupped and stepped back. Mom dabbed at her face, and Emma grabbed her hands. She'd dreamed of this moment since waking in the Little Shoppe of Colours. She'd imagined all the things she'd say, but the words wouldn't come. She cried and clung to Mom.

When she'd wished on that shooting star, it had been for Mom to find her. But the second star was for anyone to find her so she could live this moment. She closed her eyes and leaned into her mother.

"I finally found you." Mom held Emma tight, her warmth pouring into Emma, forgiving her.

"I'm so sorry."

Mom brushed the hair from her face. "You look like you could use a night in the hospital."

Emma chuckled. "I suppose I do."

"There's someone here who is anxious to see you."

"Sarah?"

"Gran, and Papa, too."

She closed her eyes. "Thank all the goddesses."

"What?"

263

"Nothing. Are they okay?"

"That's their story to tell. Let's just say, Gran wanted to run out here in her hospital gown to see you. The nurse said, she couldn't have her patients mooning the doctors."

Emma laughed, her cheeks aching from smiling so hard. She didn't want to break this spell. A stillness settled in her chest. She'd survived with the help of strangers who had become friends.

She could never view the world as she had before the storms. The devastation, the power outages, and the blocked roads, none of that mattered now. She had found her family.

Mom held her at arm's length as if taking inventory. Emma would never need her as she had two weeks ago. She had survived.

Josh walked down the sidewalk talking with his dad. Was he waiting for her? Another surge of emotions washed through her. She lifted her hand and waved, unable to name all the emotions coursing through her: gratitude, relief, love?

"Who's that?" Mom nodded in Josh's direction.

Josh and his dad approached, Josh holding out his hand. Mom clasped it. A chill ran down her spine, and she swallowed, pushing down a lump.

"Mom, this is Josh and his dad, Dr. Woolf."

"Thank you, so much for bringing her here." Mom clasped Josh's hand and held it. "I can't tell you…" Her tears fell freely.

Josh blushed. "She's strong and smart. She helped me as much as I helped her."

Did he just say smart? Emma swayed, and he took her elbow. Her cheeks burned, but she leaned on him.

"I'm Ed." Josh's father held out his hand. "My wife's here, too."

Josh's mom. His fingers were twined with hers, and she never wanted to let go. He glanced at her, all the small talk a blur in her brain.

"We're going inside now."

"Yes," she murmured.

He raised her hand to his lips and kissed it. "Until we meet again."

He'd remembered. Mrs. M's final words to her pulsed through her veins like ice then fire. She closed her mouth. How long had it been hanging open? He held her gaze then grinned releasing her hand. He turned to his dad, and together they strolled into the hospital.

Mom raised an eyebrow, a grin spreading across her face. Heat rose to Emma's cheeks and burned. He'd remembered.

"I think it is time for you to see a doctor, young lady. You're pale and a little wobbly."

"Me? What about you?" Mom could have mentioned Josh kissing her hand, but she didn't. Emma wove her arm in her mom's and squeezed.

"Maybe they can put a cot next to Gran's, so you can lie down while you visit."

"That sounds amazing."

She wanted to pinch herself. Her stomach filled with tingles that had nothing to do with drinking from the river. Josh's kiss, his, "Until we met again."

She strolled into the hospital arm in arm with Mom, a brisk November wind brushing loose hairs against her cheek as they walked into the lobby. The lights popped on, and a cheer echoed in the vast space.

"Here she comes." Mom swept a racing Sarah into her arms.

Sarah kissed Mom's cheek then squirmed from her arms.

"Emma." Sarah grabbed her hand.

Emma pulled her into a hug.

Soft clouds in a sea of blue sky reflected off the glass doors. Emma released Sarah as the intercom clicked.

"Code blue, second floor, room 312."

A word about the author…

Avis Adams writes poetry and YA Fiction. Her poems have won awards and been published online and in various literary journals, and Quilcene, a chapbook was published in 2019. Her debut YA novel is *The Incident,* published by TWRP. She lives on a small farm in the Puget Sound area of Washington State, where she writes and gardens. She teaches English at a local community college.

https://avis-m-adams.com/

Thank you for purchasing
this publication of The Wild Rose Press, Inc.

For questions or more information
contact us at
info@thewildrosepress.com.

The Wild Rose Press, Inc.
www.thewildrosepress.com

CPSIA information can be obtained
at www.ICGtesting.com
Printed in the USA
BVHW061251291221
625055BV00015B/1247